How would it feel to be kissed by him as if she were lovely, sensuous and desirable?

How might it feel actually to *be* those things to a man she wanted so badly it didn't matter about social distinctions or correct behaviour any more?

For the longest and most charged moments of her life so far those questions sang between them as if she had spoken them aloud. Her lips parted without her permission; his fascinated gaze was encouragement enough. Her entire body was aware of itself as never before. Every breath was a novelty as the scent and power and sight of him reached a curious and dangerous place inside her and whispered, *Maybe.*

A curve of almost tender amusement lifted his mouth in a wry smile. Her feet rose on tiptoe, inviting him to lower his head and let wild, reckless Eleanor Hancourt out of her cage the instant he kissed her…

Author Note

During the Regency period a governess wasn't regarded as an equal by her employers, but she didn't belong in the servants' hall either. She had to earn the respect of her pupils and employers, and teach young ladies all the accomplishments that would fit them for high society, but not turn them into blue stockings. Then she had to hand them on to a suitable chaperon and find a new position where she could do it all again with another set of strangers—if she was lucky.

The moment I began to wonder if any of them *enjoyed* taking on such a challenge Eleanor Hancourt turned up, as if she'd been waiting for a chance to have her say. With enough secrets in her travelling box to keep a novelist happy for months, and a hero who tells almost as many lies as she does, she has been a joy to write about.

So this is Nell's story. Anyone who read *The Winterley Scandal*, in which Nell's brother Colm meets the love of his life, will recognise some characters in this book, but *The Governess Heiress* is also intended to stand alone—just as bright, determined and ever-so-slightly bossy Nell Hancourt had to when her wicked uncle turned her out into the world to earn her own bread.

THE GOVERNESS HEIRESS

Elizabeth Beacon

First published in Great Britain 2017
By Mills & Boon, an imprint of HarperCollins*Publishers*
1 London Bridge Street, London, SE1 9GF

Large Print edition 2017

© 2017 Elizabeth Beacon

ISBN: 978-0-263-06800-9

MIX
Paper from responsible sources
FSC
www.fsc.org   FSC™ C007454

This book is produced from independently certified FSC paper to ensure responsible forest management. For more information visit www.harpercollins.co.uk/green.

Printed and bound in Great Britain
by CPI Group (UK) Ltd, Croydon, CR0 4YY

Elizabeth Beacon has a passion for history and storytelling and, with the English West Country on her doorstep, never lacks a glorious setting for her books. Elizabeth tried horticulture, higher education as a mature student, briefly taught English, and worked in an office before finally turning her daydreams about dashing piratical heroes and their stubborn and independent heroines into her dream job: writing Regency romances for Mills & Boon Historical Romance.

Books by Elizabeth Beacon

Mills & Boon Historical Romance

A Year of Scandal: Spin-off

The Winterley Scandal
The Governess Heiress

A Year of Scandal

The Viscount's Frozen Heart
The Marquis's Awakening
Lord Laughraine's Summer Promise
Redemption of the Rake

Linked by Character

The Duchess Hunt
The Scarred Earl
The Black Sheep's Return

Stand-Alone Novels

A Most Unladylike Adventure
Candlelit Christmas Kisses
'Governess Under the Mistletoe'

Visit the Author Profile page
at millsandboon.co.uk for more titles.

Chapter One

'I would rather be outside, too, Lavinia, but you said it was too cold to learn as we walked this morning. Now we're inside you still won't listen,' Eleanor Hancourt said sternly. 'Remind us how many rods make a furlong.'

Nell's eldest pupil went on staring out of the high schoolroom window and it took Caroline's nudge to jolt her cousin out of a daydream. 'Archbishop of Canterbury, Miss Court,' Lavinia said triumphantly.

'We have moved on from Plantagenet kings and troublesome priests, Lavinia Selford. British history was this morning.'

'Oh,' said Lavinia listlessly. 'Well, it doesn't matter, does it?'

'Kindly explain how the fate of Kings and measuring God's creation are unimportant, Lavinia,'

Nell said softly, although she wanted to let her temper rip.

'Because I don't care. Knowing such rubbishy stuff won't get me a husband and a fine house in London,' Lavinia replied defiantly.

'Being a well-bred mother to his children will be enough for you, then?'

'No, he will adore me and when I make my debut I'll dance and have fun while you sew for the poor and read improving books out loud of an evening.'

Nell mentally conceded the girl could be right about the dullness of their current lives, even if everything else she had to say showed how immature Lavinia was. It *was* dull in this half-closed-up house at the back of beyond. Even she, the girls' governess, was only three and twenty and sometimes longed for more and now it was temptingly within reach. Except nobody else really cared if they were happy or miserable, so long as they didn't cause trouble. So she would have to stay until the Earl of Barberry came to take responsibility for his wards and the estate, but that seemed about as likely as pigs learning to fly.

Her authority felt fragile even after two years

teaching the man's orphaned wards, but at least he wasn't here to challenge it. He had never been here to see if she was doing her job properly. He hadn't even bothered to meet his young cousins during the decade he'd been head of the Selford family. The Earl left the country as soon as he heard his grandfather was dead and had stayed away ever since. Even two years on from being brought in to try and drive knowledge and lady-like behaviour into the Misses Selford, Nell was too young for such a role. Now she was an heiress to add to her puzzles, but she could think about that when Lavinia wasn't as slyly confident she was going to win their latest battle.

'I am well born and pretty and I have a good figure and a fine dowry,' the girl listed smugly, the difference between them sharp in her light blue eyes.

'A true gentleman requires more than looks and a large collection of vanities in a wife,' Nell replied coolly, pushing the unworthy argument she was well born and a lot wealthier than her eldest charge to the back of her mind. 'A talent for flirting and dancing won't fascinate the fine young man you dream of marrying when every second debutante has that as well. Wit and charm, a sincere interest in those around her, a well-informed mind and a compassionate heart make a true lady, Lavinia. Youthful prettiness fades; do you want to end up lonely and avoided since you have no conversation or common interest to keep your husband at your side when you are no longer as young as you were?'

'Oh, no, Vinnie, imagine how awful it would be to end up like that lady who stayed at the manor last year. The one who bored on and on about imaginary illnesses and how hard her life was until her husband went out of his way to avoid her,' Caroline exclaimed with genuine horror.

'What sane gentleman would marry an empty-headed creature for aught but her money?' Caroline's elder sister Georgiana added with a sideways look at her least favourite cousin.

'That's enough, Georgiana,' Nell said firmly.

Lavinia was the daughter of the last Earl's eldest son and senior in status and years, but what did that matter when all four of the old Earl's granddaughters were stuck here in the middle of nowhere? None of them could inherit the earldom and Nell counted herself lucky that she could only imagine the last Earl's fury when his youngest son made a runaway marriage to Kitty Graham, still whispered of as the loveliest actress of her generation. Hastily doing some mental arithmetic, Nell supposed Kitty and the Honourable Aidan's son hadn't mattered to his paternal grandfather for over a decade. The fifth Earl's eldest son had a robust heir and never mind if his wife refused to share his bed after the boy was born and she declared her duty done. Since the lady was the daughter of a duke the old Earl didn't challenge her until the boy was killed in some reckless exploit at Oxford. Then he'd ordered his heir to mend his marriage and even the Duke agreed, so Lady Selford gave birth to Lavinia a year after she lost her son and was declared too fragile for further duty by the doctors. According to local gossip, the lady turned her back on her baby daughter and returned to her family. Nell marvelled at her indifference, but Lady Selford died when Lavinia was seven and Nell doubted the child had set eyes on the woman above once or twice.

At least Georgiana and Caroline seemed to have been loved by their parents, but a sweating fever killed Captain Selford and his wife and Nell imagined the girls had had a stony welcome from their grandfather, since the servants still gossiped about how bitterly he resented his granddaughters for daring to be born female. Only Penelope had escaped the fury of that bitter old man by being born three months after the Earl died, but as a posthumous child of his third son she had been his last hope of keeping the offspring of an actress out of the succession. The latest Earl of Barberry had carried off the family honours in the teeth of his grandfather's opposition then, but the sixth Earl had done precious little with them. Nell supposed it was better for the girls to grow up without another angry lord glowering at them when he recalled their existence. Lavinia's old nurse once told her how the old Earl cursed whenever Lavinia crossed his path, so little wonder if she grew up imagining a rosier future for herself. Nell hoped the girl would make a good marriage, but misery awaited her if she wed the first young man who asked her to so she could escape her lonely life.

'Forty, Miss Court,' Lavinia said casually at last.

Nell wondered what she was talking about, then remembered the rods and furlongs. 'Very good, Lavinia. So, Georgiana; how many feet in a fathom?'

'Even a land sailor knows there are six and we were at sea until Papa died.'

'You and your stupid sister insist on telling us about him all the time. As if we care,' Lavinia said, quite spoiling the novelty of joining in a lesson for once.

'Then why don't you go and count your rubbishy ribbons, or gaze at your own ugly face in the mirror for hours on end, since you love it so much? At least then we won't have to look at your frog face or listen to you rattle on about who you're going to marry this week, Lavinia Lackwit,' Georgiana scorned as tears flooded Caroline's wide blue eyes at the thought of what the two sisters had lost when their parents died.

Nell felt sorry for Lavinia when even little Penny glared at her for upsetting the most vulnerable of the cousins and all three looked as if they'd be glad if Lavinia disappeared in a puff of smoke.

'Georgiana, that's an inexcusable thing to say. You will stand in the corner until I say you can come out. Lavinia; apologise to your cousin, then copy out the One Hundredth Psalm twice in a fair hand. Maybe that will make you humbler about your own shortcomings and a little kinder to others, but your guardian will be displeased to hear you refuse to make any effort at your lessons and fall out with your cousins.'

'He doesn't give a snap of his fingers for any of us and I hate this place and all of you as well. You're always such good little girls for your *darling* Miss Court and she's only a servant when all's said and done. You make me sick. I hate you all, but I hate Cousin Barberry most. Why should I care what he thinks? I doubt he remembers we exist,' Lavinia railed at the top of her voice, stamped her feet as if words couldn't express her anger, then ran out of the room on a furious sob. Nell listened to the sound of her charge thundering downstairs and the garden door slamming with a sinking feeling in the pit of her stomach that her day was about to get even worse.

'I hope she took a shawl,' Caroline said with a sympathetic shiver.

'And I hope she didn't,' nine-year-old Penny argued vengefully.

Georgiana flounced to the corner she'd been ordered into with a sniff and a contemptuous glower and Nell tried to do what came next instead of feeling defeated.

'Georgiana, stay there for ten minutes without saying a word or pulling faces at Caroline and Penelope. I shall ask Crombie to sit with you. Caroline and Penelope, you can read quietly, but you will *not* tease Georgiana or speculate about Lavinia. As soon as the ten minutes are up you may read as well, Georgiana,' she told her charges as calmly as she could.

Seeing how impatient Penny's one-time nurse was about being fetched away from her comfortable coze with the housekeeper, Nell knew they wouldn't be allowed to riot in her absence. Now she only had to worry about organising a search for Lavinia with the daylight already fading. She gave orders for all the available staff to comb the gardens and parkland, then went outside to search her own section of the shadowy gardens.

Fergus Selford, Earl of Barberry, rode into the stableyard of Berry Brampton House for the first time in his life and found it strangely deserted. He hadn't expected a fanfare on the arrival of an

errant earl nobody knew was coming. Or much
of a welcome even if they did, but it felt a bit of
come down to stable his own horse. He owned
the dratted place from cellar to rafters, yet he'd
settled the tired animal in a convenient stall and
retrieved his unfashionable boat cloak from the
tack room before he met a single soul.

'We're not expecting visitors, so if you're the
new land agent you couldn't have arrived at a
better time, although you're three weeks late and
we had almost given up on you,' a rather pleasant
contralto voice told him from the shadowy doorway. 'I saw the lamp and heard someone moving
about in here as if he had a right to be here. All
the stable boys are supposed to be out looking
for one of my charges so I came to see if one of
them was shirking. Now you're here we need all
the help we can get before Lavinia hurts herself
or one of us falls into the ha-ha. You can help me
search, since you'll get lost if you wander about
on your own and we'll have to find you as well.'

'If you've managed to mislay one of the Selford
girls that's your problem,' Fergus told her gruffly,
blaming his shabby cloak for her mistake. He was
almost inclined to tell her who he was and that he

employed her to take care of his wards, so why should he bother himself with a search for one of them when he was weary and uncomfortable and didn't want to be here in the first place?

'It'll be yours if the Earl finds out we couldn't keep one of his wards safe because you refused to help.'

'Is she mad or just simple? It has to be one or the other since you believe she'll do herself a mischief in his lordship's private grounds.'

'Miss Selford is a bright and spirited young girl who has trouble keeping her temper in check. A trait I sympathise with at this very moment,' the governess said through what sounded like clenched teeth.

Now why was arguing with her in the semi-darkness more stimulating than flirting with sophisticated beauties? He heard her take a deep breath and she seemed to call on the reserves of patience his wards hadn't already tested to the limit. Reminding himself he was here to do his duty, not amuse himself at the governess's expense, he ordered himself to stop provoking her and get on with it.

'Never mind, we'll find her without your help

and I suppose you wouldn't be much use anyway,' she said haughtily. 'If you can exert yourself long enough to cross the yard and find Cook, I expect she will feed you, then direct you to your quarters. I wish you joy of the land steward's house, by the way. You should have told us you were coming—since you are so tardy we had given up on you and abandoned the attempt to make it more welcoming.' Even in the gloom he could see the glare the Amazon shot him before she turned to march back the way she came.

'Stop,' he ordered and she turned as slowly as an offended queen. He wanted to kiss the temper off her lips for a shocking moment. She would slap him and quite right, too, and he hadn't come here to prove that every hard word his late grandfather had said about him had turned out to be true.

'No, I'm busy,' she said and strode towards a path he could only just see in the fast fading light.

'Two pairs of eyes and ears will be better than one in this gloom,' he said as he caught up with her, bowed ironically and indicated she carry on leading the way. 'You know where you're going,' he explained, beginning to enjoy himself now he had such a prickly lady to annoy and this new disguise to settle into.

He told himself he wouldn't have thought of such an impersonation until she thrust it on him, but *not* announcing who he was to a household he never wanted to inherit in the first place was too tempting to turn his back on. As a ruse for finding out what was going on without putting the entire neighbourhood on alert that the new Earl was home at last it could hardly be bettered. Pretending to be the land steward would save him the huge effort of being the sixth Earl of Barberry and he could spy out the land, then decide if he could endure being here. Perhaps it was as well the Moss boy, who he'd lined up to act as land steward, had backed out of this post for an easier one since his lack of backbone had forced Fergus to come here, but taking up his inheritance in the teeth of the late Earl's bitter opposition still rasped his pride somehow.

Everything the Selfords had worked so hard to keep from a whore's son, as they so charmingly called him, was his, but it felt like a hollow victory. After living on his own terms in Canada for almost a decade the rules of a polite little English society felt petty. As a heedless and rather angry young man he had been determined to defy his grandfather and all those who made his time at Eton and Oxford a mixed blessing. There was always some aristocratic sprig ready to deride him as grandson of Lord Barberry on one side and an Irish gypsy on the other. None of them would believe he never really wanted the titles and lands hanging around his neck like a millstone, so he'd left the country when the old Earl was barely cold in his grave. There were so many things he could do elsewhere, so many adventures to have, but he'd been doing his best to ignore the voice of his conscience and his mother's pleas to come home ever since he'd fallen in love with the vastness and promise of the so-called New World. Another thing he could blame being Earl of Barberry for, having to leave a place he could have made his home if not for all the responsibilities he'd been so intent on running away from ten years ago.

Still, as Moss he could learn what he wanted to know, then go away again if he chose to and nobody here would even know he'd been. He ought to thank the woman striding along the path ahead of him as he stumbled in her wake like a rowing boat chasing a stately galleon.

Now what *was* her name? He was ashamed to find he couldn't remember it, despite the quarterly reports she insisted on sending him of the state of his cousins' health, happiness and progress, or lack of it. Still, she was the latest in a long line of governesses who'd all insisted on writing to him about their woes with the Selford girls when they were paid handsomely to deal with them. Just as well this one had no idea who he was, because he paid little attention to her meticulous lists of how Miss Lavender or Miss Patty, or whatever they were called, were progressing when his lawyers sent them on. Thousands of miles away he'd had to trust that his senior lawyer knew what he was doing when he'd insisted that young girls needed someone youthful to care for their happiness as well as teach them to paint screens and sew samplers, or whatever young ladies did until they were old enough to marry. Considering this female had carelessly mislaid one of his wards, he was beginning to wonder about the fellow's wisdom and sanity right now.

'Where are we going?' he asked as he followed Miss Whoever into a generous old orchard.

'If I told you it would mean nothing, unless you've been studying estate maps before taking up your employment?' she said with too much irony for his taste.

'I'm here now, aren't I?' he said defensively.

'And only three weeks late as well. How very diligent, Mr Moss.'

'That discrepancy is between me and my employer.'

'And he doesn't sound the most patient or tolerant of them. In your shoes I'd be careful how I conducted myself, now you're here at last.'

'Is that a threat?' he asked, with what his half-sisters said was his most annoying sneer. Annoying or not, it was wasted on this woman. She was peering at what looked like a tall hutch in the twilight as if he didn't exist.

'An observation,' she said absently. He felt like a fly so trivial it wasn't even worth slapping him. 'Don't get too close,' she warned and he instantly wanted to.

He was beginning to sympathise with his absent ward's need to escape her governess's authority.

Then he got too close and an angry buzz shot past his ear. He stepped back hastily as the persistent little creatures took exception to him but, annoyingly, left the governess alone as if she belonged here and he didn't.

'I did warn you,' she said with *I told you so* in her voice.

'What is this place?' he asked gruffly.

'A bee house, of course,' she said and followed him away as if nothing about this place troubled her, which it didn't, he supposed—she wasn't the one in danger of being royally stung.

'Oh, of course, and what an ideal place for a runaway schoolgirl to hide.'

'Lavinia is a fanciful creature and local lore insists the bees be told whatever happens in a household if they are to be part of it.'

'And they really want to know when a girl is out of sorts with her governess?'

'It was a possibility. Now maybe you'll go back to the house and ask for your dinner so I can get on,' she said as if tired of indulging him.

'While you wander about in the dark and risk life and limb? Even I'm not that much of a yahoo, Miss... Who are you anyway?' he demanded irritably, glad now he hadn't remembered her name and given himself away.

'Miss Court and I'm not in any danger since, as you pointed out just now, we are in his lordship's private grounds. And I'll get on a lot faster if you leave me be.'

'No, if the wench has done something to herself in the dark you can't carry her, great girl of fifteen or sixteen as she must be.'

'How do you know the age of my eldest charge?'

Curse the woman, but now she sounded suspicious. Fergus searched his memory for lies he'd already told her. Even the son of a country squire would know enough to guess how old the Earl of Barberry's wards must be now.

'Everyone knows Barberry was left with a stable of female cousins when he inherited,' he said and even managed to sound plausibly impatient. 'The old lord's quest for another male heir is hardly a secret and if those girls were old enough to be presented they wouldn't need a governess, so even the eldest cannot be out yet.'

'Clever,' she said flatly and why didn't he think it a compliment?

Chapter Two

They reached the end of the orchards and the interfering female found a wicket gate out into the park as if by instinct, or perhaps she came here rather too often in the dark, a jealous impulse prompted Fergus. The notion she was so familiar with his grounds because she came here to meet a lover and flit through the moonlit park at the idiot's side for a stolen idyll goaded him to the edge of fury for some odd reason. He hadn't even seen her properly yet, but she sounded just the sort of woman to order some poor besotted idiot to dance attendance on her in the dusk so they wouldn't be caught courting and risk dismissal. He employed the woman to look after his cousins, he told himself uncomfortably. She should be keeping a close eye on his little cousins, not planning to run off with a local curate or farmer's son even her family might consider a misalliance.

'Where are we going now?' he demanded rudely, but he'd ridden all the way from Holyhead and felt as if he was entitled to be a little out of temper.

Miss Court might have a lover lurking nearby *and* she was being rude to the very person she ought to impress if she wanted to keep her post. Was he more impressed by his title than he thought, then? No, he didn't want to be an earl today any more than he had ten years ago. Miss Court made him feel like a grubby schoolboy who hadn't washed behind his ears even as his inner demons tempted him to kiss the wretched female and find out if she was as headlong and determined a lover as she was as a rescuer of wild girls in the semi-darkness. And it *would* be nice to find a way to make her stand back and take notice. Not that she'd waited for him to fight his inner demons back where they belonged. She was almost beyond reach by the time he realised he didn't want to be left here like the last lame nag in a stable. He speeded up and almost fell over a tree root in the shadows.

'Devil take it, woman, will you slow down?'

'No. You didn't want to come in the first place, so I don't understand why you won't go away. I should never have made you come, you're no help at all.'

'If the girl doesn't want to go home, you won't be able to drag her back,' he pointed out rather sharply.

Had she paled at the idea of having to force her errant charge to obey her? Hard to tell in the gloom and why should he care if she endured the role of governess or loved it? Catching himself out thinking like the spoilt aristocrat he'd sworn not to be, he wondered if his half-brother was right and he was as arrogant as any Selford in his own way.

'Hush,' she whispered. 'Do you hear something over there, on our right?'

'No,' he said in a normal voice, telling himself he was bored with looking for unruly schoolgirls who didn't want to be found.

'I *wish* I hadn't bothered to find out who was lazing about in the stables when the lads were supposed to be looking for Lavinia,' she informed him crossly and strode into the night yet again.

'The wages of curiosity,' he called, then scurried after her like a tardy footman before she could disappear. 'Where are we going?' he asked when he almost ran into her standing still under a tree as if she could hear her way to what she wanted if she tried hard enough. She was warm and rather delightfully curved and he felt passion thunder through his senses until he reminded himself the woman was his cousins' governess and he was her employer.

'*Will* you go away?' she demanded as if she was oblivious to him and his unruly masculine urges, then she started off again without giving any in- dication where she was heading.

'No,' he said, grabbing the back of her cloak and holding on when she did her best to snatch it away. 'Tell me, or I'll shout a warning we're on our way.'

'Can't you hear the poor girl, you blundering great idiot? She isn't going to run in that state,' she whispered furiously as she towed him forward by his hold on her cloak.

He wondered how he'd managed to miss it as well now; self-preservation, he decided ruefully. Noisy sobs and the odd pathetic little moan car- ried on the cooling air as the girl fought for breath against all that sorrow. Fergus wished he'd left the governess to cope with a soggy storm of tears and almost melted into the darkness as Miss Court ordered. On the one hand, he would be obliging a lady, on the other he'd be a coward. He let go of Miss Court's cloak and meekly followed in her footsteps.

'It's me, Lavinia,' Miss Court said so gently he wondered if he'd been wrong to class her as an irritable she-wolf in petticoats when she'd first loomed out of the darkness. 'You must be hungry and cold, and you sound as if you need a shoulder to cry on.'

Fergus could make out a Grecian-style temple. As they emerged from the trees he saw the first stars reflected in the lake beyond it and wondered how it would feel to meet Miss Court here for a twilight tryst. Exciting, a forbidden voice whispered in the back of his mind and he uneasily tried to ignore it. He didn't even know the woman; even if he did it would be wrong to lead her on when he was really her absentee employer and never mind this odd feeling of connection to the wretched female.

'Oh, Miss Court,' the girl gasped and Fergus backed away when an overgrown schoolgirl pelted down the steps of the summer house, then flew into her governess's arms with such force he stepped forward to steady the woman and never mind feminine tears and his dread of a *scene*. 'I'm so sorry,' the girl managed to gasp out between sobs. 'I don't think I'll ever learn to behave properly or keep my temper as you say I must.'

'Hah!' Fergus muttered darkly. He felt Miss Court stiffen beside him and knew she must have heard him, but she *had* lost hers with him several times and if she was going to pretend to be a pattern card she should get her emotions under better control.

'Never mind that now. I'm so glad you're safe, even if you are more than a little bit woebegone. And it's getting dark and chilly, so why not come home and be pampered a little for once? We can talk about your troubles when you're feeling better. I only want the best for you and, whatever your cousins say when you all lose that fiery Selford temper, they love you, Lavinia. At times I'm even quite fond of you myself.' Miss Court ended with a laugh in her voice that made Fergus smile in the darkness, so he wasn't at all surprised to hear a watery chuckle from the drooping young lady snuggled in her governess's arms as if they'd never had the argument that probably caused this fuss in the first place.

How unworthy of him to envy the girl and wish he was enjoying all that warmth and welcome. Miss Court was a lady and he certainly wasn't a land steward. He hadn't even met the woman in the clear light of day, he reminded himself hastily and if this was what pretending to be Moss did to him, he might have to reconsider the plum she'd handed him when she'd made that hasty assumption about who he was. He could have been anyone, he condemned her with a frown it was as well she couldn't see. Who knew what sort of rogue could be stumbling about in the dark silently lusting after her if he hadn't found her first?

'Thank you, but I do wish Mama hadn't died, Miss Court. There's nobody left to love me,' Lavinia confessed in a whisper and reminded him they had a very effective chaperon and Miss Court had only ever seen him as an extra pair of eyes and ears to help her find her charge.

Nell knew how it felt to be lonely, but at least her brother had always loved her, however determined their eldest uncle might be to keep them apart. 'All the wishing in the world won't bring her back, I fear,' she said gently, 'but soon you'll be able to show the world how a true Selford lady behaves and what a shame to waste it on the first callow youth to pluck up the courage to ask you to wed him.'

'Heaven forbid,' Nell thought she heard muttered with heartfelt sincerity by the annoying man behind her. She turned around with Lavinia in her arms and the silence that met her glare was so innocent she knew she'd heard aright.

'Who are you?' Lavinia demanded and Nell didn't correct her manners for once because he didn't deserve any better.

'Miss Court will tell you I'm the new land steward,' he said in the lazy drawl that made Nell's palms itch.

'And are you?'

'So it would seem.'

'You are a very odd person if you need someone to tell you who you are, isn't he, Miss Court?'

'Mr Moss seems quite deaf, the poor gentleman. He certainly takes no notice of anything I say.'

'You don't look very old, sir,' Lavinia observed sagely.

Nell had to argue with herself before she corrected her gently. 'Remember what I said about it being impolite to make comments on the odd behaviour of others, Lavinia?' she said, but Mr Moss saved the girl an apology Nell hadn't quite demanded.

'I could lie and say I'm a mere stripling of five and fifty, I suppose, but it's hard enough being Methuselah without making things any worse, Miss Lavinia,' the rogue said with such self-mocking laughter in his voice Nell wanted to smile, briefly.

'Now you're teasing me, sir, and, as you don't seem offended by what Miss Court insists are my bad manners, *are* you telling the truth about yourself?'

'Oh, I never do that,' the new land steward said brazenly. 'If you choose to believe me, I'll admit to being one and thirty, Miss Lavinia. If you don't; I'm five years less because even we gentlemen have our vanity.'

'Since he has confessed to being a work of fiction, maybe we should add five years to the total

and make Mr Moss quite an elderly young gentleman instead, Lavinia,' Nell said lightly, wishing
he could see her best frown through the gloom.
She wondered how he managed to irritate her so
much when they'd only just met; it was a special gift, she decided, one she was glad most men
didn't share.

'You have my sympathy, Miss Lavinia. Your
governess makes *me* feel like a small boy with
a dirty neck and I thought I was grown up until
we met.'

'Miss Court is a wonderful governess and a very
kind person, Mr Moss,' Lavinia surprised all three
of them by saying earnestly.

'Thank you, my dear,' Nell said, giving her most
challenging pupil another hug and draping most
of her cloak around her shivering shoulders. 'But
we must get you inside before you take a chill.
Never mind Mr Moss and his poor opinion of
anyone who doesn't fawn on him as if he was
your guardian and not the Earl's new land steward, we must scurry home as fast as may be now
I've found you at last.'

'And I have travelled far today, so let's hope my
manners will mend after a good night's sleep. The

lawyers tell me I have a great deal to do if things are to be run smoothly here once more,' Mr Moss said in what Nell felt sure was a rather kind attempt to divert Lavinia from the last of her sobs and the convulsive shivers that followed them.

'They're right,' she replied as calmly as she could with the chill reaching both their bodies now. The cold was biting even through her sensible gown with Lavinia wrapped up in most of her cloak. 'Your predecessor should have retired sooner with such a large and complex estate to manage,' she went on, mainly to distract herself from her own need to shiver and in the hope it would take Lavinia's mind off her physical woes as they had to pick their way back over roots and rabbit holes in the ever-deepening twilight.

'Poor man,' Lavinia said and Nell heard the shake in her pupil's voice and pushed their pace as hard as she could without one of them falling flat on their faces.

'Aye, and if you're not set on catching a chill in order to be thought interesting for the next week, we'd best get you home faster than this, Miss Lavinia,' Mr Moss said and hefted the girl into his arms when they paused for breath.

'Gracious, you're very strong,' Lavinia said breathlessly.

'I'll run ahead to warn everyone you're on your way if you will direct Mr Moss, Lavinia? You should be safe with him, by the way. He has atrocious manners and a misplaced sense of humour, but he made no attempt to molest me on the way here,' Nell managed to say brusquely and scampered away before either of them could argue.

'Why, thank you, Miss Court,' Fergus muttered as he eyed the darkness in her wake.

'She is a very definite sort of person,' Lavinia said with a catch in her voice that told him she was fighting the last of her tears.

'Here, let's wrap you up in this cloak since she's left it behind. If you can face her wrath if you catch a chill, I'm not sure I can and don't get us lost, will you? I don't know the way even by daylight.'

'How thoughtless of Miss Court,' the schoolgirl in his arms said sleepily and Fergus suspected he'd have to get them back as best he could, dark or not.

What a good thing he didn't lead the sort of

life most idle earls about town did, he decided, finding a path through the woods almost by instinct. Slight as this girl was, he was weary from his journey and she was almost an adult. He was oddly touched when she fell asleep in his arms, but wasn't it as well she didn't know who he was? His wards probably regarded him as a devil incarnate. He changed his hold on the Selford sleeping so trustingly in his arms and marvelled at the toll too much emotion could take on a young lady. Memory of how it felt to be torn between childish simplicity and the need to find your own way in the world made him feel sorry for his young ward.

His mother had dealt with his rebellious and confused younger self with her usual common sense and his stepfather would shrug and take him on one of his adventures whenever he got out of hand. Saints, but he was lucky, wasn't he? Not for him the starch and disapproval of a Miss Court; or the memory of parents who saw their own child as a failure simply because she was born female. His mother would have loved him if he had been born a dumb, cross-eyed lunatic, but at least Lavinia's governess hadn't ripped up at her. Indeed, Miss Court seemed truly concerned that the girl felt she had to sob out her woes alone. The woman could stay until he found out more about her, he decided grudgingly. Now he would take the role she had thrust at him by mistaking him for Moss and what better way to find out if he could trust her with his wards until they were ready to be brought out in polite society? Then he could go somewhere he would like better and forget Miss Court and his stupid reactions to her in the dark.

What with racing back to the house, making sure the stableyard bell was rung to signal Miss Lavinia was safe and organising a welcome for her, Nell should have no time to think about rude and disobliging Mr Moss. So, of course, she thought of little else while she ordered a hot bath for Lavinia and a warming pan for her bed. Then there were the other girls to reassure that their cousin was in one piece and being brought home safely. The stir of the man's arrival with Lavinia seemed oddly muted and Nell went to peer over the wooden banister of the staircase leading to the nursery wing. Why did the sight of Lavinia fast asleep in his arms make her heart ache so?

Puzzled by her own emotions at the sight of the

girl cradled protectively in a stranger's arms, she ran up to Lavinia's room to announce she was on her way. 'We'll forget a bath and get her straight into bed as she seems to be fast asleep. The new land steward is on his way upstairs with her right now.'

'He's turned up at long last then, has he?' Mary said, showing more interest in the steward than she ever did in her young mistress. 'He must be much fitter than old Mr Jenks to carry Miss Lavinia here, then have breath enough to bring her upstairs.'

'Only just,' the man himself announced ruefully as the butler shepherded him into the room as if he was important. Mr Moss had impressed someone tonight then, Nell thought ungratefully. No, some were too impressed, she decided, as she watched Mary making sheep's eyes at the newcomer. The buxom little maid seemed to have forgotten she was employed to look after the young lady they must now try to get into bed without waking her up.

'Thank you, sir. Mary and I will manage now,' she told the man coolly as he gently sat his burden in the comfortable chair by the fire.

'I know I'm in the way now, Miss Court.'

'Goodnight then, sir,' she said repressively.

'I fear not; the housekeeper has insisted I stay here for dinner while my house is being hastily got ready for occupation. It seems it was got unready and left cold when I failed to arrive at the appointed time.'

'You *are* very tardy,' Nell said shortly.

'But also sharp set after such a mighty journey,' he told her with a knowing grin, then sauntered out as if he owned the place.

'Insufferable man,' Nell spluttered when the door was shut behind him.

'He's very handsome, Miss Court,' Mary said with a longing gaze at that very door, as if wishing might bring him back.

'Not really,' Nell said as she tried to decide why he was so uniquely attractive.

Not wanting to discover the secret of it, Nell set about undressing Lavinia as gently as she could and shot the maid a sharp look to remind her of her duty. Between them they coaxed Lavinia to raise her arms so they could strip off her muslin

gown, stockings, indoor shoes and flannel petticoat without rousing her fully.

'Let her sleep in her petticoat this once,' Nell
said as they each put an arm about the girl's waist
and walked her over to the bed. 'She needs rest
more than food right now,' she warned and put a
finger to her lips to tell Mary not to argue until
they were out of earshot.

'What if she wakes up hungry later?' the girl
whispered when they were out in the corridor with
the door almost shut.

'I must persuade Cook to make her something
that won't spoil. If she sends your dinner up, will
you listen for her while I go downstairs? If the
poor child has one of her nightmares I don't want
her to be alone.'

Nell could sense the young maidservant wanted
to argue, but it was her job to look after the eldest
Selford girl. Mary probably wanted to giggle with
her fellow maids at the thought of such an exciting addition to the local pool of bachelors. Nell
would stay and watch Lavinia's slumbers herself if
she didn't have three other charges and a disturb-
ing stranger to keep an eye on. Mr Moss might
regret accepting the housekeeper's invitation to

stay to dinner while she scurried her staff over to his house to give it a hasty airing. Or at least he might when he found out Nell was in the habit of instructing her pupils in the art of fine dining and good manners and he would be a tame gentleman to practice on.

Chapter Three

'Mr Moss has gone upstairs to wash and shave. Parkins showed him into the Red Room and sent Will to wait on him,' Penny told Nell when she went along to the night nursery to make sure her youngest charge was ready for the meal ahead.

'Are you sure you don't want to move into a proper grown-up bedchamber, my love?' Nell asked to divert them both as she caught Penny's sash and hauled her gently back into the room to be made as neat and presentable as she already thought she was.

'No, I like it in here and Crombie is next door if I have a bad dream.'

'Sooner or later you'll have to become a young lady,' Nell said as she brushed Penny's wavy nut-brown hair to shining perfection. It struck her that Penny might well be the most sought-after Miss

Selford one day, for all Caro's potentially stunning looks. As Penny was nine years old at least Nell could put off worrying about her future for a while.

'Not until I'm too big to have a choice,' Penny said with a grimace of distaste.

Nell knew it was wrong to have favourites, but she secretly doted on her youngest pupil. She pronounced Penny perfectly turned out even for dinner with a strange gentleman now and reminded her that her manners ought to match her appearance.

'Of course,' said Miss Penelope Selford with a solemn nod and a hop, skip and jump to show how excited she was by even this much company.

Memory of how it felt to be the daughter of a scandalous lord had kept Nell here, trying to fill some of the gaps in the girls' narrow lives, even if they were lonely for a very different reason. Now her brother Colm's fortune was restored and her own dowry doubled by her father's efforts to protect his children before he died. She wondered what Mr Moss would make of a governess with a handsome fortune and a scandalous father. As the third son of a country squire he might court her for her fortune, whatever he thought of her and her blighted family name, and that was another reason Nell refused to join Colm and his new wife for the upcoming London Season. Fortune hunters. Even the thought of men pursuing her solely for her money made her shudder with dread. Then there was the unscrupulous lecher who had been trying to force her sister-in-law to marry him on the very night Eve and Colm met. Nell knew she would find even less determined ones difficult to fend off and she didn't understand how to do it without a fuss, as Eve had learned to during her rather trying three years as a single society lady with that same scandal hanging over her. Nell had spent most of her life in the company of women and girls, so how would it feel to be put on show for the poorer gentlemen of the *ton* to decide if they could endure marrying her for her money-bags? Appalling, she decided with another shudder and snapped back to the here and now with a sigh of relief.

'Are we going downstairs soon, Miss Court?' Penny asked. 'Mrs Winch will not be happy if you leave her to make sure that Caro and Georgie behave like proper young ladies in company.'

Nell shot a look at her own reflection in the small mirror. She was neat enough in a dark blue stuff gown and at least her hair had stayed in place. It took a legion of hairpins to keep it neat and she had no intention of making a special effort so that would have to do. Mr Moss would have to endure the sight of her everyday clothes. How silly to have a vision of dazzling him in a fine silk gown with her hair arranged to flatter instead of disguise her charms. Even if she had such a gown she wouldn't wear it for Lord Barberry's land steward.

'We had best hurry before they go down without us,' Nell said and braced herself for the ordeal ahead, wishing they could have nursery tea in the schoolroom and retire betimes instead of having to meet Mr Moss again today.

Before they went downstairs she had to make Georgiana remove the pins from her hair, then take off her late mama's second-best pearl necklace and do up the buttons of her gown all the way to the top. Drat him, but the man was disruption in breeches, she decided with a long-suffering sigh. As she plaited the girl's tawny mane neatly she tried not to be disturbed by the idea of dangerous adult company herself and sincerely hoped he was less intriguing by the light of several wax candles than he was in the dark.

Oh, confound the man, she decided when they finally got downstairs; he looked every inch the gentleman. How on earth did a lowly steward afford to have his coats made by a master tailor? Scott had crafted her brother's fine new coats and was a firm favourite with former military gentlemen. Perhaps Mr Moss had engaged Weston instead, but that midnight-blue superfine coat wasn't the work of a provincial tailor. Nor did his snowy linen and spotlessly sleek knee breeches seem quite right on the younger son of a country squire. Nell frowned as her charges meekly curtsied to him, rendered almost speechless with awe for a few brief moments as they took in the splendour of their unexpected guest. There was something very much out of kilter about a hired man appearing here in clothes that must have cost most of his annual salary before he had even begun to work for it.

'Good evening, sir,' Nell managed coolly, as all the reasons for his unexpected style clamoured in her head and she couldn't find one that didn't spell trouble. 'Miss Georgiana, Miss Caroline and Miss Penelope Selford, meet your guardian's new land steward, Mr Moss.'

'Good evening, ladies,' he replied with a courtly bow. Now thoroughly out of sorts, as she worried about the reasons Moss had left his last post, Nell had to whisper a sharp aside to Caro and Georgie before they remembered their manners and returned his greeting.

'You look very fine, sir,' Nell said as her eyes met his and he seemed to mock her conclusions some besotted lady had paid for her lover to appear every inch the gentleman in her company. She wished she had someone ready to whisper good conduct in *her* ears and tried hard to ignore a sharp pang that couldn't be jealousy. Why didn't she have the wit to invent a headache and excuse them all this supposedly quiet dinner with his lordship's new land agent?

'My godmama pays my tailor's bill once a year, so I can present a better appearance than a younger son is usually able to do,' he replied smoothly.

Nell looked for mockery in his acute blue eyes

and met bland innocence, but did she believe him? No, yet she could hardly challenge him in front of the girls. She gave him a polite, insincere smile and waved the girls to sit on a sofa the other side of the fire from their unexpected guest. She didn't approve of him looking so at home by his employer's fireside, but the Earl didn't want it, so she had no real reason to object. If he took advantage she would deal with him in private, but she suspected he was far too subtle a man to do anything so obvious.

'Were you waiting for your new clothes to arrive before you came?' Penny asked innocently. Nell was ready to rebuke her, but Mr Moss shook his head and smiled at her youngest pupil.

'A land steward needs gaiters and homespun more than a fine coat and expensive boots, Miss Penelope, but the Earl had another use for me so I did as I was bid. I hope my workaday clothes turn up on the carrier's cart soon, because I certainly can't ride about the countryside in my town finery if I wish to be taken seriously as Lord Barberry's steward,' he said.

Nell hoped the girls didn't notice his mocking look in her direction, as if he'd read every doubt in her mind about that tall tale. He could have as many lovers as he needed to keep him in style, so long as he didn't impart his dubious morals to her pupils, she concluded, with a militant frown he ignored with annoying ease.

'That would be sensible, considering the dire spring we have endured so far,' she agreed as if she almost believed in his doting godmother instead of a foolish lover.

'I promise to be ill dressed and muddy next time we meet, ma'am. You Misses Selford have a very conscientious governess. I doubt you get away with putting a foot wrong without her knowing about it almost before you do.'

'Miss Court is kind and looks after us very well,' Penny said loyally.

Even Caroline nodded and Georgiana looked as if she was disappointed in him and Nell would have hugged them all if he wasn't looking.

'I'm sure she does all a good governess should,' he approved with a sly smile Nell didn't trust one bit.

'Thank you, Mr Moss,' she said calmly, although it sounded more of a challenge than a compliment. 'I do my best.'

'And who can ask for more?' he asked and she wasn't sure she could endure much more of being laughed at by an estate manager who looked more like a society rake without telling him exactly what she thought of him.

She couldn't do anything of the sort, but his questionable standards of behaviour felt like a betrayal and what was between them for him to betray? Nothing; she was Miss Hancourt and he the son of a country squire with a living to earn and never mind any side benefits he had fitted in along the way.

'I feel quite famished tonight,' Caro said quietly.

Nell was concerned enough about her least gar-rulous pupil to look for signs of girlish infatua-tion in her eyes. No, from the spark of anger when she eyed the man warily, Caro was trying to stop this exotic newcomer mocking her governess. It warmed Nell's heart to think shy Caro wanted to defend her from this puzzling stranger.

'I expect dinner will be served as soon as Mrs Winch is able to join us,' she said with a fond smile at Caro to say she was excused the minor faux pas of admitting to hunger in public.

'Lavinia will be very sharp set by morning,' Penny said cheerfully.

'I asked Cook to make something cold for her to eat if she wakes up hungry,' Nell said with a slight frown at her youngest pupil to warn her not to gloat about Lavinia's exhausting bout of tears.

'Good, because she really can't help it,' Georgiana said earnestly.

'I know, Georgiana, and I'm sure Penelope will forget what her eldest cousin said in the heat of temper, especially if she wishes to take dinner with us tonight,' Nell said firmly.

'She said...'

'There are faults on all sides,' Nell pointed out. 'Your cousins were rude to each other and the slate is clean now, unless you would like to do penance for your own hot words and uncaring sentiments?'

'No,' Penny said with a sidelong look at her cousins to confirm she would be an idiot to work out a grudge against Lavinia when the alternative was dinner and far more exciting company than usual.

'Miss Court the peacemaker, who would have

thought it?' the company said as if he had every right to pass judgement on her.

'And Mr Moss, the peace breaker, what of him?' she replied so quietly the girls couldn't hear when she crossed the room to find Parkins and get him to tell Mrs Winch dinner was overdue. The lady's services as chaperon to her and her pupils felt more important than whatever was delaying her and the sooner this meal was over the better.

'Oh, him. He's a rascal,' Moss murmured when she was on her way back to the stiff-backed chair as far away from him as she could get and still feel warmth from the fire. She had taken it because she disliked him, she reassured herself, and gave a little nod of confirmation she hoped he'd take so badly he wouldn't tease her again.

The girls needed practice at polite dining and proper topics of conversation when gentlemen were present and she would usually admit she needed more adult company. As a single lady who might end up alone and at her last prayers, the whole neighbourhood would assume Miss Court was doing her best to marry any spare bachelor who came along. No doubt everyone in the area would assume she was intent on catching the wretch now he'd turned out to be vigorous and well looking. The thought of speculative eyes watching them at church every Sunday made her shudder. The last thing she intended to do was break her heart over Moss and she doubted he had one to break if she was so inclined. She would stick to the schoolroom or wait for the paragon who might inspire even half the love and passion in her as her brother Colm and his new wife Eve had for one another.

In public the newlyweds acted like a very proper young couple. There was no sitting gazing into each other's eyes and sighing for a bed and just a bit more privacy for them. Yet they showed how much they loved each other by small glances and little touches. One always knew where the other was without having to watch every little movement and, whereas most people grew heavy eyed and weary the later it got in the day, those two glowed with delicious anticipation of being alone again at last. Nell had never seen two people so silently and discreetly delighted at the idea of being wrapped up in the night when nobody else would expect them to be polite for a few precious hours.

Something told her Moss would never let his

cynical detachment drop long enough to allow a female that far into his life. What would she find if he did offer to share it with her? A hardened heart and calculating mind? Or perhaps, a protected heart—because he had such a tender, ardent spirit under all that cynicism? *And look where misplaced love got your late father*, Nell reminded herself, resolving to get on with real life before it got out of control.

A suitably bland topic of conversation eluded her. She doubted Mr Moss would let the mild amusement of speculating who the new rector of Great Berry might be run for long. It was impolite to wonder who was up or down in local society when he didn't know them; which left the state of the nation or the arts. Nell opted for the latter until Mrs Winch finally tore herself away from other duties and they could go in to dinner and get this difficult evening over with the sooner.

'I'm so sorry,' Mrs Winch said breathlessly as she hurried into the room a few minutes later. 'One of the maids has managed to scald herself *and* tip half the fish course on the floor,' she murmured in Nell's ear before greeting their guest graciously and signalling to Parkins it was time to announce dinner was served.

Nell hoped that part of the meal went to the pigs, however spotless the kitchen floor was before it fell. And what would Moss make of the simple dishes they were used to in the Earl's absence? The girls were too young for elaborate sauces and the clever touches of a French chef and Nell and Mrs Winch were happy with Cook's beautifully cooked but simple meals. If the man usually took his dinner in the sort of company his evening attire indicated he must, he'd be disappointed. He seemed to enjoy it though, so perhaps he really was a simple man in dandy's clothing. If so, his godmother's folly in outfitting him so splendidly was no kindness when he must earn his own bread. Why, he could sit down to dinner with the Earl and not be outshone and what a mistake that would be in an underling.

How had she got from hoping her food had never been on the floor to worrying about the social niceties of Moss's wardrobe? The man was old enough to look after himself and if he chose to ride around the country fine as fivepence or dressed in the meanest homespun it wouldn't matter to her.

'Surely a fine novel can outshine the shady reputation of its kind, Mrs Winch?' she intervened in the conversation she had started earlier, before Georgiana could recite a list of those she had read and enjoyed. That might reveal the fact Nell had allowed her to read books many would consider unsuitable for a young girl.

'A fine novel might, but the occasional triumphs are lost in the morass of sensation and fantasy,' Moss answered before the worthy but upright lady could condemn the whole genre and Georgiana might argue hotly for her most-loved examples and let out their secrets. 'I have neither the time nor patience to work my way through stacks of three-decker novels to find the occasional gem. Poetry and plays are an established form and I can trust time to sieve out the worst and keep the best of them,' he added as if dropping stones into a pond just for the pleasure of making ripples.

'Some might say that makes you a lazy reader, sir, but I hope you will concede that Dean Swift and Mr Defoe tower above their imitators,' Nell argued because she couldn't seem to help herself.

'I grant you those excellent examples, ma'am, and Sir Henry Fielding's works, although these young ladies must be ignorant of all but *Amelia* now society thinks the rest improper, which says more about society than Sir Henry if you ask me.'

Hiding a smile as Mrs Winch tried to decide if she should argue, Nell shot Georgiana a warning look. It had seemed a good idea to let her read *The History of Tom Jones* as well as *Amelia* at the time, to show her the world wasn't always kind to an innocent abroad. Luckily Lavinia had no interest in any but the popular novels Moss was being so scathing about, so Nell needn't worry she would let Mr Jones's name out unwarily. Caro was worried enough about what lay outside the gates of Berry Brampton House not to burden her with such vivid misadventures.

Luckily talk soon moved on and Nell could relax while they argued for this or that favourite poem. It was a chance to listen instead of having to instruct her pupils. The elder girls seemed much like any on the verge of womanhood and, considering what a pair of hostile little savages they were when she'd arrived here, Nell was proud of them. Penny was confident enough to sit and listen when she had nothing to say, but Nell couldn't rest on her laurels. Even Penny would soon feel the changes in mind and body that transformed little girls into women. The others were well launched on that stage when Nell arrived and she tried not to shudder at the memory.

For once Mr Moss was a welcome diversion. He was a strong man, she decided after a few furtive glances at him to take in what the shadows hid earlier, long-limbed and oddly graceful, despite his air of suppressed energy and to-hell-with-you manner. Something about him recalled Lavinia for an instant, but she looked again and thought it was a trick of the light. They both had intensely blue eyes, but he was dark as the devil and Lavinia was fair and the shape of their faces were quite different.

And what did an almost-handsome man think of the governess? That she was a middling sort of person and quite unremarkable, she concluded. Her once angelically fair locks were halfway between gold and brown and her eyes were plain brown. She was neither tall nor short and even at seventeen Lavinia outdid her in womanly curves. All Mr Moss's worst fears must be realised by candlelight, not that it mattered; once he settled into the agent's house he'd be in such demand among local society they would not meet except by chance.

It was no small thing to be land steward to the Berry Brampton Estate and, as the Earl did not live here, some of his status would fall on Mr Moss. Genteel young ladies would badger their fathers and brothers to call and invite him to dinner or an informal party so he'd soon be too busy charming the local beauties to dine with four unfledged young ladies, their plain governess and Mrs Winch. The Selford cousins were above his touch and Nell beneath it. What if he wasn't Mr Moss and she wasn't Miss Court, though? With a fortune like hers he could buy his own estate to manage. Revolted at the idea of being courted for her money, Nell decided if she ever married it would be to a man who loved her for herself. She came out of her daydream to find the others all but done with their meal and Mrs Winch more than ready for a cup of tea and half an hour nodding by the fire.

'Parkins will bring in the port, Mr Moss,' the lady said. 'It's time we left you to it and Miss Penelope looks half-asleep and ready to say goodnight.'

'It is early for the other young ladies to retire, don't you think, ma'am?' he said as if he was the master here and not his man.

He must have seen Caro's wry grimace at the thought of another early night and Nell couldn't let herself be charmed that he seemed to be trying to save Caro and Georgiana from dull routine. It seemed a simple act of kindness, but was anything about him truly simple?

'Mrs Crombie is waiting to take Miss Penny up, Miss Court,' Parkins told her when he came in with the decanters, treading the fine line between housekeeper and governess with his usual impassive gloom.

'Are you happy to take that sleepy head of yours up to bed?' Nell whispered to her smallest charge.

Penny nodded and smothered another yawn behind her hand. 'I'm half-asleep,' the girl said with a smile that won Nell's heart anew. 'I know you must stay and help chaperon Caro and Georgie, so goodnight, Miss Court. Goodnight, Mr Moss,' she said with a curtsy to gladden any governess's heart. She kissed Nell, wished her cousins goodnight and seemed likely to tumble into bed and sleep as soon as she was undressed.

Chapter Four

Fergus watched pupil and teacher bid each other goodnight. The dragon seemed almost soft-hearted so perhaps Poulson wasn't as far abroad in his judgement as he'd first thought. Of course, she was still too young for the post and two years ago could hardly have been long out of the schoolroom herself. Take away the spotless wisp of lawn and lace perched on her shining golden-brown curls and he could take ten years off the ones he'd first put in her dish. Her assured manner and limited patience fooled him at the time, but a very different person was revealed by candlelight. This Miss Court might pretend to be at her last prayers, but her mouth gave her away. It was less certain than he imagined when he met her in the gloomy stables. The young lady under the front of a no-nonsense governess had soft and expressive lips to go with her pert nose and brown-velvet eyes. Miss Court was a shade under the average height for a woman and slim as a whip, with the sort of slender yet intriguing womanly curves even a blue stuff gown made high to the neck couldn't quite conceal. A connoisseur of feminine beauty might not rank her a diamond of the first water, but she would be very pretty if she threw away that dire gown and ridiculous cap. It wasn't right to long to discover the vulnerable and generous woman under her would-be stern exterior. He usually liked his lovers buxom and bold and wished his mistress was nearby to visit when the need arose, because it might arise right now if he wasn't very careful where his thoughts wandered in Miss Court's presence.

'I promise to restrict myself to one glass, ladies,' he said as Mrs Winch and her chicks rose, looking uncertain about this whole enterprise. As well they might, he told himself sternly. He blinked away a vision of the lovely young woman under Miss Court's armour and stood up politely.

'Very well, Mr Moss, we shall see you shortly,' Mrs Winch said.

He caught a sceptical governess look from him

to decanter and was tempted to live down to Miss Court's low expectations and get roaring drunk before he staggered into his smallest drawing room and gave himself away as the owner of all this faded glory. He wasn't prepared to do that, he decided, and if the truth ever came out he must remember to thank the starchy female for the disguise she'd thrust on him, because he wasn't sure he wanted to be 'my lord' now he was here. His grandfather might have found the vast portrait of a Cavalier ancestor and family an aid to good digestion, but he did not. The Baron Selford portrayed so skilfully had an arrogance that must have had recruits rushing to join the Parliamentarian Army in order to escape his tyranny. A master painter had caught hints of rebellion in the man's son and heir and a sidelong glance from the old lord's lady said she didn't blame her eldest one for wondering if he wanted to die for the same cause.

God forbid any child of his would ever look at him with such cool dislike in his eyes. If it wasn't for his uneasy conscience about shirking his duty as Earl of Barberry for so long, he'd turn tail and catch the next tide to Ireland and his stepfather's comfortable home. No, he had a chance to observe his estate and mansion as he never would in his own shoes. He girded Mr Moss's loins and took him back to the Small Drawing Room by proxy.

'Do continue, Miss Caroline,' Fergus said as the piano playing stopped the instant he pushed opened the door. 'I am very fond of Herr Mozart's sonatas, at least when they are played with such a delicate touch,' he added and the obviously very shy girl smiled and carried on.

He had expected his cousins to be haughty and aloof, but they were brighter and more thoughtful than most of their kind, which he put down to their own spirit and Miss Court's influence. According to Poulson's reports, the laziness of a junior partner he had dismissed the moment he found out how negligent he'd been meant these girls had had little real guidance before their young governess arrived to try and bring sense, order and a little compassion into their lives. Once more he found himself oddly drawn to the young woman who sat as far away from him as she could. The sooner he was installed in the land steward's house and busy about the estate the better. Miss Court and Mrs Winch had his wards and his house in order and it was high time he could say the same for the land, and that would keep him out of Miss Court's way until it was time to go away again or reveal his true identity.

'Do you think Mr Moss will like the steward's house, Miss Court?' Caro asked Nell sleepily as they finally went upstairs, at long last.

'I'm sure he will and he can't stay here with us. That would be dreadfully improper in the Earl's absence, or even with it now I come to think about it. For either gentleman to move into Berry Brampton, we would have to leave.'

'I suppose so, but it's such a long time since Mr Jenks decided to retire and live with his daughter. I know the house was cleared out and dusted when we were told a new steward was coming, but that was weeks ago. The whole house could be damp after this dreadful weather and all sorts of things might have happened while it was lying empty, don't you think?'

'Not if I can help it,' Nell said with a weary sigh. 'If Mr Moss couldn't send a message to warn us he was coming, at long last, he must accept the fact his house needs airing before it is quite comfortable. Mrs Winch will have kept an eye on the place, so I doubt it will be as difficult to sleep there as you imagine. Mr Moss will not find the land in good heart, though. I suppose I should have found a discreet way to let his lordship know how bad things were before Mr Jenks admitted his sight was failing and left.'

'Oh, no, Miss Court, Jenks said he owed it to Grandfather to carry on managing the estate and he was so loyal to the family we couldn't betray him, could we? He has such old-fashioned ideas—perhaps it's as well Jenks had to go all the way to Yorkshire to live with his daughter so he can't argue with everything Mr Moss wants to do,' Georgiana said with a wise nod that left Nell trying not to smile at her unusual interest in estate management.

Georgiana enjoyed a combative relationship with the local squire's eldest son. One day it might grow into something more and Nell thought them well matched. Persuading Lord Barberry that the heir of a mere squire would make a good husband for one of his wards would be a challenge, but not one she need worry about now Georgiana was fifteen and the lad a year older.

'Yorkshire is not so very far away,' she teased

gently as she urged the sisters upstairs to the modest room they insisted on sharing, despite the many splendid bedchambers in this grand old house.

'It is as far as Mr Jenks is concerned,' Caro put in and smiled her thanks when Nell loosened her laces and helped her out of her simple round gown, then began brushing Caro's thick blonde locks while their maid undid Georgiana's gown.

'You can't help wondering why he agreed to go there in the first place though, can you?' Georgiana observed with a frown and Nell wondered if it was odd that the man had finally left in such a hurry.

'The love of family can lead us to the most unexpected places,' Nell said with a shrug and a last look around. Becky had everything in hand and her charges looked so tired they should sleep soundly. Wishing them all a good night, she went to check on Lavinia and found Mary nodding in the dressing room.

'Miss Lavinia hasn't stirred all evening, miss. I've never known her so quiet or so little trouble,' the maid admitted sheepishly.

'You might as well go to bed now, Mary. If Miss

Lavinia was going to take a chill, we would know by now and no doubt you'll hear if she wakes up and needs you in the night,' Nell told the maid with a nod at the truckle bed already set up in the narrow little room for her to sleep in and still be close if Lavinia needed her.

'Thank you, miss,' the young maid said dutifully.

Nell wondered why nobody found it odd Mary was Lavinia's age and yet a maid had to be far more sensible and self-disciplined than the girl she was employed to wait on. 'This isn't a fair world,' she murmured when she shut the door on her responsibilities for the night. 'You ought to know that by now.'

She was only three and twenty herself and had taken responsibility for four young girls when she was barely of age. Looking back, she wondered why Mr Poulson picked her from the list of mature and experienced applicants for this job and decided it could only be because she wasn't either of those things. Add Miss Thibett's hard-won praise for Nell's five years spent as a pupil teacher at her school and she supposed Mr Poulson thought she would understand her charges better and perhaps grow up with them. She recalled her giddy, schoolgirlish rush of excitement when she'd met Mr Moss's deceptive blue eyes for the first time tonight and wondered if it might not be better if she knew a little more about men and their odd quirks and unlikely preoccupations.

Nell had grown up apart from her brother and she wondered why aristocratic gentlemen were so harsh with dependent children as she recalled the servants' gossip about how little time the last Earl of Barberry had for his female grandchildren. Her uncle certainly didn't have any for her. Parting her and Colm when her brother was old enough to be sent to school at eight years old was cruel. The more she pleaded with her uncle for one holiday a year or even Christmas together, the less he was inclined to grant them even a day. The memory of being desperately lonely in her late uncle's house made her shudder even now. She'd cried herself to sleep for months after Colm had gone away and memories of how it felt to be alone and unwanted in an echoing house was one reason she'd agreed to apply for this job when Miss Thibett suggested she should. The thought of four lonely and aban- doned girls got her here when Mr Poulson chose her for the post of their governess and memories of being unwanted by her own family made her grit her teeth and stay, although she wanted to run as far and as fast as her legs would carry her as soon as she met Lavinia's hostile glare and re-alised the younger Selford cousins took their cue from her and had very good glares of their own.

Was she sorry she had stayed now? It had taken months of patience to wear their hostility down, but she truly wanted the best for them. She re-called the feel of poor Lavinia sobbing in her arms and letting out so much pent-up unhappiness and at least she understood her a little better now. If she didn't have responsibility for these lonely girls she might have agreed to join Colm and Eve for the coming Season in London, though. Maybe there she would have found a gentleman quiet and steady enough to marry and make the family she'd always longed for with. Oddly enough an image of Moss interrupted her daydream and mocked her with a cynical smile. He might be right, if he was actually here and knew what went on in her head, because by the side of him her paragon did sound dreadfully dull.

With thoughts like that jostling about in her

head wasn't it just as well she wasn't about to join the polite world as Miss Hancourt, heiress and elderly debutante? She stared into a mirror softly lit by the candle in the nightstick. Imagining what the so-called polite world would say about her behind her back made her shiver. They would laugh and call her a quiz, she decided, and glared into her looking glass as if they were already on the other side being airily amused by her.

Her father was wild Lord Chris Hancourt, lover of the most notorious woman of her generation and her partner in reckless death when they'd raced to a party in a land at war with Britain. What would Moss make of her shady history if the truth came out? Never mind him, the Earl of Barberry would dismiss her, heiress or not. The mud that stuck to her father's name would finish his daughter's career as guide and mentor to young girls. She hated the thought of all the snide whispers that would do the rounds wherever she went if she did as her family wanted her to and tried to ignore them for a Season.

In a decade or so, when Penny was old enough to be presented as the last of the beautiful Selford orphans, it might be time to consider what she would do with the rest of her life, but until then she had a job to do. Nell unpinned her flimsy cap, managed to unlace her dull blue gown without the aid of a maid and sat at the dressing table to unpin her hair and brush it the vast number of times Miss Thibett had always insisted on to transform it into a shining, silken mass that fell heavily about her shoulders and reached as far as her waist.

Was this the true Nell at the heart of Miss Court's dreary plumage? The girl looking back at her seemed far too young to be the guide and protector of four vulnerable young ladies. She looked too uncertain to resist the charm and experience of a gentleman who wasn't anywhere near as humble as the third son of a country squire ought to be. Her brown eyes were soft and dreamy as she stopped brushing and felt the silky thickness of those tawny waves tumbling around her like a shining cape. Her workaday locks felt sensuous and heavy and a little bit wicked against her shift, as if a lover might loom out of the soft shadows of this familiar room and run his hand over the silken ripple of it at any moment, then whisper impossible things in her eagerly listening ears.

Nell shivered, but it wasn't from cold; the hand she pictured adoring and weaving a sensuous path through her thick pelt of shining hair to find the woman underneath was firm and muscular, but gentle and a little bit reverent. The owner of that hand was intent on her, his blue eyes hot as he watched the way her creamy skin looked through fine lawn and a veil of glossy golden-brown hair that didn't feel ordinary any more. As she went breathless with anticipation his touch would get firmer and his gaze even more intent and wickedly sure she was ready for more.

No, here she sat, shivering with hot nerves and anticipation—like the caricature of a frustrated, dried-up spinster governess, longing for a lover in every personable man she met and never finding one to watch her with heat-hazed eyes as he stepped into her dreams and took them over. Nell snapped her eyes shut, squeezing her eyelids so tight it almost hurt. Then she took up her comb to part her heavy locks, ready to make plaits for the night ahead and forget imaginary lovers of any sort. She swiftly wound it into two thick tails of hair without looking at herself in the mirror, her fingers deft and driven to tighten the silky mass as her thoughts raced. Argh, but that hurt. She couldn't sleep with hair that pulled at her scalp like a harsh saint's scourge for sinful thoughts. She must begin again and pay attention to what her fingers were up to this time. That was it, her hair was tied easily enough for sleep and just tight enough to remind her to sin no more, even in her dreams.

Now for her formidably proper nightgown. Plain and buttoned sternly to the neck, made up from warm and practical flannel, it was a garment without a hint of sensuality. Let anyone find a hint of seductress in such a respectable get-up and she'd shout her true identity from the rooftops. She gave herself a severe nod, knelt to say her prayers and begged to be delivered from such silly fantasies, then got into bed. Staring into the night, she ordered herself not to dream of dark-haired, piratical gentlemen who could raise such silly fantasies in a spinster's heart without even trying as she snuffed her candle and hoped for quiet sleep against the odds.

In a faded corner of the great city of London another member of the nobility was finding it impossible to sleep. 'Thought I'd never get away from the jackals, Lexie,' Lord Derneley told his wife as he settled into a grim corner of a wine cellar in this rotten old house on the Strand with a sigh of relief. It might not be much for a man born to splendour and great wealth, but at least it wasn't the Fleet Prison.

'So did I, my love,' she whispered back, as if their creditors might manage to hear them even down here if she wasn't very careful. 'Lucky for us that my Aunt Horseforth is such a misery nobody will believe you're here. I think she expects me to be an unpaid companion and skivvy for the rest of my life,' she added gloomily.

'She's a dour old trout, but it's the only port we have in a storm. At least everyone knows she can't abide me and wouldn't have me in her house if she knew I was here. I could always come out of hiding and scare her into an apoplexy.'

'No, no, Derneley, don't do that. Her grandson will come down from Scotland and put me out on the street before she's cold if you do and you'll starve to death down here without me. There's nowhere else for us to go now the creditors are after you as if you murdered someone instead of taking their horrid loans when we ran out of things to sell. Heaven knows I got nothing but snubs and refusals to acknowledge they even knew me for my pains when I tried to visit my friends,' she said mournfully and even her selfish, careless lord looked humble and almost defeated for a moment, before his true nature reasserted itself.

'Have you found anything worth selling yet?'

'No, her grandson's man of business has everything locked up that isn't already in the bank. He doesn't trust me,' she said, sounding very put out.

'If we could only lay hands on a few hundred guineas we can slope off to Italy and at least be warm while we think what we're going to do next. Right now I can't even afford a decent bottle of wine, for if there were ever any in here someone drank it years ago.'

'If only Lord Chris hadn't deceived poor Pamela so badly we'd have all the Lambury Jewels in our possession now and none of this would have happened.'

'Except if he wasn't dead she wouldn't be either and if you think we'd have got a single jewel out of her, you're more of a fool than I thought. Chris was a lot more cunning than we gave him credit for being once she'd got him under her spell though, wasn't he?' Lord Derneley sounded almost admiring for a moment. 'Who would have thought he'd be able to palm her off with paste versions of the emerald and sapphire sets after she had the rubies tested to make sure they were real the moment he handed them over.'

'Everyone said the rubies were cursed and it turned out to be true, didn't it? My poor sister was dead within six months of wheedling the wretched things out of him. And he never even pretended to hand over his wife's diamonds to her, so he must have put them somewhere for that horrid little girl to find.'

'We could make far better use of them,' her lord said thoughtfully, 'but nobody said a word about the Lambury Jewels turning up when young Hancourt came into that blind trust thing, did they? You could be on to something, Lex,' he added and his wife stared at him in wonder.

'You mean *we* could find them?' she said.

'I daren't show my face, but that tough your sister used to play with when Chris wasn't looking might track them down for you if we promise to share.'

'No, he's dead and I was too frightened of him to go anywhere near him if he wasn't. I might be stuck upstairs waiting on my nip-cheese aunt most of the time, but I suppose I could find out when they were last seen if I get her talking about the old days long enough, but are you sure we'll be able to find them, my love?'

'Why not? And we have nothing to lose, do we?'

'No, we've already lost it,' her ladyship said gloomily, the fabulous wealth her lord inherited the day he came of age seeming to haunt her for a moment. 'They only let me leave Derneley House in what I stood up in *and* they searched me for anything valuable before they even let me do that,' she remembered mournfully.

'You can keep a ring and one of the small neck-lets when we sell the rest,' her lord said almost generously.

'Thank you, my love,' she said meekly.

'Hmm, it might work, but Hancourt's too tough a customer for us to get anything out of him and he knows us too well.'

'Yes, and he must be dangerous with all those scars and fighting in all the battles he survived when Gus Hancourt sent him off to be killed in the army,' her ladyship said matter of factly, as if she saw nothing very wrong in the late Duke of Linaire's heartless scheming to gain his nephew's fortune.

'Cunning as well—think how he deceived us. He was only a secretary when he came to Derneley House to take my father's books away. He must be hiding that sister of his somewhere though, because she certainly ain't doing the Season, is she?'

'No, I would have heard. Aunt Horseforth may not go out much, but she corresponds with half the old dowagers of the *ton*.'

'I dare say the Hancourt wench is as plain as her mother was then, or he'd have insisted she came to town by now.'

'I wish Pamela never met their father, but she and Chris would have had far more beautiful children together if he'd been able to marry her.'

'You're the aunt of the wench Hancourt married though, ain't you? You must call at Linaire House when she and Hancourt get back from the north and make sure he feels a pressing need to write to his sister. That way we'll be able to find out her address and somehow get her to lead us to the jewels. Chris must have realised how plain she would turn out to be and he knew a man needs a good reason to wed an antidote. Lady Chris could never have hooked the son of a duke without the Lambury Jewels and the old man Lambury's fortune as bait. The diamonds would set us up nicely and the old man gave them to Chris's wife after the marriage, so they weren't part of the settlements and he could leave them to his daughter if he wanted to.'

'You're so clever, Derneley,' his wife said with an admiring sigh. 'I can't imagine how I'm to make that horrid boy of Chris's so worried he'll give her address away by writing to her, though.'

'Oh, really, Lex, do I have to think of everything?' her lord said sleepily and waved her away so he could sleep after a strenuous day of escaping his creditors and looking for new money to waste.

Chapter Five

'Oh, do stop the carriage, Binley!' Georgiana shouted before Nell could check her. 'Good morning, Mr Moss.'

Nell managed a sickly smile for the man who had been haunting her dreams.

'Good morning, Miss Georgiana, Miss Court,' he said politely.

'But we are keeping you standing in the rain, Mr Moss,' Nell said in the hope he'd agree and hurry on without further ado.

'A mere drizzle, Miss Court. We land stewards have to accustom ourselves to the whims of the English weather.'

Now why did she think he was mocking himself as much as her this time? 'All the same it is another cold and dreary day—can we take you up as far as Brampton Village?' she offered as politely as she could manage when she didn't want to be shut in a closed carriage with him even for that long.

'That is very kind, ma'am. My horse is being re-shod so it will save me a half-hour's walk to collect him from the forge,' the man said cheerfully and Nell bit back a protest she was being polite and didn't mean it.

At least he sat with his back to the horses, but that meant she must look at him instead of feeling his muscular male limbs next to her and it was only marginally better. He had acquired more suitable clothes in the three days since he appeared out of the night to plague her. In practical leathers and countryman's boots and coat he should be quite unremarkable, but somehow he was nothing of the sort. His linen was spotless and his plain waistcoat was cut by a master, but it wasn't his clothes that made him stand out, it was the man underneath them. His masculine vitality seemed almost too big for a confined space and Nell felt she couldn't even breathe without taking in more of him than she wanted to. And she didn't want to, did she? Her doubts about that had been creeping into her dreams. Every morning she had to tell herself they were nightmares when she woke up with those fading rags of unthinkably erotic fantasies shaming her waking hours. How was she to look him in the face with the thought of them plaguing her with impossible things?

'The others are sewing with Mrs Winch this morning,' Georgiana informed him happily. 'I share Maria Welland's music lessons and Miss Court comes with me to have tea and a comfortable coze with Maria's Miss Tweed while our teacher shouts at us in French.'

'You unlucky creatures, no wonder the other Misses Selford prefer their embroidery frames.'

'Lavinia has no ear for music; Madame says she would rather—'

'Never mind her exact words, Georgiana,' Nell interrupted hastily, having overheard the lady's agonies before she'd declared Georgiana the only Selford girl with even the suggestion of a voice and refused to hear the others sing ever again.

'I was only going to say she would rather teach cats to sing than Lavinia, Miss Court,' Georgiana said with such mischief in her eyes that Nell would usually have to laugh, except she refused to do so in front of Mr Moss.

'Well, don't,' she said crossly instead. 'Lavinia can't help being about as unmusical as possible without being tone deaf.'

'I know and she does embroider exquisitely,' Georgiana admitted. 'She can paint far better than the rest of us as well. But that's why we're out and about on our own this morning, Mr Moss,' she went on with an expectant look at him that said it was his turn to recite a list of engagements for the day.

'I am engaged to meet several of your guardian's tenant farmers at the market in Temple Barberry, so I shall have to hurry there as soon as my horse has his new shoe, Miss Georgiana,' he replied obediently.

Contrarily, Nell felt excluded as they chatted about the market and how most farmers were gloomy about prospects for the harvest, whatever the weather. They conceded this was a very peculiar spring and this time they were right to be pessimistic. Being brought up in London, and then Bath, Nell had had to learn even to *like* the countryside when she first came here and she was the first to admit she didn't know its ways and habits as well as her pupils. She felt like a town mouse as Georgiana and Mr Moss happily discussed the difficulty of sowing crops and getting them to grow when it was cold and the skies so grey nothing seemed likely to thrive. Sunshine was now needed to make it all work and Nell felt she might be withering for the lack of it herself by the time the carriage rolled into Brampton and pulled up at the smithy.

'You seem unnaturally quiet this morning, Miss Court,' Mr Moss observed as he gathered up his crop, hat and a leather case that must contain tenancy agreements or leases, or some such dry stuff it was as well not to be curious about.

'I have nothing to say, Mr Moss. I am an urban creature and know little of agriculture and country lore.'

'Then it was rude of me to bore you with them.'

'Not in the least, sir. I hope I can still listen and learn as well as hold forth about what I do know.'

'Then I shall send over one of the agricultural reports on this county for your further education, ma'am, since you want to know it better.'

'Only if you are not using it, sir,' she said coolly. She could imagine nothing more likely to send her to sleep so perhaps it would have its uses.

'Oh, no, I'm a quick study when a topic interests me and the state of land is important. I suppose that's one reason my wider family disapprove of me and mine,' he said, then seemed to regret his frankness and his expression was closed and formal as he jumped down and gave them a fine bow, before waving goodbye to Georgiana and nodding stiffly at Nell as the carriage drove past on its way to the Wellands' manor house. Why would a country squire regard his interest in the land as undesirable? Mr Moss might not be able to inherit the family acres, but not all younger sons were destined for the army, the navy or the church. Becoming a land steward was a perfectly respectable ambition in a gentleman of slender means. On a large estate like Berry Brampton the position was often filled by a junior line of the family who owned it. So why was Mr Moss so defensive about his chosen way of life?

By the time Brampton Village was behind them at least Georgiana had stopped speculating about Mr Moss and the reception he would get from the notoriously close-mouthed farming community, so that was a relief, wasn't it? Hearing her most lively pupil shift her attention from the steward to what her friend Maria might have been about since they last met might make her head spin, but Miss Welland's sayings and doings were a much safer subject and she let her pupil chatter on unchecked. It didn't matter how well or badly the man got on with his family, he was here, at last, and Nell hoped the injustices and oddities Jenks had closed his eyes to on the estate would come to an end. Anyway, she could hardly condemn Moss for being so late to take up his post when she had deserted hers twice in the last year. Governess or not, responsible for the girls as she was with no resident guardian to look out for them when she was gone, nothing could have stopped Nell finding her brother after Waterloo and, six months later, attending his wedding to the love of his life. It had been a joyous marriage ceremony, despite the time of year and the rough weather and terrible roads. At last Colm had looked as joyous and carefree as a man of his age, birth and fortune ought to when he stood up so proudly to wed his unexpected bride. The last marriage in the world anyone would have predicted for the children of the Hancourt–Winterley scandal and there they both were, as shiningly happy as any couple Nell had ever met. It felt strange coming back here from Darkmere Castle and those bright celebrations to be Miss Court again and pretend nothing had changed. Until Mr Moss arrived she'd been plagued by a feeling this world seemed dangerously unstable after the bustle and common purpose in Lord Winterley's northern heartland. If she left Berry Brampton House as her brother and sister-in-law wanted her to, what would become of the girls? Without a competent manager, the estate had been like a rudderless ship in these hard times. The war was over, but the whole country sometimes seemed about to plunge into chaos as they floundered from one crisis to the next. Now her worry about the lack of a strong man to keep all steady here was gone, she realised how uneasy she'd been before he arrived.

Mr Moss was an unlikely protector of a pack of schoolgirls, but he would still do it if he had to. The footmen and butler were tall and strong and the formidably respectable Mrs Winch gave the household gravitas, but nobody else had the status of my lord's land steward. She didn't have to like him for it, though. He had sat opposite her and talked to Georgiana of matters she didn't understand, then offered to lend her a book. Well, she'd read the dratted thing if that would stop him doing it again. As for that habit he had of calling her *ma'am*—there might be more exasperating ways to address a lady not yet four and twenty, but she couldn't currently think of any.

'Mr Moss was right; you are quiet today, Miss Court. Do you have the headache?' Georgiana asked as the carriage turned towards the next village and the Wellands' neat manor house.

Not yet, Nell thought, *but I soon will have if I brood about the impossible man for much longer.* 'No, but I couldn't get a word in when you two were chattering nineteen to the dozen.'

'Papa always said my tongue ran on wheels when we were little...' She paused and looked out of the small carriage windows at the dull grey sky before sighing heavily. 'I know I was only a child when he died, Miss Court, and I was so lucky my parents loved me and Caro, but will I ever stop missing them, do you think?'

'Now that really is a hard question.'

'I know I shouldn't pry into the feelings of my

elders, since you told me so, but do *you* still miss your mama and papa?'

'At times; although my mama died when I was little more than a babe, so I don't really remember her, and my father was more often away from home than in it during the last few years of his life. I do still miss him though, yes. I found it very hard to be parted from my brother when he was sent to school as well, so I'm glad you and Caroline are together and can share your feelings as well as your memories. Lavinia and Penny love you both as well, however little they choose to show it at times. I suppose the pressure on the heir to produce a boy was so strong in your family that Lavinia has always felt herself at a disadvantage and she is unsure of herself and a little jealous of those who seem to be more fortunate.'

'I will remember that and try to make allowances, but you don't like to talk about yourself, do you, Miss Court?' Georgiana responded with a direct stare that made Nell feel she was the younger of them for once.

She had hoped nobody would notice her habit of turning the subject and not giving anything away about her past that she didn't have to, but

Georgiana was a lot more perceptive than most people realised. 'I'm not a very interesting topic,' she replied warily.

'Now there you are quite wrong, Miss Court. Mr Moss finds you as much of a mystery as we Selfords do. All the time we were talking about farmers and cows and fields at least half his attention was fixed on you.'

'No, it wasn't. He thinks me an antidote and was very happy to talk to you this morning instead of me, so please don't start imagining otherwise, Georgiana. Your matchmaking efforts are unwelcome at the best of times and Mr Moss would laugh himself hoarse if he could hear you now.'

'Which would be very ungentlemanly of him, don't you think? Although I doubt he would; he seems a kind man under that teasing manner of his.'

'I don't think we know him well enough to say if he is kindly or not yet, Georgiana, and if I did want more to do with the gentleman than I have to because we work for the same employer he'd be horrified. I doubt I ever came across a gentleman less likely to be in search of a wife than that one and I'm certainly not the woman to make him change his mind.'

'If only you would wear something that doesn't make you look centuries older than you truly are and throw away that silly cap, he'd soon make a liar of you. He's a single gentleman and you're an unattached lady; what would be so terrible about him taking an interest in you as a person instead of a governess, Miss Court?'

'The fact I have a job I enjoy, despite the occasional bouts of nonsense my pupils indulge in. It's impertinent of you to even ask that question as well and some governesses would punish you severely for it. I don't want to hear any more of such silly speculation from you or your sister and cousins on the subject and I have no desire to marry the man. Even if I did, neither of us earns enough to be comfortable if I had to stop work. I don't think your cousin, the Earl, would be pleased to hear you plotting to deprive him of one or other of us either, do you?'

'I suppose not, since he hasn't even bothered to meet us and, now his estate will be run as soundly as his house, he can stay away until we're ready to be married off. I dare say he'll come home the instant the last of us leave for London.'

'Lord Barberry will probably find himself a wife and need his grand home sooner than that, my dear. Penny is not ten years old and will not be marrying for another ten if I have anything to say about it.'

'You think eighteen is too young for a young lady to wed?'

'I think not many young ladies have seen enough of the world to know what marriage will entail by then. A woman should be able to love and trust a man before she commits all she is and can be to marriage and I hope you are mature enough to make an informed choice when the time comes.'

'You have little time for the Marriage Mart, then?' her pupil asked as if she was still more interested in Nell's future than her own.

There were odd little corners in all four of her young charges' hearts. Nell hoped against hope they would find happiness when they became part of the pairing off into brides and bridegrooms the *ton* organised for their young twice a year. 'I always thought that such a repellent term and hope you won't use it in public, but in private I admit there seems little difference between the sort of market Mr Moss is off to observe this morning and this habit of selling off well-bred young ladies to the highest bidder. Marriage is more than bargaining for titles or money and so many other things ought to be taken into consideration. I shudder to think how huge a shock it must be to innocent young things who end up married to a virtual stranger.'

'Me too, so don't worry, Miss Court; the Earl probably wants to marry us off as fast as he can, but I'm not minded to oblige him. Caro is quite stubborn under her quiet manner as well and we all know Penny has a mind of her own. Lavinia is the only one of us eager to wed in a hurry, but Lord Barberry will find the rest of us a much bigger challenge, if he ever bothers to meet us.'

'Best if he stays away perhaps, at least until you are old enough to argue for your chosen future.'

'True, so you had better keep sending him pages of boring reports on our excellent progress as pattern cards of dutiful obedience, Miss Court.'

'How did you know about…? Oh, you dreadful girl. Now you've made me admit I've been lying to the man since I stepped over his threshold.'

'Tut, tut, Miss Court, what a dreadful example to us Selford girls. No wonder we're going to disappoint our cousin when he finally deigns to meets us.'

'True, now all I need do is persuade Lavinia to frustrate him as well and perhaps the wretched man will sit up and take notice. If he bothered to come and meet you he'd soon realise you have feelings and hopes he has no right to trample over so he can be rid of his responsibility all the sooner,' Nell declared too forthrightly and was glad when they reached Welland House and she could stop her tongue saying outrageous things without permission from her sensible governess's brain.

Chapter Six

Fergus watched the carriage he had ordered from afar to make sure his wards travelled in comfort draw away and sighed at his own idiocy. Being here incognito had proved distinctly uncomfortable so far. He'd had no idea until he'd pretended to be Mr Moss how much he enjoyed the comfort he could expect as a gentleman of wealth and importance, even when he went under an alias. Instead of the best bedchamber of the best inn he had to endure an old-fashioned house with chimneys that smoked and windows that let in nearly as much chilly spring weather as they kept out. Not that he spent much time there, he supposed philosophically. His days were taken up with walking fields with his tenant farmers, inspecting tumbledown cottages and all the obligations Jenks had neglected. It was a wonder he wasn't in for re-shoeing instead of his horse, he decided, with a rueful glance at his once spotless and very expensive riding boots.

'He looks to be in fine fettle again,' he told the smith and enjoyed a genial argument over the slightly inflated price the fellow wanted to charge because Fergus was new to the area and might be fool enough to pay it.

Having won that battle, he reviewed the bigger ones he must fight before he left here, with or without admitting who he was, as he rode to Temple Brampton. So far his predecessor's failures as land steward seemed understandable, given old Jenks's failing eyesight and other infirmities. The man had lied about his age from the day Fergus inherited the estates, but he should have come here and judged it for himself. Jenks claimed to be not quite sixty when a report on this estate was made for the new Earl ten years ago, so he could have found the old rogue out years ago, if he wasn't still so sore about being the heir his family had moved heaven and earth to keep out of his grandfather's shoes. Jenks probably was capable of carrying on a decade ago, but why hadn't he admitted that he was failing sooner? Now Fergus had to undo all the abuses the old man was too weary to notice were happening under his nose and drag the whole estate into the current century.

He frowned at the horizon and hoped he recalled the route into the nearest town from the sketchy estate map his new housekeeper had found when she turned out the long-disused front parlour. Jenks used the framed map as a makeshift fire screen, but he knew the place like the back of his hand and had no need of it. Fergus sighed wearily and wondered if he would ever overcome the prejudices of his grandfather's tenants. At the moment he was too busy learning the differences between land here and land everywhere else and getting the estate back in proper order to confront them as his true self, but the sooner he found a suitable replacement for young Moss the better. At least then he could decide if he was ready to admit to being Earl of Barberry or not and stay or go as the fancy took him.

Which brought him back to the puzzle of the last ten years. He'd begun them a furious young lord with a burning need to put as much distance as possible between himself and Berry Brampton and all he was never supposed to inherit. Wrong and irresponsible of him to stay away, but he had been absorbed in his new life and all but forgot this other one for too long. His fascination with a new world kept luring him on to explore the Canadian wilderness until he was entangled in the lives of those who sought to tame or live with its trackless wildness.

He'd stayed too long and got caught up in a senseless war between the United States and Britain, so how could he slide out of Canada like a coward when both nations were fighting over it and the native tribes losing more than any people should? His mouth set in a bitter line as he thought of friends who'd lost homes and families and turned into killers. Now there was a ceasefire rather than peace he could mourn and celebrate a land he had come to love. During those ten years he had lived through many adventures; loved a wild and generous woman and lost her to a better man; then fought against men his instincts screamed should be comrades and not enemies. The whole war felt like brother fighting brother and soured the promise of the new world he'd fallen in love with as a rebellious and angry boy. He'd learned so much and spent those years living and loving and exploring as Mr Ford, a man of modest means, but a stern voice he'd tried to ignore had been whispering he should go home ever since he'd got there.

So what now, Fergus? Now you're here at last and still not your true self?

It wasn't quite home though, was it? he excused himself. His stepfather's rambling manor felt like his real one, but it would go to his half-brother Brendan one day. Fergus Selford had far grander houses and even more fertile acres to call his own. Yet the temptation to not quite commit himself to Berry Brampton and the life of an English nobleman had been too strong to resist when Miss Court offered him an easy alternative. Every day that went past showed him what a coward he had been that night and how far he was from calling this place home.

Then there were his wards to consider and how had he managed to close his eyes to their needs for so long? They were little more than babes when he'd turned his back on them as if him having to be the Earl of Barberry was their fault. He *was* the reason at least two of them existed though. Lavinia would never have been born if the true heir hadn't done something so reckless that he'd died in a hastily hushed-up scandal and her parents had reluctantly reunited to try to put him out of the succession and produced a daughter instead of the longed-for son and replacement heir. Fergus suspected Georgiana and Caroline's parents had made a love match, but from all accounts little Penny's birth was something of a wonder. Even in Ireland there were whispers that the old Earl's third son was not interested in the fair sex, yet the man wed some accommodating girl at his father's command then died before his child was born. The old lord hadn't been able to hang on to life long enough to be disappointed yet again, but silly, immature Fergus Selford had still walked away from a babe only days old when he left Britain, knowing he was the new Earl of Barberry after all and be damned to every Selford who thought he'd ever lusted after his grandfather's coronet.

Well, he could sit here on his fidgeting horse and feel more and more guilty about what he'd done and not done ten years ago, or do his best to get a true picture of all that needed to be done here before he admitted who he really was and got on with doing it. The past was done with, now he must get on with finding out what could be salvaged from such youthful idiocy. The girls were safe with their fierce young governess and protector for the time being and he would make sure they stayed that way. There was so much to do he barely knew where to start. At least Miss Court cared about her charges and he could go on leaving her to that while he got the measure of them.

He glanced at yet another stand of woodland that ought to have been thinned and coppiced years ago. A fierce frown knitted his brows and he imagined his mother telling him they'd stick like that if he wasn't careful. His hard gaze softened as he pictured Kitty, Lady Rivers, ordering him to solve his problems instead of puckering the perfectly good brows she and his father had given him at great personal cost and giving himself premature lines.

'Yes, Ma,' he'd murmured, then chuckled at an image of quiet and respectable Berry Brampton under the onslaught of his nearest and dearest, intent on protecting it, and him, from all invaders. The fact they were the biggest invaders of all would pass them by, but at least his half-brother was five and twenty now and capable of keeping a still tongue in his head if he absolutely had to. All Fergus needed to do was persuade Brendan to do just that and they could both be in and out of here a lot sooner than if he had to work alone. If it could be done without having to admit he was the Earl of Barberry until he was ready, then so much the better.

His horse jigged at a crow flapping raucously out of the woods. They were nearly at Temple Brampton and none of the problems he'd been brooding on since parting from Miss Court and Georgiana needed solving today. He'd tried to be an idle gentleman when he got back from Canada, but now he'd spent time with his mother and stepfather and visited the finest tailor in London he needed to be busy again. He ought to be happy with at least a decade of neglect to make up for and, less than a week after arriving, he hardly recognised the man looking back at him out of the pitted and watery old mirror Jenks had made do with when he shaved of a morning.

Which reminded him, he must put repairs and

modernisation of the land steward's house at the top of the long list he was assembling. He'd never keep a real replacement for Jenks longer than a few days if he didn't. It might not even take that long for the next candidate to decide his old-fashioned and neglected quarters were not up to scratch. He imagined Miss Court looking down her rather fetching nose at him for putting his own comfort first, but if he was really going to do that, she and her precious girls would be out in the cold looking for respectable lodgings right now. There, he was thinking about his wards' governess again and he had far too much to do to bother himself about the stubborn woman. He rode to the Angel Inn, handed over his horse to be pampered after his cold ride here, then strode inside to find paper and whatever ink the landlord could come up with in order to write to Brendan without delay. At least with his half-brother around he wouldn't have time to brood on how different his life would be if he really was Edward Moss and Miss Court was her usual prickly self. She might be a good match for the third son of a country squire but he was an Earl, like it or not, and way above her touch.

* * *

'Don't get up, dear niece, although you must tell that delicious young husband of yours to have words with his uncle's butler. The impudent wretch insisted that you were not at home. I told him I am your aunt and even then he tried to leave me in the hall like some common servant.'

'Aunt Derneley,' Mrs Colm Hancourt said coldly, 'what do you want?'

'Must I want something? You're the only family I have left,' the faded lady said in a die-away tone that implied she probably wasn't long for this world.

'And I'm so dear you stood by while my mother tried to kill me with neglect in your own house when I was a baby? Add your scheme to make money out of me last autumn and even you ought to know by now that you can't rely on that accident of birth to get you a welcome under this roof.'

'What a hard-hearted creature you are,' Lady Derneley said with an elegant sniff into her lace-trimmed handkerchief. 'So like your father.'

'Yes, I'm very proud to agree with you, for once,' Eve Hancourt said with a sceptical glance at her supposedly weeping relative.

'He drove her to it, you know? With his stiff-necked pride and that ridiculous expectation of his that she would agree to live in that dreadful Gothic castle of his miles away from civilisation for months on end. Poor, dear Pamela. She swore there wasn't a party to be had from one week to the next and she was used to living at Derneley House and there was never a dull moment with us in those days. No wonder the poor child pined away for some life and laughter, shut away as she was in the wilds of Northumberland with only proud and stuffy Winterleys and all those wretched sheep for company.'

'I have no interest in my mother's excuses for leaving my father; if you've come here to plead her case, then you're twenty years too late.'

'No, I mustn't do that, must I?' Lady Derneley said rather distractedly. 'I doted on my little sister and miss her to this day, but I can tell that you were only ever told hard things about her.'

'Perhaps there were only hard things to say,' Eve said warily.

'Not from me. She had such energy, such charm and wit,' her aunt explained and her faded features warmed into a shadow of the girlish loveliness that netted her such a dashing young husband nearly three decades ago. 'And she was such fun.'

'At least one person loved her then,' Eve said gently.

'Lord Chris Hancourt adored her, don't forget,' Lady Derneley objected, then covered her mouth with a delicately gloved hand as if to remind herself nobody under this roof would want to be reminded of that uncomfortable fact.

'Good afternoon, Lady Derneley,' Lord Christopher Hancourt's son said smoothly from just inside the door of his uncle's newly refurbished drawing room. 'Are you receiving this afternoon after all then, my love?'

'You know very well I'm not, Husband,' Eve said with a smile of welcome.

'Then how may we be of service, Lady Derneley?'

'Since Winterley has forbidden any of you to help poor Derneley you cannot, but I don't see why I shouldn't visit my niece,' the lady replied, sniffing delicately at the thought of her lord in hiding from his creditors.

'My wife might have welcomed one in the past,

but you're more than twenty years too late,' he said implacably.

Lady Derneley started as if she'd found a viper in her reticule instead of a handkerchief. 'Pamela was my sister; how could I go against her wishes?'

'Because she was wrong in every way I can think of. Is there anything else?'

'No…that is, yes,' the lady said as she shredded her lawn and lace handkerchief and avoided Colm Hancourt's level gaze. 'We are family. It's our duty to show the world a united front,' she said like a well-rehearsed child repeating her catechism.

'Your husband is still under the hatches, then?'

'Yes,' she admitted baldly.

'I'll give you a cottage on one of my estates and a pension if you agree to live apart, but Derneley's not having a penny piece of mine or Eve's.'

'How can you be so mean? You have so much.'

'He tried to sell Eve into slavery for the sake of a share of her dowry and *you* schemed to leave her alone with a contemptible rogue last autumn. You're lucky to be offered so much, madam. I'd let you join Derneley in the sponging house but for my wife's tender heart. You are her mother's sister, although most nieces would turn their back on you after what you tried to do to her.'

'I refuse to be parted from my husband for ever,' the lady said in a quavering voice.

'Then I'm sorry for you, but Colm is quite right, Aunt Derneley. I won't pay a penny towards your husband's upkeep. He did his best to trick me into marriage with a monster and even if I could forget what he did, Colm never will. If you change your mind our offer of a home for you alone still stands, but until then I wish you good day.'

'You'll regret this; family should stick together. You should remind your sister how badly it looks when one does not do so, young man. It does none of you good for the wench to stay in the countryside now she's an heiress and can catch some sort of husband, even if she is a quiz and too long in the tooth to take properly. Rumour has it she's ugly as sin or not as virtuous as she ought to be and hiding her in the country now she has a fortune in her dower chest won't help. Derneley says they're taking bets in the clubs on which of those reasons for her staying away is most likely.'

'I'm amazed he's welcome anywhere in St James's,' Colm said.

Eve frowned at her aunt for prodding her husband where he could be most easily hurt, through his family. 'Goodbye, Lady Derneley,' she said coldly. 'Despite your spiteful gossip a letter to this address will suffice, if you ever decide to take up our offer.'

'And one to my aunt's house will tell me that you have recalled your duty to me, Niece,' Lady Derneley replied, then swept out of the room as if she was still a rich and secure peeress and not the wife of a fugitive bankrupt.

'She'll have to walk back to the Strand; her carriage was seized by her husband's creditors weeks ago,' Eve said.

'I'm not sending her home in one of my uncle's carriages or your new town chariot, love. Derneley probably thinks we'll tow him out of River Tick if he drowns in it showily enough and he's not having a penny after what he did to you.'

'She seems determined to drown with him, though.'

'Then let her; at heart she's as cold and unscrupulous as Derneley. She would have let you die as a babe and schemed to get you raped and forcibly wed the night we met. If you hadn't foiled that plan, I'd have had to kill the brute to free you and look where that would have got us.'

'We probably wouldn't have met at all,' Eve said with a shudder.

'Unthinkable,' he said and took Eve in his arms to reassure them both they had and were now blissfully happy, despite the Derneleys' worst efforts.

'You must write to your sister though, Colm,' she said hesitantly as soon as she had breath to spare.

'Aye, I must,' Colm replied with a frown that emphasised the scar high on his forehead and might make him look almost saturnine to someone who didn't love him to distraction. 'I'm not sure Nell will change her mind and come to town for the Season because of the scandalmongers though, love, she's more likely to dig her heels in and snap her fingers at the gossips than listen to what they have to say about her.'

'Then maybe you should hint how satisfying it could be to prove them wrong. She is a Hancourt, after all, and therefore stubborn as rock.'

'And you think we're all like that, do you, Wife?' her own particular Hancourt asked softly. Eve did her best to reassure him she liked him exactly as he was and they forgot the Derneleys and even Colm's sister for a blissful hour or two.

Chapter Seven

Nell carefully folded her brother's latest letter and put it in her writing box to read again when she had time. While she was genuinely fond of the Selford girls, such snatched moments were more precious than gold. She was glad Colm was content with his new life and had his darling Eve to share it. He deserved such happiness, but she did feel lonelier at times when she compared her life with his. It made her feel guilty to sit and long for the sort of love Colm and Eve had found together. She had made a useful life here, but sometimes the longing for a lover and family of her own was so strong it felt almost like a physical pain. Ridiculous, she told herself sternly, she had chosen this existence. The fortune she inherited the day Colm was five and twenty gave her alternatives she never dared dream of until now, but she was still here.

If the former Duke of Linaire had been as good a man as the current one Nell would have been the wealthy and pampered Miss Hancourt all her life, or maybe even Mrs Somebody or Lady Self-Important by now. In that life her gowns would be of the finest wool, silk or velvet; she could wear a jewel-bright spencer jacket or pelisse. She preferred the simple graceful lines of gowns fashionable at the start of the century and an image of herself reclining gracefully on a fine *chaise* appeared in her head, despite the reality of her drab wool gown and tightly bound hair. She would look charming and seductive as she gazed at her chosen lover, like an engraving she had once seen of Madame Récamier as painted by Baron Gérard. Her watcher; the man who commissioned this fantasy picture, now *he* would want her so urgently his brilliantly blue gaze would be almost molten with heat as he gazed past the artist as if he wasn't even there and soon he would dismiss him and make love to his wife until…

Until nothing, Eleanor, the voice of her stern

conscience interrupted, followed by Caroline's voice calling her back to reality.

'Miss Court, where are you?'

'Up here, Caroline,' Nell finally made herself reply even as she remembered why she had stopped reading Colm's letter and blushed rosily.

In that other world her husband had looked a lot like Moss. Why on earth was she taking the man into her fantasy world when she didn't even like him? She sighed and waved that very different version of him smiling mistily at his lovely, fashionable wife a sceptical goodbye.

'Here I am,' she said, after a look in the small mirror on the landing outside her room to make sure her improper thoughts about the land steward didn't show.

'Oh, good, because the strangest thing has happened, Miss Court.'

'I am on pins to know what it is, Caroline.'

'A gentleman has called and he is asking for you or Mr Moss.'

'And why is that so strange?'

'Because he says he's our cousin's half-brother.'

'Which cousin does he claim to be related to, then?

'Why, our guardian of course; the Earl.'

'Goodness,' Nell heard herself say faintly and wondered what on earth she was supposed to do with such an unlikely visitor and whether he had come here to test the ground for his very tardy half-brother.

'He seems very polite and he is really rather handsome.'

It got worse, Nell decided, with another panicked glance at her reflection in that scrap of looking glass. Nothing to show her front of a calm and competent governess was as fragile as glass today, she decided with a sigh. But wasn't Mr Moss trouble enough without this latest disaster? If they had to contend with the Earl's younger brother as well, Nell almost wished the Earl was here to take command of his own household for once. Although if he were, she supposed she and the girls would have to take up residence elsewhere. Even Mrs Winch wasn't enough to stop the gossip if the elusive Earl of Barberry, his wards and a young governess lived under the same roof without a stern and aristocratic chaperon to squash any hint of scandal.

'Never mind handsome,' she muttered as she hurried after her much more eager and rather awe-struck pupil. 'What on earth are we going to do with him?'

'Good afternoon,' the young man waiting in the small drawing room greeted her with a smile and rather a gallant bow, considering she was only the governess.

'Good afternoon,' Nell managed faintly in reply and blinked owlishly at their 'really rather handsome' guest. She tried to recall her manners as she managed not to gape at him openly and wondered if it might be a trial for a young man to be born so dazzlingly good looking. Not that he didn't seem perfectly at ease with his golden hair, dark eyes and all the other outward perfection of an Adonis in breeches and a superbly cut riding coat.

'When Miss Caroline said she would fetch her governess I was picturing a stern grey lady with twice as many years in her dish as you, Miss Court.'

'We governesses come in mixed ages and I believe we can be found in all the usual variety of heights and temperaments as well, sir.'

'Maybe you do, but I haven't come across one I wanted to spend *more* time with until today.'

'Flattery will not do you any good with me, sir—rather the opposite, in fact.'

'That wasn't flattery,' he said with such an admiring look Nell was tempted to find another mirror and make sure she hadn't been turned into a ravishing beauty by a passing fairy godmother on the way downstairs.

'I beg to differ and if I am to remain here until the last of your brother's wards is old enough to be out of the schoolroom we must do better than this, sir. Please treat me with respect and spare me such empty compliments in future.'

'They are not empty and I'm not sure I'm ready to admit that my lordly brother and his wards have a right to stand between us quite yet either.'

'Then please hurry up and do so, sir. It will sit very ill with me if you make my task here impossible and I am forced to leave.'

'Since your standards are undoubtedly much higher than my darling brother's I shall concede you take your post as mentor to four young ladies very seriously. Will you not at least tell me your name before I go and get ready to eat humble pie at the inn in Temple Brampton?'

'Can you not stay for dinner, Mr Rivers?' Caroline interrupted impulsively and Nell frowned at the suspicion her shyest pupil was besotted with the man.

'I doubt your governess or cook will thank you for that impulsive invitation, Miss Caroline, but I am grateful for it and very sorry to refuse it,' he said gently and went up a peg or two in Nell's estimation. He seemed genuinely concerned to make sure Caro didn't feel snubbed for speaking out of turn.

'Perhaps another night, Caroline, when we can ask Mrs Clennage and the Vicar to be present and make us all so respectable nobody can talk scandal about us,' Nell said in a probably vain attempt to make Caro's disappointment easier to bear. First infatuation could be painful for a young girl on the edge of womanhood and she was glad Caro wasn't given to melodrama like her eldest cousin.

'Mrs Winch is every bit as respectable as Mrs Clennage and she lives here. Mr Moss dined with us when he first came here, so I really don't see why Mr Rivers can't have dinner with us as well,' Caro argued stubbornly.

'I doubt my brother's new land steward would

be viewed as a suitable chaperon for four young ladies of quality and his employer's little brother by your neighbours, do you?' Mr Rivers asked with a careless shrug.

Nell was relieved to see some of the stardust leave Caro's dreamy blue eyes as she took in the gentleman's arrogant implication that the brother of an earl was far above a land agent in so many ways he didn't need to list them. Such a high opinion of his own consequence would not sit well with Caroline, who seemed to regard Moss as a friend for some reason that escaped her governess.

'I shall make sure I ask if the Vicar and his wife are free to dine with us one evening very soon, Caroline, but perhaps we could ask Mr Moss if he is ready to share his house with a guest yet. If you would prefer staying in the village to riding back and forth to Combe Brampton every day that could be a solution to at least some of our difficulties, Mr Rivers.'

'Mr Moss says the windows in his house don't fit and most of the chimneys smoke,' Caroline said rather sulkily before Mr Rivers could speak.

'Your Mr Moss sounds a very fastidious sort of land agent to me, Miss Caroline. Luckily I'm a hardy Irish peasant and not nearly as finicky about my surroundings as he seems to be,' Mr Rivers said cheerfully in direct opposition to his top-loftiness a few moments ago. 'So long as the roof doesn't leak as well and any ghosts have moved on since he took up residence here, a share of his quarters would suit me very well, if Moss agrees to tolerate my company for a few days while I attend to some business of my brother's that he's too idle to come and see to himself.'

For some reason Nell thought the gentleman was on the verge of laughing even as he tried to sound as if he was having to make the best of a bad job. Did he know more about Moss than he was willing to admit? How could he? He was obviously a gentleman in Ireland, whatever high society had to say about his one-time actress mother behind her second husband's back, and Moss had grown up as a squire's third son from the north of England. A bustle in the hall spoke of another arrival and even when she couldn't see him, Moss's impatient footsteps gave him away before she even set eyes on him. Wasn't it a bit worrying she knew it was him, come to find out what was going on, before she could even see him? She didn't have time to think too deeply before he strode into the small drawing room so abruptly it seemed as if news of Mr Rivers's arrival had interrupted important business and he was eager to be off again.

'Here is Mr Moss, so we can ask what he thinks, can we not, Miss Court?' Caro said brightly.

'We should introduce Mr Moss to our visitor before anything else, Caroline,' Nell reproached her, trying to grab control of this situation back before someone else ran away with it.

Mr Moss was frowning and muddy around the edges when he stalked into the room as if he had a God-given right to say who could stay or go under this roof, as well as his own humbler one across the garden from the great house.

'Yes, indeed,' that visitor said with a mocking smile at the land steward's hastily wiped riding boots and splashed leathers. 'I've heard so much about you since I arrived that I almost feel I know you already, Moss,' he added with a languidly offered hand.

'Good day, sir, you have the advantage of me,' Moss said gruffly.

'Rivers, d'you know? Half-brother to the Earl of Barberry,' Mr Rivers drawled.

'So he really does exist, then?' Moss asked disrespectfully.

Nell marvelled at his effrontery and wished she could afford to share it. She put the girls' welfare first and kept a still tongue in her head about her true opinion of the absent and neglectful Lord Barberry. This post might be even more of a challenge than it was before rude and abrupt Moss arrived to add a pinch of adventure to their dull existence, but she was beginning to question things that had seemed unchangeable until now. Such as what right did the Earl have to shrug off all responsibility for his wards on to her shoulders? And should she stay here and let him keep on doing it? Not sure she wanted to come up with an answer right now, she waited for two very different gentlemen to finish sizing each other up like a pair of wolves getting ready to fight. They must have reached a silent agreement not to give battle though, because Mr Rivers suddenly grinned like a schoolboy at his potential adversary, possibly in the interests of harmony or perhaps because he needed somewhere convenient to stay for a few days.

'He does indeed,' the Earl's brother said with

deep chuckle that didn't do much to endear him to his unwitting host from the look of Moss's austere expression. 'My half-brother is far too big and awkward to be the product of even the most disordered imagination.'

Caroline was staring at the Earl's brother as if he was a fabulous being from another world again, which Nell supposed was hardly to be wondered at. The biggest wonder was she was immune to his looks and charm herself. She was a relatively young and acute female and Mr Rivers was an exceptionally handsome man, so it really was a wonder. Instead of being bedazzled by the Earl's half-brother, Nell's attention kept wandering to the dour and work-stained land steward and not even his mother could call *him* classically handsome without crossing her fingers behind her back first.

'What do you want to ask me, Miss Caroline?' Moss said, with a disapproving glance at the newcomer, as if he was concerned about the dreamy smile on Miss Caroline Selford's face as well and thought the man needed a stern warning not to play with her youthful emotions.

Perhaps he was also wondering if Mr Rivers's arrival would disrupt the smooth running of Berry

Brampton House. Nell told herself not to find the idea he cared about Caro's gentle heart touching; the people on the estate might be uneasy and a bit rebellious if the Earl's handsome brother charmed too many young women into losing their wits over him and Moss was here to get everything back in good order as fast as he could. Any distraction from that task was a burden he probably didn't want to even think about shouldering with so much to do already.

'Ah, yes,' Caroline said, as if his question had shocked her back into everyday reality where she was only thirteen and this god in human form was at least a decade her senior. Nell sympathised, but refused to rescue her shy pupil so Caroline could lapse back into her daydream of being three and twenty and fabulously beautiful instead of thirteen, coltish and terribly shy with anyone she didn't know well. 'Mr Rivers can't stay in the house with us, so we were wondering if he could stop with you at the land steward's house instead, Mr Moss,' Caro finally managed to say in a rush.

'Were you now, Miss Caroline? And you, too, Miss Court?' Moss asked, as if her possible infatuation with Mr Rivers's good looks and charm was a gap in her armour he didn't approve of one bit. As if he had any right to disapprove, Nell chided silently and glowered at him to prove he didn't.

'Mr Rivers is the Earl's brother. We can't expect him to live in the nearest inn, even if his brother does own it and practically every other stick and stone for miles around.' She excused herself as if she needed to, which she didn't, of course.

'He might well be more comfortable there,' Moss said, casting a critical eye at Mr Rivers's impeccable Hessians and exquisite pantaloons. He raised an eyebrow at the fanciful waistcoat which even Nell knew marked the Earl's brother out as a member of the dandy set. Mr Rivers's coat was so beautifully cut that her annual stipend would very likely buy a sleeve and maybe a lapel of it and no more.

'But so very far away,' Mr Rivers drawled, as if Temple Brampton and the Angel Inn were fifty miles away instead of a mere five and even less as the crow flies.

The otherwise polite and sociable Mr Rivers seemed intent on annoying his brother's steward and Nell wondered why, when it had been so hard to get Moss to come here at all that the Earl would surely be annoyed with his little brother if the man upped and left. The younger man didn't seem so impressed by his own looks and attire he was vain or obnoxious with anyone else, so why taunt a man who had to earn his living as Moss had been doing since his belated arrival?

'Shall I ask Mrs Winch to send a couple of maids and the boot boy to help your housekeeper get your house ready for a guest then, Mr Moss?' she offered with a warning glance at their unexpected guest to stop making himself the least desirable one a man could resent having thrust upon him like this. She was beginning to wish Mr Rivers had stayed in Dublin or Belfast, or London, or wherever he was before his wretched brother persuaded him to come here and cause an upheaval for some reason best known to himself.

'If she can spare them, they will be most welcome,' Moss said with a warm smile of thanks that made Nell's knees knock as Mr Rivers's easy grin never would. 'My new housekeeper is a diligent soul, but it took Jenks so many years to neglect it that the house is still hardly fit for his lordship's brother to inhabit.'

'Then we had best go and ask Mrs Winch to order as many of her staff as she can spare to go and help her make it so, Caroline. We must leave Mr Moss and Mr Rivers to become acquainted, since they seem fated to live with each other for the next few days, whether they like it or not.'

'It may even be weeks,' Mr Rivers said sunnily.

'Do you think we all ought to pack up and go to stay at the Angel instead, so Mr Rivers can take up residence here on his brother's behalf?' Caro whispered with a doubtful glance back down the enfilade towards the small drawing room as Nell scurried her away.

'No, Caroline,' Nell said firmly, 'if Lord Barberry wished to live here he would have made arrangements to do so. I think we can safely say this is the last place in the world he wishes to take up residence, since he's not even been to visit you and your sister and cousins once during the ten years he has been your guardian.'

'I suppose so, although Mr Rivers's arrival could argue his brother is softening towards us and this poor old place, don't you think?'

'It could, or maybe Mr Rivers is curious about

Berry Brampton House and his brother's wards and has come to see for himself.'

'We're not so bad we need to be inspected like wild ponies, are we?'

'Of course not; you are wonderful girls,' Nell said hastily before the picture of Lavinia in one of her tantrums or a fit of overwrought tears could cast a shadow on that happy picture.

By seeking to distract Caro from the dazzling Mr Rivers she had put doubts about her place in the world into Caro's head again instead. Feeling out of sorts with herself for damaging Caro's fragile confidence by accident, Nell tried to persuade her to charm Mrs Winch into releasing two of her maids and stores as well as bedding from the Berry Brampton House linen cupboards, since Caro was the housekeeper's favourite Miss Selford. Somehow they needed to furnish a room in the steward's house in fit style for the Earl's brother to stay there for as long as he chose. Moss might have to endure patched and sides-to-middle sheets, but Mr Rivers could not be expected to share an upper servant's discomfort when he was obviously used to the best of everything.

Chapter Eight

'**W**hy the devil did you come here looking as if you've never done a day's work in your life?' Fergus demanded the moment he was alone with his brother on their trip from the great house to the one he was making do with for the time being.

'I'm lulling your enemies into a false sense of security,' Brendan returned as if Fergus was an idiot not to see the logic of his plan straight away.

'Which enemies would those be?'

'I don't know; you summoned me here to smoke them out, so you must know more about them than I do.'

'I don't even know if I've got any yet. I only asked you to find out if there's good reason to worry about leaving my wards and their governess virtually alone in that great rabbit warren when I decide to go away again.'

'And you're planning to do that soon, are you?'

'Of course I am; you know I never wanted to be here.'

'Hmm, but how can I guess what you're going to do next when you're pretending to be your own land steward?'

'As Moss I can find out what's going on here without everyone being wary of telling me the truth. My tenants and neighbours are eagerly lining up to tell me their woes right now and Lord Barberry wouldn't hear the half of it. Why should I look such a gift horse in the mouth when the governess presented me with it before I could even open my mouth?'

'Nevertheless, I'm surprised my dour and upright elder brother is behaving so badly. In your shoes I would have come here ten years ago and to hell with your stiff-necked family and whatever they had to say about me and mine, but you're too stiff-necked yourself to accept what they didn't want you to have. We both know Ma's worth a hundred of every other Selford but you, for all they called her foul names and tried to take you away from her when your father died.'

'And I hope they're rotting in hell for what they

tried to do to her, but I still have the care of four young girls on my shoulders and you know how Ma's been nagging me about them since I got home. Now I'm here I know she's right to worry.'

'She usually is, it's one of her worst habits,' Brendan said with a rueful shrug. 'But it's not the girls' fault they were born Selfords, any more than it's yours you were as well. You're going to be busy if you're about to become their true guardian though, Caroline Selford is going to be a beauty and you'll have no peace at all when she makes her debut. I'll give you my expert opinion on the rest after I've met them.'

'If I catch you flirting with any one of them I'll string you up by your balls,' Fergus said with a fierce protectiveness that surprised him nearly as much as Brendan.

'You'd have to catch me first,' his brother replied with a lazy grin.

'That shouldn't be hard, considering you're too idle to ride here and back from Temple Brampton every day and I've walked and ridden half the county since I arrived. I'm heartily sick of corn and cabbages and can count sheep in my sleep, but I'm fitter than a poacher's dog.'

'Ah, but I only *look* like a Bond Street Beau.'

'And if you ever *look* at my eldest ward the way she's going to want you to, I'll black both your eyes and send her to a nunnery until she's learnt some sense.'

'Like that, is she?'

Fergus felt a terrible urge to wipe the smile off his little brother's face before Brendan could even meet his eldest ward and wondered what the devil had come over him. He felt like the girl's father with a dangerous predator in his sites, for heaven's sake, and he'd never asked to feel anything for these girls who had been thrust upon him along with the title he didn't want either. He wondered if the Fergal Ford of a few months ago would recognise the confused idiot he'd become since he came here.

'Yes, she is,' he finally admitted on a gusty sigh and wondered why it mattered so much to him that Lavinia had the airs and talents of a hardened flirt and turned into a lost little girl the moment she forgot to be so rebellious. 'God knows how I'm going to protect her from the wolves when she'd far rather be gobbled up by the first one who comes her way.'

'Maybe you should let her scare herself on a tame one,' Brendan suggested with the modest look of an expert in the art of flirtation and seducing willing women that Fergus knew was a little too well-deserved for comfort.

'I might, if I thought she wouldn't fancy herself in love with you. I doubt you want to land at the altar with her, but that's what'll happen to you if she throws her reputation away haring about the country chasing after you as she would probably love to do.'

'That's the last place I want to be for a good while yet,' Brendan almost yelped in horror at the idea of marriage to a rebellious schoolgirl.

He followed it up with a colourful curse at the very notion of marriage that made Fergus feel a lot better. At least his sometimes careless brother had been reminded to take care with the confused and confusing young woman Lavinia was about to become. He was doing his brother a favour by warning him off, he reassured himself, as that protective instinct argued any young man who wanted to wed one of his wards had best be close to perfect. If Fergus didn't take him apart for playing along with Lavinia's fantasies, their mother would flay Brendan alive for raising a young woman's hopes if he was reckless enough to do anything of the kind after that warning, then she'd weep because her beloved boy had broken a young girl's heart. Her impressive fury followed by abject misery at any bad behaviour they were forced to own up to could outdo a synod full of bishops saying a stern *No* when they were younger. Yet he could rely on any member of his family to fight for him to the death and Fergus realised how lucky he was now he'd met his true father's family. The more he saw of what his late grandfather had done by putting the succession before everything else, the less he minded being the Selford family outcast. Set against the deep love he had always had from his mother and the patient good humour of his stepfather, the Misses Selford were poor indeed. Miss Court tried to make them feel valued and unique, but even she couldn't blot out their grandfather's contempt for them as mere girls, or his own indifference.

'We're nearly at the steward's house, so kindly remember you're not my brother and we never set eyes on each other until today,' he warned Brendan after the rest of their stroll through the parkland passed in thoughtful silence. He supposed the generous garden of the quaintly foursquare Queen Ann house in front of him ought to say how much the Earl of Barberry valued his land steward, but its current state did the exact opposite.

'What a fine old place this should be, big Brother. You have yourself to blame that it's nothing of the kind, so don't glare at me as if I've been wilfully neglecting it for a decade, Moss,' Brendan said, raising his eyebrows at Fergus's muddy boots and well-worn working clothes as if he couldn't imagine why the brother of an earl had agreed to share the quarters of such an out-and-out son of the soil.

'As if you don't spend most of your days on the gallops looking a damn sight worse than I do now,' Fergus said grumpily, contrarily longing for the fine clothes he'd once thought so disposable as he eyed his brother and wondered if Miss Court was as impressed by them as she seemed to be by the rest of his confounded brother.

'Ah, but that's what I do when I'm in Ireland. We all know what a heathenish place that is, don't we?' Brendan asked as if he didn't love the place passionately.

* * *

'Did you do as I bid you and bribe the post boy for a look at one of Hancourt's letters?'

'Of course I did, Derneley,' Lady Derneley replied triumphantly.

Her fugitive lord looked reluctantly impressed by his wife's unexpected talent for subterfuge. 'Good, that was the last half-crown I had; so, where is she?'

'At Berry Brampton House, working for the Earl of Barberry, of all people. I could hardly believe it—that milk-and-water creature in the employ of one of the most eligible men in England. If I was thirty years younger, I'd marry an earl.'

'You're not and he doesn't even live there,' her spouse said impatiently, reverting to his usual bare tolerance of his wife's butterfly thoughts as she flitted from one topic to another without much connection between.

'No wonder the clever little minx doesn't come to London, though. She must be waiting for him to get home so she can catch him by hook or by crook before anyone else can get there first.'

'Shut your chatter, woman. I need to think.'

'Remember, I'm the only one who recalls how

life was when we were young and you were handsome and more fun than the rest of my suitors.'

'Aye, and you were a damned fine woman, thirty years ago,' he conceded. 'But that was then, so be quiet and listen to what you must do if we're to get out of here. I can't venture out without being caught by the vultures and put in the Fleet, so you'll have to go to Berry Brampton and get Chris's daughter's papers off her somehow or another.'

'I certainly can't live with my aunt's nip-cheese ways for much longer, so it might make a nice change. I've no pretty gowns and she expects me to sew and clean and even wash my own laundry and cook for us both. You know perfectly well I don't know how to do any of that; I'm a lady.'

'If you don't learn you'll starve or stink,' her lord told her abruptly, 'now listen to what we must do if we're not to be stuck here for the rest of our days.'

'Ooh, no, Derneley, don't even think of it—I swear I'll go as mad as my aunt quite soon if we don't get away.'

Her lord muttered something about that not being much of a leap, then perhaps he reminded himself she was his only ally, because he went on to explain his plan for tracking down the fabled Lambury Jewels and making off with them before anyone worked out he hadn't been able to have them broken up years ago, because Pamela never got the real ones out of her lover in the first place.

'You're so clever, Derneley. I wouldn't marry Barberry even if I could.'

'Seeing you've no money or brains and you can't cook, sew or clean to make up for the lack, it's as well he ain't even in this country to get in my way, then,' her doting lord said under his breath.

'How am I to get to Berry Brampton and do what you say though, my love?' his lady asked, in blissful ignorance of her husband's true opinion of her.

'There must be something left in this dusty old mausoleum the witch or her lawyer haven't locked away. Isn't there anything worth selling?'

'I haven't looked.'

'Why not, woman? How else are we to get out of this mess than by cashing in our assets?'

'But they're not ours.'

'Then you stay here and endure the old woman. Somehow I'll manage this business without you if you're going to be a witless fool.'

'No, no, Derneley, you can't leave me here on my own with her. I'll die without some life about me and my own pretty things, and some new gowns, and hats and...'

'Then be quiet and do as I say,' her lord demanded roughly before her list of requirements could get any longer.

Chapter Nine

By the time her afternoon off came around Nell felt as if she needed peace and quiet even more than usual. She thanked Mrs Winch for the house-keeping lessons she had organised to keep the girls out of mischief in Nell's absence and went out into the parkland armed with her sketchbook. It was urgent with new life, despite the grey and cheerless weather so far this year, but she couldn't seem to find the right place to settle. A stile or tree stump would offer her a subject; she'd open her sketch book and find her thoughts ran on so busily she'd wasted half an hour doodling before she knew it. Sighing impatiently at another draw-ing of nothing much, she got ready to move again and find some wonder that might finally hold her wandering attention.

'Now here's a dilemma,' the deep masculine

voice she told herself she least wanted to hear drawled from behind her.

She turned to glare at Moss, because somehow she couldn't endure being written off as a quiz today. 'You made me jump,' she accused quite unnecessarily; he must have seen her start half an inch in the air. 'Must you creep about like a cat on the prowl, Mr Moss?'

'I do know a true gentleman is not supposed to argue with a lady, but a troop of land stewards could have marched along this path in step with me and you were so lost in thought you wouldn't have heard us, Miss Court.'

'What a nightmarish idea,' she grumbled, then snapped her drawing book closed as she got ready to jump down off the stile and wait for him to pass by.

'You have no time for us sons of the soil, do you?' he said as if he knew the inner workings of her soul and found them narrow and rather petty.

'Your profession has nothing to do with it,' she said, stowing her precious pencils more carefully than usual because she didn't want him to know her face was flushed at his faulty judgement.

The awful truth was he intrigued her and neither Miss Court nor Eleanor Hancourt could afford to be drawn to the Earl of Barberry's land steward. As a governess, she was probably beneath *his* touch. She had to set a good example to her charges and falling at his feet like a besotted schoolgirl would not be one of those. As the granddaughter of a duke and a lady of birth and fortune she truly was, he was an unequal match for *her.* Not that he showed any sign of being bewitched by her, so she needn't worry his tender heart would be trampled by her real status in the world as he clearly didn't have one.

'Why *do* you look down your nose at me whenever we cross paths, Miss Court?' he asked, like a boy taking a clock apart to find out how it worked.

'Maybe I am simply a cross-grained creature, Mr Moss,' she replied primly.

'Hmm, I doubt you're anything as straightforward as that.'

'Of course I am, you remarked on it just now.'

'If you revise our conversation you'll find out I did nothing of the sort. I have the evidence of my own ears and eyes on my first night here to argue with that stiff and unyielding image of a lady who doesn't care for anything but her own comfort. You are a fraud, Miss Court,' he accused, his gaze steady as he met hers with a challenge to argue and prove it.

'Am I?' she asked as lightly as she could when her heart was racing at the very idea he might have found her out and now she would have to tell the truth about herself.

'Yes; you pretend to be stern and unbending to an outsider like me, yet you cherish and protect the girls in your charge so fiercely I suspect you'd walk barefoot across Britain for them if it seemed the right thing to do at the time. If you ever dreamt of setting yourself up as a strict and uncaring educator, you veered wildly off course the day you agreed to take on the welfare of those girls of yours virtually alone.'

'This is plain speaking indeed, Mr Moss. I shall return the compliment and ask what I should think of a gentleman who was outfitted nearly as grandly as the Earl the day you came here, yet you stay in a rackety old house as if you don't care for your own comfort and we're not supposed to find that odd?'

'No,' he said gruffly, as if she had trampled on his pride by pointing out the facts of his life.

'Then maybe I am as ideally suited to my position here as you are to yours,' she lied. She wasn't born to this sort of life and now as an heiress in her own right again there was nothing ideal about it. He was right the first time; Miss Court *was* a fraud and no doubt he'd be the first to denounce her as such if he ever found out who she really was.

'I don't think so,' he argued. 'Something about you says no to that notion, Miss Court. I wonder if you have a secret you're half-afraid one of us will stumble upon if you don't hold us at a distance?'

'What nonsense. Of course I haven't,' she said briskly, afraid that he might see into her very soul if she let him. The idea that he'd already looked harder than she wanted anyone at Berry Brampton to look made her even more uneasy. She should be eager to get away from him, instead of standing here as if he'd put a spell on her feet so she couldn't make them move until he set her free. 'I was fortunate to receive an excellent education so I can earn my keep by passing it on to Lord Barberry's wards. I'm a simple soul and such fanciful speculation is ridiculous.'

'Hmm,' he murmured with a hint of a smile in

his eyes. 'I don't doubt your learning, but a simple soul? You seem rather complicated to me, ma'am.'

'I wish you wouldn't call me that, *sir*. I'm not in my dotage,' she said to try and divert him from his doubts about her.

'Of course not; you're nowhere near it,' he scoffed as if she had managed to irritate him without even trying this time. 'I doubt you're much older than Miss Lavinia Selford. I can't imagine how you came to be appointed governess here two years ago, when you can hardly have been long out of the schoolroom yourself.'

'Of course I was; I'm a competent and experienced teacher. If I thought *you* had a right to question *my* status I'd refer you to my former headmistress in Bath, as I was a pupil teacher at her school from the time I really was Lavinia's age.'

'I really can't imagine anything less likely than Miss Selford teaching small girls their alphabet. You must have been far too young to teach much at such an age.'

'That's how we schoolmistresses begin. Access to our universities being denied to us women, how else can we learn our trade?'

'Not at seventeen,' he said, as if he knew far more about the education of young girls than she did.

Perhaps he had little sisters, she speculated. Was he too young to have a daughter of his own, but if he had a wife or child he'd have brought them with him, wouldn't he? Nell felt a chasm open up in her heart at the very thought she might have been having hot and forbidden fantasies about a married man. She told herself to stop having them this very minute and it wasn't as if she intended to *do* anything about this feeling that he could be far more important to her than the Earl of Barberry's land steward ever should be. He'd laugh if he could read her thoughts and hastily decline the honour of fulfilling those wicked imaginings of hers, she decided, with a feeling deep down that might easily be regret if she thought about it.

'We do if that's the only way we can pay our fees,' she replied absently.

The horrid thought of Moss with a wife and child outran Nell's irritation that he doubted her suitability for this post. She'd spent two years battling with the Selford girls' defiant ignorance when three more experienced teachers had declared them impossible before she came. Clearly it was unreasonable to expect a man to take the challenges she faced every day seriously, she decided waspishly.

'What were you doing at such a prestigious school if there wasn't enough money to pay the fees?' he asked as if he knew the costs of Miss Thibett's exclusive school were beyond a penniless orphan. What right did he have to question her, but for some reason she answered him anyway.

'When my grandmother died my guardian said it was foolish to educate me above my station. He informed Miss Thibett that he wasn't prepared to throw good money after bad and that I would have to find work.'

'What sort of guardian was he?' he said scornfully.

For some reason Nell felt her temper strain against the restraint of years. He didn't seem to believe her and this part of her story was actually true. 'Just the run-of-the-mill sort who cared as little how I felt as my current charges' guardian does about *their* hopes and dreams. He was as hard and indifferent to me as Lord Barberry is to four girls who have lost their parents through no fault of their own. They didn't ask to be thrown on his mercy, any more than my brother and I wanted to be dependent on our uncle. As his lordship takes as little trouble as he can over his wards, it seems to me a common enough way for guardians to behave. The Earl gives instructions to keep his charges fed, clothed and alive and as far out of his orbit as possible. No doubt he would rid himself of his wards as rapidly as my guardian did of me, if society would let him turn his back on them and get away with it. So there really must be safety in numbers; four girls cast out into the world to earn a living couldn't go unnoticed as one seems to have done when my guardian decided to disown me.'

'You are very hot against a man you don't know,' he said as if her outburst was personal and not directed at the employer he claimed not to know either.

'And you seem determined to support the Earl against the accusations most of his staff and tenants would throw at him if they dared,' she replied angrily, narrowing her eyes against a rare glimpse of the sun to glare up at him.

'Don't look at me as if I've been supping with the devil, Miss Court, neither of us know Lord Barberry, so how can we judge him? He may feel he's done his best for his wards by stopping away, so they can grow up in peace under your care. No doubt you could teach the instant you left your cradle so he may have done all he needed for them on the day he agreed to appoint you.'

'Don't be ridiculous,' she said stiffly and wished she could break the spell he seemed to have cast on her and walk away. He was mocking her as well as changing the subject and she made herself look into the middle distance while she wondered about Moss and his peculiar failure to arrive here until they had all but given up hope he was coming. His post was one most young men of his birth and station would have galloped here to grab with both hands. 'You clearly doubt I can find my way around a primer, let alone being able to teach them suitably ladylike accomplishments.'

'Spare me a list; my mother's vast numbers of friends line up to provide me with a list of what to expect of a truly accomplished young lady whenever I rashly put my head inside her drawing room of an afternoon.'

'Goodness, I thought you lived in a remote neighbourhood.' Nell allowed herself to be diverted and wonder how big a manor house his father resided in.

'It sometimes seems entirely made up of young ladies who insist on playing pianofortes and flutes very badly, or displaying pages of indifferent watercolours as if they were inspired. Perhaps a man needs to be deaf, short-sighted and oblivious to the frippery nature of most young ladies' accomplishments to be a true gentleman.'

'You are too severe. Perhaps you should consider how it feels to walk in a lady's kid slippers next time you judge one so harshly. A woman may have the acute mind and cunning instincts of a Duke of Wellington in petticoats but, for all the good they will do her, she might as well be born a fool.'

'You long for the smoke of battle and the smell of slaughter then, Miss Court?' he asked with such pointed irony she longed to smack his unfashionably tanned cheek or, even better, plant him a facer in true manly style.

'I doubt any woman does,' she said, her very real memories of the terrible aftermath of Waterloo making her shudder. 'Most of my sex have too much to fear for those who fight and die for our safety to think war anything but a tragedy. We sit at home and hope our loved ones survive, all the time knowing we can do nothing to stop the slaughter but pray for peace. Maybe I chose a clumsy example of how hemmed in and confined the female sex is compared to the masculine one, but how would you feel if every path you chose, every talent you truly possessed and longed to follow up and expand upon was closed off to you by an accident of birth, Mr Moss?'

'Frustrated and angry,' he admitted slowly. He looked thoughtful about his dismissal of half the world though and that was something, wasn't it? 'Do *you* secretly long to join the Royal Society, or mount an expedition to hunt for pirate treasure?'

Nell looked for mockery, but saw only interest in his eyes as she blinked back at him and almost forgot the question. Being alone with him under the budding oak trees lent a dangerous edge to their conversation and she should have bid him a chilly good day and moved on. If they could meet on equal terms, how irresistible he might seem next to the idle fops and rakes of the *ton*. Ah now, wasn't that the timely reminder she needed not to dream of this man kissing her in the shadow of my lord's venerable oak grove? She wasn't only Miss Court and he was Lord Barberry's steward. Even if he could lower his pride to live off his wife's fortune, she didn't know if she could endure an unequal marriage like the one her parents had made. Look what happened when you let your inner dreamer run away with you—one minute you were standing here wondering how it might feel to be thoroughly kissed by a fit and vigorous gentleman you had done your best not to admire from afar; the next you were marching him up the aisle and wondering how you could live together in harmony when your fortune was so much greater than his.

'No,' she replied as if that was all she was thinking of while she considered the biggest intimacies there were between a man and a woman and decided they were impossible for them. 'I don't have a scientific bent or long for wild adventures. Surely even you will admit I've a right to be bitter about the lot of women in our supposedly enlightened times though, Mr Moss?'

'Will I?' he asked contrarily.

'Of course; in a fairer world I could have attended a university if I was clever enough and never mind male or female. A scholar can't have too much scholarship.'

'Now there I can disagree and refuse to feel guilty. Who would want you to spend years hunched over your books until you grow a dowager's hump and need to wear spectacles, Miss Court? Not I, for one,' he said with far too much masculine interest in her currently clear-eyed and straight-backed form for comfort.

'Complimenting me won't change me into a fluffy female who simpers and agrees you know best because you're male, instead of thinking for herself. What if I heard the music of the spheres or found the cure for all ills? No matter if I am man or woman, such knowledge could be of infinite use to mankind.'

'Do let me know when you're close to tracking down either wonder, won't you?' he replied cynically as ever.

Nell knew she was clinging to an argument to shield herself against the glimmer of masculine interest in his eyes and that half-smile of his that threatened to make her heart flip over. She couldn't afford to stare boldly back at him or enjoy the novelty of not being invisible to a vigorous and personable gentleman for once.

'You know very well I'm too busy and too poor to indulge in serious and expensive study,' she said as briskly as she could. Shivers of something she didn't even want to think about were racing up and down her spine.

'And yet I heard this was your afternoon at leisure,' he murmured from far too close and the words on their tongues seemed to have very little connection to the hot thoughts in their heads if the fire in his gaze was anything to go by.

Had he sought her out deliberately? A flush of pleasure and something a lot more complicated threatened to give her away as nowhere near as indifferent to him as she ought to be. 'Yes, it is,' she said breathily and the small freedom of that half-day of leisure tugged her inner rebel to the fore and threatened to tempt her into the impossible after all.

The girls were occupied; she was not expected to supervise or teach them for the rest of the day and there was nobody to frown and shake their heads at the sight of the governess and the steward so deeply absorbed in one another. She remembered Colm and his beloved Eve and the stolen afternoons *they* spent together when everyone pretended not to notice they had sneaked off to their rooms yet again. The unexpectedness of their passionate love still seemed to surprise even them. They would laugh and agree with each other how unlikely their marriage was and wasn't it the most delightful wonder anyone ever came across that the Winterleys and Hancourts were now united by marriage instead of scandal? For a moment Nell longed to visit the same exotically unknown and fascinating territory they went to together with a most unlikely lover of her own.

No, love did neither of her parents any good and somehow she knew her mother had loved the dashing young husband who only wed her for her father's fortune. And after she died Lord Christopher Hancourt blindly loved a wanton, a renegade viscountess who blithely abandoned her husband and child to live the wild life she chose with any personable man who could afford her, until she bled him dry and moved on to the next fool in line. It felt so lonely inside the safe, dry little world Miss Court had made for herself today, though. Nell's father, besotted lover of a notorious woman, dared his very life for Pamela, Viscountess Farenze. Yet even with that warning example of how far Hancourt folly went, his daughter felt the thunder in her blood at the thought of letting all the passion inside her roar. Horrified by her own frailty, she still stood and wondered about the notion she could enjoy being a passing fancy for this man, if only she dared.

How would it feel to be kissed by Moss as if she was lovely, sensuous and desirable? How might it feel to actually *be* those things to a man she wanted so badly it didn't matter about social distinctions or correct behaviour any more? For the longest and most charged moments of her entire life so far those questions sang between them as if she had spoken them aloud. Her lips parted without her permission, his fascinated gaze encouragement enough. Her entire body was aware of itself as never before. Every breath was a novelty as the scent and power and sight of him reached a curious and dangerous place inside her and whispered *maybe*. Had her mouth actually shaped the word to cause his gaze to sharpen on these suddenly rather full and needy lips of hers? His guard seemed to have fallen nearly as far as hers as he looked back at her with sharp interest and something gentler and warmer in his eyes. A curve of almost tender amusement lifted his mouth in a wry smile. Her feet raised on tiptoe, inviting him to lower his head and let wild, reckless Nell Hancourt out of her cage the instant he kissed her...

'Ah, there you are, Moss,' Mr Rivers's genial tenor voice drawled from far too close for comfort. Nell sprang back as if she'd been stung and the land steward stepped away as if he and the governess were always poles apart.

'Indeed I am, sir,' he said blandly with a not very respectful bow, as if the Earl's half-brother was intruding and ought to know better.

'Good afternoon, Mr Rivers,' Nell greeted the newcomer with a hasty curtsy and saw how horrified Moss was by how close they'd sailed to the disaster of being caught together as lovers by this inconvenient gentleman. Well, if he thought it a disaster, Miss Eleanor Hancourt should be congratulating herself on a lucky escape. So why did she feel something rare and precious had been snatched away?

'My brother's lawyer has sent those maps and

deeds on, Moss. No doubt he will expect us to pore over them until we resolve the northern boundaries he's so concerned about all of a sudden. Best get on with it as soon as we can, hey?'

'Very well, sir. I'll join you in the muniment room as soon as I've escorted Miss Court to her destination,' Moss said rather shortly, considering the gentleman might get him dismissed if Moss was as awkward and abrupt with his employer's brother as he was with her.

'Miss Court can get there without help, thank you,' Nell snapped because it hurt to be only an obstacle in his path now they'd been brought back to earth so abruptly. 'I am not yet in my dotage, Mr Moss.'

'Indeed you're not, ma'am, but with these rumours of down-at-heel strangers in the area looking for mischief any sensible lady must be wary of roving about alone.'

'Even the governess?' she said bitterly. His refusal to meet her eyes or be other than stiff and correct in front of Mr Rivers felt like a slight, however hard she told herself she hadn't really wanted his sensual attention in the first place.

'Especially her,' said the man who charmed her one minute and disclaimed any interest the next.

'Perhaps we could both escort you, Miss Court?' Mr Rivers asked more politely when she shook her head and stepped back from the man who had her senses so confused they were still yearning for his touch. 'As we're on our way to the estate office anyway it's a good excuse not to talk business until we get there.'

'I'd best agree to be escorted back to my duties then, sir. Mr Moss seems disinclined to move out of my way unless I do,' Miss Court said with her best smile for the Earl's gilded brother and a cool look of disdain for his land steward.

'We had best prove agreeable company then, Moss, since we're reordering Miss Court's leisure,' Mr Rivers said with an odd, mocking look at the man that gave Nell something else to think about as he offered her his arm and they strolled back towards the stately old mansion with Moss following behind like a bad-tempered hound.

'I'm not doing well at my drawing today, so I suppose it is not a hardship to be interrupted,' Nell managed to say lightly enough.

It was the peace and leisure to think that she

regretted. Back at the house she was always listening out for the girls; out here she was free to consider the dilemmas her restored fortune and Colm's marriage had thrown her way and now there was Mr Moss and his not-quite kiss to consider as well. The contrary man was stiff and reserved to a fault as she strolled towards the great house at Mr Rivers's side and she decided she didn't understand the opposite sex and didn't particularly want to right now.

'Whatever are you be about now, Fergus?' Brendan demanded the moment they were alone in the ancient muniment room with the stout oak door shut.

'I'm getting ready to read a pile of dusty documents in a room I never saw the inside of until Miss Court thrust the role of land steward on me all those weeks ago and what an idiot I was not to correct her.'

'Don't try and sidetrack me; you've been leading that poor girl astray since you got here. You were about to do something unforgivable until I came along and stopped you.'

'Which poor girl would that be?' Fergus said

in the mocking drawl he knew would annoy his little brother most.

He didn't want to be reasoned with about his bothersome fascination with a lady unlike any other he'd come across. So, *did* she seem unique because he wasn't his true self here, or even the modest Mr Ford he'd pretended to be on his adventures? Moss was a working man. Could that be why a much quieter and plainer young lady than he was usually attracted to had come fully into focus and made the rest seem dull and frivolous? Brendan was right, though; it *was* cruel to raise false hopes. Moss could be Miss Court's way out of the life of hard work and responsibility she was trapped by now. Yet she was still so young it pained him to see her frown over Lavinia's antics or look tired and pale at the end of a long day doing her best to teach his wards to at least act like proper young ladies.

'You know perfectly well which lady I mean— don't try to goad me into a temper or change the subject. You can't change the facts. Lord Barberry can't wed a governess and you know it as well as I do.'

'Aye, I do,' Fergus admitted with a heavy feeling

in his chest that felt oddly like loss. He couldn't lose something he'd never had and didn't particularly want—Moss was a convenient disguise, but he didn't want to wear his workaday boots for ever.

'Although you pretend not to care a fig for the wider world's opinion of my Lord Barberry, I know you couldn't make a refined and proper lady like that one your mistress and live with yourself afterwards, Fergus. Only imagine trying to meet Ma's eyes over the breakfast table after ruining the girl without your sins being obvious to her and tell me that I'm wrong.'

'You're right,' Fergus admitted reluctantly.

He imagined the brilliance of Miss Court's intriguingly fathomless brown eyes dimmed by shame and an even deeper loneliness than she endured now, if she lowered herself to be an idle aristocrat's plaything. Her current path in life was a hard one, but at least it left her some self-respect.

'Maybe I ought to send for a doctor, big Brother; you can't be well.'

'Worse; I think I might have to grow up,' he said ruefully.

'You mean come here as your real self? Truly

be the Earl of Barberry; after you swore not to step into your grandfather's shoes when he died?'

'Hmm, well, maybe one day I might do that,' Fergus half-agreed.

A mental picture of the governess's face when she found out the truth made him squirm at the deception he'd set out on that first night, even if she did offer it up to him on a platter with an apple in its mouth. If he wanted to stay here he'd have to confess sooner or later, but he wasn't sure he could face blank contempt in Miss Court's fine eyes when he admitted to being Earl of Barberry when even the idea of it made him feel slightly sick. No, he became Moss to get a true picture of how things stood here. His lordship could still be fobbed off, so he had at least one good reason to stay as he was.

'This year, next year, some time, never, then?' his brother asked as if he could read all his basest motives for staying quiet and didn't approve of a single one.

'You think I'm being a coward?' Fergus asked haughtily, wondering if his little brother wasn't right.

'I think you don't know who you truly want

to be and it's high time you made up your mind. You've been Earl of Barberry for a decade and refused to admit it whenever you can get away with pretending to be someone else. Until you decide to live comfortably in your own shoes, you'll be a danger to yourself and any stray governesses who expects more of you than you're capable of giving.'

'I hate the fact you're probably right, little Brother. You're five years younger than me and nobody seems to have told you I should be the wise one.'

'Natural genius trumps ageing cynic,' Brendan said smugly, but Fergus knew his brother was worried and why wouldn't he be? He was quite concerned about himself as well.

He had a brother and two sisters a prince of the blood would envy him, as well as a mother and stepfather who'd have gone to the stake to protect him when he was young and vulnerable. His mother even tried to forgive and forget the fact she and her baby could have starved when his real father died for all the noble Selfords cared. She pitied them for refusing to meet her son unless she agreed to relinquish him, but Fergus grew up hating them anyway.

All there was left of the mighty Selford family to be angry with when he inherited were four young girls who would have outranked him if they had been born male. His young cousins were more vulnerable than he'd ever been and he turned his back on them. He'd failed them as badly as his grandfather and uncles did him when his father died. He had a lionhearted mother to love him and they'd had nobody until old Poulson employed Miss Court to be their lioness.

He caught himself comparing Miss Court with Kitty, Lady Rivers, and smiling foolishly at the idea he'd hate to come between Miss Court and anyone she truly cared about as well. The old Earl's dead hand was all that had stopped Kitty dashing to England and gathering his orphans under her wing. That was another vile act to lay at the old devil's door instead of blaming the victims. Fergus was the girls' guardian only as long as his mother had no contact with them that had not been sanctioned by their trustees. And Miss Court wasn't bound to stay here and care for the Selford girls. Any day now a real land steward or curate would do his best to marry her and even the idea of her walking down the aisle and into another man's bed made him feel queasy. Yet as a wife she would be mistress of her own home and mother to her own brood, so why would she stay here and risk an uncertain future when her last pupil left the schoolroom?

All the clever, questing spirit would be knocked out of her if he seduced her because he wanted a woman in his bed, though. It was more than that, he knew it deep down even if he didn't want to. Miss Court fascinated him. He looked for her when he was near the house or in the Brampton villages. His day seemed brighter when he met her out and about with her charges, or busy on some errand in the shabby gig drawn by the placid old horse kept for her use. Although she would greet him stiffly and go on her way as fast as she could, his day improved on first sight of her awful bonnet and dreary pelisse in the distance. Not many ladies owned up to having any brains at all, but she was employed to use hers and had no reason to keep it a secret.

Admit it though, Fergus, his inner cynic whispered, *it's not only her inner beauty you're drawn to, is it?*

Not even Miss Court could completely hide her natural assets under those awful gowns and old-maid caps and bonnets. His mother and sisters could spend hours choosing frivolous hats and poring over fashion plates and he tried to picture Miss Court joining them, but it didn't work, so he must have been right all along—she would never fit into his real life if he was fool enough to pursue her with honourable intentions. He was about to kiss her just now, so he owed Brendan for stopping him committing such delicious folly with his wards' governess.

He spent the hours before dinner deep in estate business so his brother didn't have to. At least then he couldn't wonder how Miss Court's generous mouth would feel under his, if she didn't slap his face for taking liberties and storm off in a huff.

Chapter Ten

Nell let the most recent letter from her brother Colm drop into her lap and stared out of the latticed window at yet another dull spring morning. She wished it would get on and rain, but instead they endured day after day of grey skies and chilly gloom. Local farmers were shaking their heads and making dire predictions about the harvest; seeds couldn't sprout and grow without warmth or water to sustain them and only the crows seemed likely to grow fat this year. Colm said nothing of his own worries about this unremitting gloom in his letter, but between his recently inherited estates and those he oversaw for their uncle, the new Duke of Linaire, he must be anxious as any right-thinking landowner about the dire state of the land. The ducal acres were sadly neglected and Colm's own estates without a true master for a decade and a half, so Nell read between the lines and concluded that Eve had got him to London to enjoy the life of a wealthy and recently married aristocrat for a few weeks to escape all that heavy responsibility for a while.

Nell smiled at the thought of her beloved brother charmed into doing what was good for him by his new wife. Even when he knew she was doing it, he let Eve think she had got her way by stealth because he loved her so much and Eve almost glowed with happiness. Nell sighed and felt guilty about the nag of envy she tried hard not to feel. Colm was long overdue some joy after all those weary years of war their late uncle had inflicted on him by buying a commission in the most dangerous regiment he could discover and insisting Colm join it as soon as he was sixteen.

It must be wonderful to build a family with someone you loved and trusted so truly, Nell thought dreamily. Sometimes she longed for such a love so much it hurt, but she refused to make the Earl of Barberry's land steward the heart of those dreams. Moss would never fall headlong in love with a plain governess and she told herself she didn't even want him to. She sighed and tried to put the wretched man out of her thoughts, but the dull day outside her window offered no distraction from wondering what sort of young lady *would* tempt him. To fend off the shocking stab of jealousy such a smugly perfect female could cause her, she let her mind drift back to her childhood instead. Colm's letter had reminded her how she would read and re-read his every word to enliven the dull days back then. When Colm was sent to school the nursery governess her eldest uncle engaged to keep her out of his way was so stiff and unyielding Nell soon learned not to show her feelings. Tears brought a stern rebuke and an hour in the darkest and most spider-infested cupboard on offer.

Thank goodness Nell was sent to school herself at the age of eight. She might have gone mad locked in that dull world with her stern governess. Colm's letters and Nell's discovery that Miss Pitch dosed herself with laudanum most nights saved her from the endless greyness of that stark suite of rooms at the top of Linaire House. Tiptoeing down the backstairs once she could hear Miss Pitch snoring, Nell would creep about the largely closed-up house, discovering the luxury of her uncle's rooms; the now shabby watered-silk walls of the ladies' withdrawing room or the leather and velvet of His Grace's State Dressing Room, and her imagination would run riot. She might tremble at the idea of being caught in her uncle's private sitting room even when he was far away, but somehow it still fascinated her.

The last Duke of Linaire never came to London in summer when the city was tired and dusty and stank of too much humanity. Nell wondered if he hoped she would be carried off by one of the epidemic fevers that swept through the capital when heat sweltered in narrow courts and over-crowded rookeries. He was so proud and selfish any hint it wasn't Colm or Nell's fault their father had brought scandal on the family name would have been greeted with blank incredulity. He was a stupid man born to a great title and hadn't cared the snap of his fingers for anyone's comfort but his own.

His next brother, the current Duke of Linaire, was his exact opposite and that was probably why Nell could persuade Uncle Horace to travel to Brussels with her last summer to search for her injured brother on the battlefield at Waterloo. The stench of blood and death and all the appalling sights and sounds would haunt her to her dying day. For most of the day after the battle she and Uncle Horace peered into piles of the sightless dead and tried to avoid looters so eager for plunder they would kill anyone who stood in their way. They asked dazed survivors if they'd seen Captain Carter of the Rifles with desperate hope Colm had survived the carnage. When they were on the point of despairing and going back to the relative safety of the city for the night they finally found him; wounded and already in a high fever, but blessedly alive.

Futile hatred for the last Duke burned in her gut at that terrible memory. The late Augustus Hancourt, Duke of Linaire, might be dead, but she wasn't a fine enough Christian to forgive him for putting her brother in harm's way for eight years of the late war. No… Stop, she couldn't think of the spindle-shanked monster without being sucked under by hatred and fury even now. She refused to let him matter that much, so where was she? Oh, yes, tiptoeing about Linaire House in the dark and never mind her obsession with Moss the steward that constantly threatened to lure her into an impossible daydream of being a poor gentleman's wife and forgetting Eleanor Hancourt altogether.

She could still smell the dust and stale air of that grand town mansion when too few servants were kept on to keep it immaculate in the Duke of Linaire's absence. She could still imagine herself back there, listening for a sign her night wanderings had been discovered. Luckily she was too frightened of the dense shadows of the great city by night beyond the shuttered windows to venture outside, but saw some of it when she stood on a rout chair to peer through a gap.

Sometimes she would creep down the back stairs to listen to the other inhabitants of the half closed-up house. The servants kept on to protect it and wait on her and Miss Pitch would be dozing by the fire or talking in the smaller kitchen where the housekeeper baked her cakes when she and the Duke were in residence. Listening to them discuss when the Duke might return, Nell would wonder why she never went to Linaire Court, deep in the fertile Midlands and far away from dusty, smelly London. She had only seen true countryside from a hackney Miss Pitch hired to visit her parents in Hampstead on a day when the maid who had promised to look after Nell for the afternoon took to her bed. The Pitch family lived in a cottage on the Heath, but seemed happy and less wooden than their eldest daughter. Nell enjoyed Mrs Pitch's good-natured fussing, until Miss Pitch bundled her back into another stuffy coach for the return journey to grey and gloomy Linaire House. After that the governess seemed to dislike Nell even more and perhaps a woman forced to earn her living resented a child born to privilege, even if there were few signs of it by the time Miss Pitch began her stern rule.

She wasn't doing well at putting the past behind her and going on with her life as best she could, was she? Folding Colm's letter to be read again later, she frowned at the dull grey skies outside again and blamed Moss. His arrival here had woken something in her that was better left sleeping. She was content until he came, even if her duty to her charges was an excuse not to accept Colm and Eve's offer to stay with them and live the life Lord Chris Hancourt's daughter should have had all along. That duty still existed, but she wasn't so sure she was the person to carry it out.

She had blossomed at Miss Thibett's school

and perhaps her pupils would do better there as well. Once she was here Nell was too occupied with the struggle to get them to learn anything to wonder if she was the right person for the task. It took news that Lord Chris Hancourt was a very different father to the one his eldest brother had painted and the spectacular fortune Colm inherited at five and twenty to make her think again. Miss Hancourt was a catch on the marriage mart again, or she would be if the *ton* knew where to find her. Her father added her more modest fortune to the blind trust he had set up to protect her maternal grandfather's riches from his greedy eldest brother and Lord Chris's last gamble had paid off spectacularly well. Nell had a dowry that put all the Selford girls' portions added together in the shade. Now Moss was here another layer of uncertainty was plaguing her and he'd laugh himself hoarse if anyone suggested she might have a voice in his future, so why was she so reluctant to bid him goodbye if she went to the capital and forgot about Miss Court's duty?

'Miss Court, where are you?' Caro's voice sounded anxious. 'The carriage is at the door and we're all ready for church,' she called and Nell felt guilty about even thinking of leaving Berry Brampton House. Pushing the girls' absent guardian into sending her charges to Miss Thibett's Academy for Young Ladies instead of looking for a replacement governess could be a betrayal and she hastily pushed Colm's letters back into her writing slope.

'Coming, Caroline,' she called and tied the ribbons of her dull bonnet before taking a glance in the square of mirror on the mantelpiece to make sure she looked as dull and unremarkable as ever before picking up her prayer book.

'I was afraid we'd be late. Do you think Mr Rivers will attend church this Sunday?' Caro asked when Nell appeared in the hall. Bad enough that Lavinia sighed over every man she came across without Caro becoming infatuated with Lord Barberry's dashing half-brother.

'If he follows the Roman Catholic faith he will not be able to,' she answered, wishing him and his reluctant host at Jericho right now.

'Oh, no, all his family are Protestant—I asked him.'

'Are they indeed? That makes your family's attitude to his mama even less understandable,' Nell said before she could stop herself.

'That's what I always thought,' Caro agreed quietly.

'I expect they were good and right-thinking people otherwise,' Nell replied and wondered where such clumsiness would take her next.

'Grandfather used to shout a lot and call us girls names. I'm so glad Papa took us to sea with him because Grandfather used to say no girl was of use or decoration and he'd rather be dead than cost a dowry when some fool wanted to wed one of us.'

'Then he needed to beg forgiveness on his knees before he met his maker and was forced to account for his sins. Poor little Lavinia.'

'Vinnie tries to pretend it wasn't so bad being left here by her mama. It was wrong to leave her child with a bad-tempered old man if she didn't have to though, wasn't it, Miss Court?'

'Between you and me, yes, Caro. You can be very wise sometimes.'

'I'm quiet, Miss Court, I notice things and people often forget I'm there,' Caro said with a shrug that said a little too much about her life here since her father's death.

'Maybe, but not everyone puts what they over-hear to such good use. I shall try to be a little more patient with Lavinia in future.'

'And goodness knows, you'll need to be,' Caro admitted with a fleeting hug for her governess that warmed Nell's heart as they walked to the side door to wait for the other girls to finish dressing in their best for church.

'Good morning, Miss Court,' Moss greeted quietly and made Nell jump. She had found out the carriage was about to drive away to the inn yard down the street with Georgiana's prayer book and best handkerchief on board. 'Your footman asked me to give these to Miss Georgiana, but I expect you feel the lack of them more acutely than she will until she has need of them.'

'True, she does tend to live in the moment,' she said absently and wondered why, even blunted by gloves, his touch sent a *frisson* she didn't want to think about through her when he passed them over with a perfunctory bow and a shadow of his usual mocking smile.

'Where else is there?' he observed lightly and offered her his arm.

'There is the future and all the unforeseen consequences leading away from what we do today. Thank you for your offered escort, but, no, thank you, Mr Moss,' she said primly, ignoring his offer to help her into the Selford family pew as if she was precious to him, or many years older than three and twenty.

Much good it did her to refuse his escort, she decided crossly. She could almost feel his amused gaze on the back of her head as he meekly took his place in the lesser box pew allotted to Berry Brampton's upper servants behind this one and all that kept them apart was an inch or two of good English oak. She tried not to know he was scrutinising her best bonnet above the partition as if its fearsome respectability amused him. If Mr Rivers had a lady Nell could remove herself from the Selfords' box and sit with Moss the steward, Parkins the butler and Mrs Winch, housekeeper and her official chaperon. Since that gentleman was young, handsome and free as air Nell had to join him and her charges in the family pew. Somehow Mr Rivers didn't feel a threat to her good reputation. The Earl's little brother was like a large and amiable young dog, not quite fully grown and only half-tamed, but well disposed towards the world and ready to believe it felt the same way about him.

Mr Rivers sang lustily, prayed dutifully and listened as patiently as any man could to Mr Clennage's rambling sermon, so she couldn't blame him for this feeling of being uneasy in her own skin. It was the sound of Mr Moss's rich baritone voice that sent a flutter of prickly consciousness down Nell's back. Then there was her irrational suspicion his attention was fixed on the back of her head again, despite the day and the place. She sat rigid and uncomfortable in her well-cushioned seat and, try as she might, couldn't recall the thread of the vicar's homily to save her life. And that meant she would have to think of a diversion when Mrs Winch tried to discuss it with her and the girls tonight.

Lingering outside the church door when the service was over was a price a governess must pay for having four young charges with friends to greet and exchange news with, amidst the quieter gossip and making of plans their elders indulged in. Nell felt as if the whole congregation knew how hard she must try not to look at Moss. She made sure they went opposite ways through the groups of parishioners waiting for carriages or husbands, or wives and children. At last she managed to get all her charges shepherded into the largest of the Berry Brampton coaches for the journey home, long after the other servants had left and Mr Rivers and Mr Moss mounted their fine steeds and headed back to the land steward's house for whatever food such fit and healthy young gentlemen needed after a hearty breakfast.

'Faith has been wicked,' Mrs Winch whispered in Nell's ear once the girls were upstairs putting off their bonnets and shawls and finding indoor shoes. 'You had best come to my sitting room and find out what she's been up to, Miss Court, if that's convenient.'

Mrs Winch was a lady superior to most governesses in breeding and status, but Nell's position here was better than most young women forced to earn their own keep. She suspected his lordship's lawyer had made it clear the governess must be treated with respect, so his provisions for the Selford girls' improved well-being were not undone the moment the Nell arrived, suffered a frosty reception and turned tail. She was made of stronger stuff, but it was a relief not to be bullied and ignored by the servants and the family she worked for, as one of the pupil teachers at Miss Thibett's school was when she left to look for excitement. Nell hoped she had earned respect for at least staying in the face of the girls' determination to make her go, but Mrs Winch had never truly unbent towards her. Maybe she thought Nell would presume if she didn't subtly put her in her place now and again.

'Of course, the girls are busy putting themselves to rights and at least none of us need worry about lessons on a Sunday,' she replied and wondered what the girl had done that Mrs Winch could not deal with sternly then forget.

Faith was standing in the middle of the Housekeeper's Room, twisting her apron between her fingers and looking very woebegone. Mrs Winch briskly ordered her to stop ruining her uniform to add to her sins and the girl burst into tears. The housekeeper told her to stop it this minute and to Nell's surprise the young maid did exactly that. Nell wondered if she should try such stern tactics on the Selford girls next time one of them indulged in a storm of tears and imagined Lavinia's scorn or Penelope's surprise and nearly laughed at the wrong moment.

'I could hardly believe my eyes when I caught Faith searching the papers in your writing slope when I went upstairs to check the beds had been properly made. I heard an odd noise in your room and thought the stable cat had got in again, but it was even worse than that,' Mrs Winch said with a stern glare that threatened worse than being scurried outside by the scruff like the poor cat was last time it got ideas above its station.

'I didn't mean no harm, Miss Court,' Faith managed woefully.

'Then why do such an odd thing, Faith?' Nell asked.

'Well, you see, miss, it was because our mam ain't been well, the baby needs medicine and Pa can't get no work.'

'I'm very sorry to hear it,' Nell said and it sounded a tale of woe and all too familiar in these hard times.

'That's no excuse, my girl,' Mrs Winch put in coldly.

'Well, the lady said she'd pay me five pounds if

I found what she wanted when I saw her yesterday on my way back from the village,' Faith said defiantly. Mrs Winch glared even more ferociously at her and the girl looked about to cry again.

'What did this lady want you to do in return for such a vast amount of money, Faith?' Nell asked, wondering when this odd tale was going to make sense.

'Your letters and papers and any writing in books I could see apart from what should be in them, miss.'

'Good heavens, what use could any of that be to her?' Nell said, horror at what her correspondence could reveal making her feel quite faint, but nobody outside her family knew who Miss Court really was, did they? And why would it interest them if they did?

She wondered if Faith had bothered to look inside her neatly folded papers before she did her best to steal them and her heart did a panicked rat-a-tat-tat at the idea she wasn't as well disguised as she had thought. Moss would see her as a fine lady slumming while she made up her mind how to play her delayed entry into polite society if the truth came out like this.

'I dunno, miss,' Faith admitted after a pause for thought. 'I wouldn't have agreed to do it, but the apothecary said he'd have us put out on the streets if we didn't pay him. It's only a few bits of paper and a book or two, after all, and we do need the money awful bad.'

'If it wasn't going to hurt anyone, why did this woman want you to steal Miss Court's private letters?' Mrs Winch pointed out with another hard look that said Faith was about to lose her job, whatever Nell had to say about the matter.

The maid wasn't much older than Penny, who seemed so many years away from adulthood the notion of *her* working hard from dawn to dusk seemed ridiculous. Poverty brought maturity long before it was due, Nell decided, thanking God her grandmother hadn't allowed her to be put to work at the same age. And how could she save Faith and her family from being thrown on the parish?

'Perhaps it would be best if we don't let this strange woman know you were found out,' she said, with a warning glance at Mrs Winch to say this was more her business than the housekeeper's. 'How did you meet her?'

'At the Maying, Miss Court. She said she'd

come specially to see us dance at dawn and asked if anyone else had read about it in the paper last year. I did, when everyone else was finished with it and it was waiting to go out for the ragman. She said I was a clever girl and walked most of the way back here with us. Then she said she was here to find out something important for the Government and what a pity I couldn't work for her as I was already working for his lordship.'

'Five pounds is too much even for a key to his lordship's strongroom and I'm sure you wouldn't give her that even if you knew where to find it,' Nell said.

The quality of her unknown enemy seemed shoddy as she wondered who would think such an outrageous bribe could go unnoticed if Faith succeeded and her family suddenly paid off their debts. It sounded like the work of a pampered lady, used to casually splashing out large sums of money to get the best service. Might such an exotic creature be behind this odd business? Nell had nothing worth stealing and she shifted uneasily as it occurred to her that a bored society lady might be curious enough about the Hancourt heiress to step outside her luxurious life for a few days to unmask her.

'No, miss, that I wouldn't. Our mam will be fit to be tied when she finds out what I've done as it is.'

'Well, you let her down very badly, Faith. I shudder to think how hard it must be for her to feed your brothers and sisters already and if you lose your job it will be even harder.'

'I know, miss,' Faith mumbled miserably.

Nell reminded herself she was dealing with a child and the woman who had approached Faith to carry out such furtive mischief should take the blame, not an urchin barely old enough to be let out from behind her mother's skirts.

'If I overlook this disgraceful affair and beg Mrs Winch to keep you on, will you promise me not to tell anyone you were caught searching my room? If this lady asks, say you haven't been able to get into my room without being caught and tell me at once.'

'I ain't very good at lying, miss.'

'You seem a little *too* good at it to me, Faith, but perhaps you'd rather Mrs Winch sent you home?'

'Oh, no, miss,' the girl said with an uneasy look

at the stony-faced housekeeper. 'We'd be put in the poor house in two shakes of a lamb's tail.'

'I suggest you bear that in mind if you ever see this lady again,' Nell warned with a pleading look at Mrs Winch to persuade her to agree.

'And you'll swear never to do anything wicked again if you want to stay in this house another minute, Faith Roberts,' the lady ordered, presenting the girl with her own bible to make it a sacred oath.

'I swear, ma'am,' the girl said, her hand on the holy book and as solemn an expression as even Mrs Winch could wish on her tear-streaked face.

'Then go about your duties and don't say a word to anyone,' the lady said briskly. 'I shall be watching you like a hawk from now on.'

'Thank you, ma'am, Miss Court,' the girl gasped and bolted for the door before either of them could change their minds.

'Give me one good reason why I should not turn her off anyway,' Mrs Winch demanded as soon as the door was shut behind the shamefaced girl.

'It would alert this woman her plan has been thwarted and I'm afraid she'll try again by some means I may like even less.'

'It's very odd. Have you many enemies who take such a close interest in your private affairs, Miss Court?'

Nell felt she was under as much suspicion as poor Faith. 'I have no idea who is behind this folly, but I must find out if an attack of mania or mistaken identity led her to move against me like this.'

'I don't see how keeping Faith in a position she has shown herself unworthy of will do that.'

'Nor do I at the moment, but it will give us time to think.'

'I'm not sure I want to. We live in dark times, despite the peace, and there are rogues enough in the world without a thief living under his lordship's roof. I hope none of your relatives are Jacobins to account for it if the Government really do need to see your correspondence, Miss Court.'

'You know very well that my brother was an infantry officer for many years and was wounded at Waterloo. I took French leave to find him and drag him off the battlefield, so my family would never side with anyone intent on overthrowing our Government when he put his life at risk every day of his service to his country.'

'True; and I'm sorry to have doubted you, but this is a very strange business. We need wise masculine counsel if we're ever to sleep easily in our beds again.'

'You think I should write to my brother?'

'No, that would take too long. We must consult Mr Moss. He is his lordship's representative and has a strong arm and a clever mind. He may see something in this dark business we cannot. Don't shake your head at me like that; if you wish me to keep that girl on after she agreed to search your belongings for money, I insist you confide in Mr Moss.'

'Very well, but I can't meet a man in private and I refuse to discuss it in front of the girls.'

'Leave it to me,' the formidable housekeeper said with enough iron in her voice to steel a whole regiment of nervous housemaids.

Chapter Eleven

'Whatever can you want with me, Miss Court?' Moss asked impatiently later that day, once he'd ghosted into the housekeeper's room and shut the door very quietly behind him.

'It's not a tryst if that's what you think,' Nell said defensively.

'Just as well; they're supposed to be voluntary,' the man said grumpily.

Nell immediately wished she hadn't agreed to this condition of Mrs Winch's for going along with her scheme to find out what was going on. Faith badly needed to keep her place though, so Nell would tell the brusque, annoying man about the stranger after her secrets without revealing them to him either.

'It certainly wouldn't be so on my part,' she muttered and thought she saw a hint of hurt in the contrary man's eyes for a moment. 'And I don't want to be caught in here with the door shut and only you for company,' she added for good measure.

'Then stop wasting time and tell me what you and Mrs Winch think so urgent she got me here under false pretences and shut the door on us like a conspirator in a bad play,' he replied impatiently. After a militant glare at him for being infuriating, she did what he asked and told him Faith's odd tale. 'Have you been through whatever papers and books you have with you and looked for anything that could give a clue to this woman's purpose?' he demanded.

'Not yet. I thought her mad and have had no leisure,' she said defensively. Four lively girls and a day when cards, dancing and games were frowned upon meant she needed all her ingenuity to keep them from quarrelling and setting the whole household on edge of a Sunday. Bad enough that hers, Mrs Winch's and Faith's nerves were stretched tight without everyone else catching the ailment.

'Then you'd best hand them over to me so I can

look at them for you,' he said as if it was her only logical course of action.

'Certainly not,' she snapped, almost overwhelmed with horror at the thought of her letters from Colm and old friends at Miss Thibett's being combed through and all her secrets revealed.

'Then how do you expect me to find out what this mysterious woman wants and track her down?' he demanded impatiently, one eye on the door as if he couldn't wait to leave her alone again.

'I don't; I didn't want to tell you, but Mrs Winch insisted I must before she would agree to keep Faith on. I don't want the poor child turned off and her family put out of their house for the sake of a few shillings. In her shoes I'm sure I would have done the same thing if it meant paying off my family's debts.'

'Then you would have to be put out as well; what's the use of a servant who can't be trusted?'

'A master or mistress can lie and manipulate, but a girl not much older than my youngest charge must be beyond temptation? What an unjust world you live in.'

'It's the same one everyone else inhabits,' he said with a wry smile that almost disarmed her, until she remembered what he wanted and hardened her heart.

'That doesn't mean there's no room in it for change. If we don't want riot and rebellion running rife, then the poor should be less poor and their bread cheaper.'

'Lord Barberry won't be pleased if you impart such ideas to his wards.'

'How would he know? No, don't answer that for I'm quite sure I don't want to know what you say in your reports to our absentee employer. And please don't take me for a fool, Mr Moss. I know debutantes are supposed to be blithely ignorant of the state of the nation they live in and I have no intention of setting the Selford girls up for a fall when their lives are difficult enough already. They can still visit the less fortunate of his lordship's tenants and do their best to see their houses and larders are improved without causing a scandal. Surely even you won't argue his lordship's wards should be brought up in ignorance of how privileged they are? I'm sure the Earl would approve of them being grateful for their comfortable lot in life.'

The irony behind that seemingly obedient and

governess-like statement wasn't lost on him. She should remember he was acutely intelligent and might have the ear of their employer, but he'd made her angry with his assumption she'd put radical ideas into her charges' heads then expect them to flourish in the very limited sphere their sex and birth confined them to. She might privately rail against the fact a young lady must seem docile and almost stupid to make a good catch on the marriage mart, but she did want the Selford girls to be happy and accepted when they got there.

'As well for you that I'm Moss and not the Earl of Barberry, madam. He is your employer, yet you speak as if you hold him in contempt,' he said with one of those fearsome frowns that made her search her conscience.

'Reckless of me if you are devoted to his interests. Would you prefer me to pretend he is a good and diligent guardian and will you report me for refusing to lie, I wonder?' she asked defiantly.

'Say what you like about me, I'm not a spy,' he snapped back, then seemed to think about his own words and shook his head as if he had to deny it all over again.

She had certainly tweaked his temper and she eyed him warily. Was she trying to cover her unease at his order to turn over her secrets for his inspection by going on the attack? Possibly, she decided. 'I never said you were,' she said with a weary shake of her own head to admit she might have gone too far. 'Forgive me, this has been a difficult day. I'm tired and let my tongue run away with me.'

'Don't apologise, Miss Court, it's so rare for you to let your true feelings past the stern guard you put around them. I ought to be honoured.'

'You don't look as if you are,' she said with a wry smile and he chuckled as if she had surprised him yet again.

'Then looks can be deceptive,' he said and suddenly the heightened tension between them had nothing to do with his loyalty to their absent employer and her rudeness about the Earl.

'I'm still not handing you my personal correspondence,' she warned lightly, using their argument as an excuse to head for the door, because now the air was crackling with possibilities that really were impossible and she had to get out of here fast, before his charm overcame her caution.

'Love letters?' he asked, half-joking; almost condemning.

She stopped and turned to eye him warily once more. 'Certainly not, but they are private and written only to me.'

'Something you should remember when you're thinking about the odd events of the day,' he warned, but their voices were stating facts while their eyes were busy elsewhere.

Nell found time to shiver at the idea of those letters in the hands of some malicious rogue bent on harming Colm or his wife. Maybe it was that too-revealing gesture, or the fact she couldn't bring herself to break the contact of their eyes that drew Mr Moss to come closer; whatever it was they were suddenly standing toe to toe, studying each other intently. Nothing her sensible everyday self could say would make her back away and turn the doorknob behind her to break a spell she didn't fully understand. One minute they were about to snarl challenges at each other, on opposite sides of a battle about their noble employer. The next their almost-argument only added to tension of a very different kind. If she was going to be honest with him Nell might admit something new and reckless walked into her life the night she met Moss in the twilit stables, but it was best not to be too truthful when you weren't exactly who you were pretending to be, wasn't it?

Moss, how absurd to have to think of him that way when he felt so much closer than a stranger, but it was all he must be, mustn't it? Whatever he was called by those he loved, he had proved himself physically strong and he had an air of power that seemed natural as breathing. Despite his position as a nobleman's land steward, nobody owned this man; not even Lord Barberry. She breathed in the outdoor scent of him and wondered why she wasn't repelled by so much untamed strength and masculine heat so close to her it ought to burn such a respectable governess as Miss Court. For a long moment it felt like waiting for a force of nature to break over them; she was breathless and in awe of whatever was coming, but shivering excitedly about what it might turn out to be at the same time.

'Kiss me, you idiot,' she whispered at last and felt his shoulders shake a little as he laughed softly and it seemed to warm the very air between them.

'Wasp,' he whispered before he lowered his head and did just that.

Their first contact lip to lip was almost disappointing—gentle and bland—asking what she thought about this and waiting for her to remember Miss Court and Mr Moss, two respectable people supposedly going about their duty. She responded with a silent demand for more and that tidal wave she'd been waiting for hit her with even more force now she'd almost forgotten it was on its way. Oh, it was bliss, she thought, as she was swept under it and didn't even want to fight. It was rich and powerful and new and she wanted to stay lost in feeling like this for ever. More than mouth to mouth, it felt as if their whole bodies were kissing, exploring, yearning, owning each other between one second and the next. She shifted in his arms; trying to find her way inside his very skin so she would know everything, see all he was right now, feel at one with him. Sensation burned on sensation in a banquet of taste, touch, scent and small gasped sounds that were all either of them could spare. There was something missing; she prodded her sluggish mind to recall it—ah, yes, *sight*. Opening her dazed eyes was a mighty effort, but there, his were blazing back at her with hot blue fire in his compelling gaze that made him changed and yet so wonderfully the same it didn't matter who they really were. She felt so alive it was as if anything was possible for them right now. If she sprouted a pair of wings and flew out of a window to soar into hot blue skies with him, as if they were a pair of courting eagles, it would feel almost normal. She gasped a huge breath in and wanted to laugh joyously, to squirm ever closer until they saw through the same eyes, felt with the same touch, learnt one another's every last breath and sinew.

His long limbs were the only way a man's limbs should be. The power of the hard muscles under her urgent hands testament to the fact here was no idle beau or nobleman, sitting about his castle in luxury whilst the rest of the world worked to keep him. His rein-callused hands on her soft curves and narrow waist were bliss, but even that wasn't quite enough for the hungry wanton within. That Nell knew there was more than even this wonder. The everyday one felt the world battering away at her certainty here was her mate, her given man, the one. In protest at this sense not everything was as it should be between them, she explored his jaw line, her hand gliding over supple tanned skin tight on his high cheekbones and down. Who would have thought the feel of a man's beard about to sprout would be the stuff of fantasies under her fingertips as she ran them back down towards his fascinating lips and padded them against his skin? He opened his mouth and suckled on her index finger and she gasped at the wild heat searing through her as his hot blue eyes held hers with a promise to forget everything but her and him for a long, sensuous moment.

Willing to give him that promise back with interest, she fell back against the nearest support her body could find at short notice and felt the cold brass of the door knob at her back. She flinched away as if someone had stuck a knife in her. Heavens above, but they were kissing like lovers in Mrs Winch's very respectable sitting room. She, the governess, and Moss, his lordship's steward, were locked in each other's arms as if they'd been born to love each other. Except she wasn't simply Miss Court the governess, was she? And he didn't love her. Did he? She peered up at him almost fearfully now, unsure if she was delighted or wounded to the heart when he seemed to catch her caution and looked a cool question back at her, despite the sound of his breath coming fast in his labouring lungs and a tremor in his long-fingered hand as he felt the knot in his carelessly elegant cravat for damage.

'I shall leave you to compose yourself, Miss Court,' he said, avoiding her gaze altogether, now he'd put that sensual wildness behind him so completely she wondered if she imagined the impassioned lover of a few seconds ago.

'How can you be so cold, so, so…oh, I don't know…so careless about kissing me and everything?' she managed incoherently.

'Ask me again tomorrow, when we're further from me throwing myself on you and begging for a night in your arms, Miss Court. Right now I'm not quite safe for you to be around; by then maybe I can be tame and Mr Moss again.'

His voice was hoarse and he looked as if it had cost him a great deal to stand back when he'd felt her jolt of shock and instinctive horror at what they had almost done together without love. She wanted to explain it wasn't horror they could have been lovers if they hadn't woken up to where they were in time. Part of her was mortified to say it wasn't that at all, it was because she wasn't being honest about herself, or any of the reasons she was still here being Miss Court instead of Miss Hancourt, with her splendid marriage portion and embarrassment of noble connections. It was the huge lie Miss Court was that stopped her tongue and made her shuffle her feet as if they'd be better off on the other side of this confounded door. A confession trembled on her lips, she even opened her mouth to start it, but he got there first.

'Promise me you will go through your papers as if you are seeing them through the eyes of a stranger as soon as you can? I can't imagine what you and your family or friends have been up to in order to attract the attention of a felon, but if you don't find some clue why this idiotic female thinks your correspondence is worth five pounds to her, then I will. I won't have the Selford girls endangered because you brought a maniac here and refuse to let me see what makes her think she can bribe and corrupt the servants to get hold of it without answering to me.'

'*You* won't have it?' she asked, startled by the steely purpose in his cold blue eyes now, almost as if she was in league with the woman who wanted to see her letters because she wouldn't meekly hand them over for him to read.

This was the man who kissed her as if his life depended on it moments ago. His eyes had blazed passion and what she took to be even deeper feelings only moments ago, when he gazed at her as if she was the centre of his world. She probably had been as well, for that fleeting instant. Bitterness blotted out her guilt about deceiving him. He didn't care for her, so why should she be uneasy about Miss Eleanor Hancourt and her fine fortune and the distance that ought to set her from the Mr Mosses of this world? None of it mattered, because she didn't matter to him.

'*You* won't let me endanger the girls I spent two years of my life trying to guide and teach to the best of my ability when nobody else cared a snap of their fingers what became of them? *You* accuse me of putting myself first when you have been here little more than a month and know nothing of the struggle I have had to even persuade them to be civil to each other, let alone learn anything? *And* you think me capable of some underhand scheme because someone I have never set eyes on has decided she has the right to single me out as quarry for no good reason? Mr Moss; judge and jury of lords and governesses; mentor and protector of my lord's despised wards and guardian of Berry Brampton's morals—what a fool I was to think you were a man in your own right. You're only a puppet dancing to your master's whims and what a master you chose to caper for; I'd rather sup with the devil than bend the knee to the Earl of Barberry myself,' she finished and took one last, dismissive look at the tall figure of Moss, Lord Barberry's faithful estate manager, before opening the door as coolly as if her hands weren't shaking almost too hard to grip it and stalking out like an offended dowager duchess.

If only she knew, Fergus thought darkly as he listened to Miss Court's petticoats rustling stiffly down the corridor and the fading echo of her soft slippers as she climbed the schoolroom stairs.

She was off to her room, alone and on her dignity, and he felt responsible for that and so many other wrong turns he'd made since he met her. He'd arrived almost ready to admit he was the errant Earl of Barberry and it was her fault he'd been diverted. Her fault he was braced like a trooper about to ride into battle at this very moment. She had no idea how harshly a man roared and ached and tore at his tethers for satisfaction of the sort of urgent, desperate need she'd roused in him just now by responding so passionately to his kiss. If she despised the Earl of Barberry, he *loathed* the man right now. The lord of all this faded splendour would get short shrift from stubborn Miss Court with very good reason. Even if he wasn't the man standing here needing her so hungrily he wanted to lock them both inside her bedchamber until she admitted she wanted him back, then satisfy them both with infinite pleasure, that lord couldn't want a governess.

Except he did and how had he let that happen? Fool, he raged at himself. How could he have been furious with her one minute for refusing to let him see her dratted letters, then step into another world of wanting and needing with her the next? It felt almost as if a cliff had dropped away in front of them and he'd grabbed hold of her eagerly as they both plunged off it into thin air together and learnt to fly. He might as well admit he'd been intrigued by her one moment and infuriated the next since he'd got to Berry Brampton and met her in the gloaming now though, hadn't he? She wasn't like any other woman he'd ever come across and she certainly wasn't a beauty. After ten years wandering the earth as Mr Ford, a gentleman of means but not quite fortune, he'd met enough beautiful women to compare Miss Court's unique features to several patterns of perfection and find it wanting. But it wasn't about symmetry and classical proportions, was it? Not when the woman you were thinking about was Miss Court, governess to the Earl of Barberry's wards and a disaster in petticoats.

He told himself her mouth was too big and her nose was pert and her dark brows too strongly marked and they didn't go with that seductive mass of potentially unruly honey-brown hair she tried to keep under such stern control. The whole shape of her face was wrong as well, he decided, warming to his subject in the hope of breaking the spell she seemed to have him so firmly under right now, beauty or not. Instead of an oval model of classical perfection it was heart-shaped and that firm chin of hers must have been especially formed to defy him—since she'd been raising it to look down her tip-tilted nose at him since the first moment they met. So how was he doing at teaching himself indifference to Miss Court and the delicious feel of her coming vividly alive in his arms when she intrigued him in so many novel ways? Very ill, he decided and began to pace the room like a caged animal as he tried to find a way not to visibly want his wards' governess. He wasn't doing well; this need to teach her to gasp out her wildest extremes of passion under him right now felt so desperate it hurt.

Now, where were all those reasons why that couldn't happen? Ah, yes, there they were; waiting for him to list them and teach himself self-control. One, Brendan was right: he couldn't make her his mistress. Two, he couldn't marry her, even if she would have him once she found out who he really was and how badly he'd been deceiving her all this time. Even if he wanted to play king to her beggar maid, she would refuse him and flounce off in an insulted temper because she despised the Earl of Barberry and was almost reckless about making that fact known to his land steward. An almost tender smile tipped up his mouth as he pictured her blaming him for the fact she must find another place because she wouldn't work for such a charlatan if he offered her ten times her current stipend to stay here. Not that he would, he promised himself faithfully.

Three—or was it four—the only way he could make this right and not ruin her was to find her another position on the other side of the country from Berry Brampton when Moss had to ride away as unexpectedly as he'd arrived. He couldn't stay here and pretend to be his own estate manager for much longer. It was only ever an impulse he ought to have resisted to pretend he wasn't really *my lord* for a little longer. Of course he'd learnt far more about the house and estates than he would have as master of it. Try telling Miss Court that when she found out who he really was; she'd be incensed at his deception and under all her bitter fury would be a deep and abiding hurt. He could picture the mix of contempt and distress in those depthless brown eyes of hers even as he thought about confessing to her who he really was. What a shame he was still too much of a coward to bring this farce to an end right now, before she was hurt even more badly.

And they would both hurt if he didn't tear himself away very soon. He'd seen his mother hiding her humiliation at the slights and mockery of her so-called betters too many times to delude himself that Miss Court would be accepted as his Countess. Maybe she was a governess and not an actress, but she was still poor, vulnerable and working as a servant. He'd promised himself as a small boy he would never do what his father did and persuade the best woman in Christendom to wed him, then die and leave her to suffer all those sneering comments and slights when he claimed to love her so dearly. It wasn't a particularly rational way of looking at the world, but the example of that love affair still stood like a stony barrier between him and a woman he might love, if he truly was Moss and not a very reluctant earl indeed. What if he wed her, then got himself killed, so some distant cousin of his could mock and slight his Countess for not producing a son in time to supersede him and grab the title of Dowager Countess for herself when her foolish lord died? It hurt nearly as much to imagine Miss Court refusing to flinch in the face of such contempt as Kitty had every time someone repeated the last Lord Barberry's spiteful words about her and his own grandfather swore he'd kill her brat before he let him stand in his shoes.

He couldn't go yet, though—Lord Barberry couldn't chase down the woman after Miss Court's papers. He would be too conspicuous as his true self, especially if everyone knew he was here and trying to fit in a place he'd cut himself off from for a decade. He couldn't leave that thread loose and let Miss Court walk off into the world with a villain on her tail either and wasn't it absurd he only knew her by her surname? He wondered what her given one was. Was she a simple Jane or Ann or a complex Clarissa or Augusta? Ah now, wasn't that exactly what he'd promised himself he wouldn't do? No good lingering on her and the fascinating inner self under all the starch. Her odd conundrum had given him a very good reason to be Moss for a little while longer though and wasn't that a relief? He gave himself a mocking grin in Mrs Winch's mirror as he mentally seized that excuse with both hands. Brendan could despise him all he liked for cowardice, but at least as Moss he could creep about the estate unchallenged when the Earl or his half-brother would be remarked on and gossiped about. It was his excuse and he was going to stick to it, because Miss Court might suffer a lot more than a bruise to her pride and a little more knowledge of a man's passions than she wanted if this stranger had good reason to track her down and take her life apart for her own ends.

Chapter Twelve

Nell couldn't see a good reason why anyone would want her letters and what few personal papers she had. Of course there were one or two bad ones, but if someone wanted to blackmail her for pretending to be Miss Court why not simply get on with it? And how would a stranger pick up her deception when she had been here two years without a soul suspecting she wasn't the quiet governess she appeared? It was a small enough leap if anyone found her interesting enough to track down as her true self, she supposed. Colm knew; her uncle and aunt, the current Duke and Duchess of Linaire, agreed to give her time to think about her restored fortune and they were too kind and vague to prod her into the open with a devious scheme they would never consider fair. The Winterley family knew who she was as well, of course, but Colm and Eve had a quiet wedding at Dark-mere and the wider public didn't know his sister had been there, so what about her friends?

Her fellow pupils at Miss Thibett's Academy had either become teachers themselves or drifted so far from Nell's orbit they lost contact. Uncle Augustus had insisted she became Helen Court the moment she'd set foot in the school so, even if they wanted to, her friends couldn't betray her secrets. Yes, she was living quietly in the country, pretending to be dependent on her earnings as a governess, but it was a small deception that did no harm. If his lordship was here even a hint she spent time alone with him would have the gossips on the edge of their seats, eager for every detail their busy tongues would make up if it didn't exist. As well the Earl of Barberry was far away, then, so she could cross one disaster off her list.

She sighed and lit all the candles in the branch on her desk for once. Hard to admit to herself Mr Moss was right, but she had to go through all the letters and papers in her writing slope and the locked box of personal belongings under her bed. Looking for any clue that might account for a stranger's odd behaviour would keep her busy.

As she pulled the familiar old box out and put the key in the lock she decided it was going to be a long night, but she didn't want to sit and dream of ineligible gentlemen with sense-dazzling kisses and a cross-grained temper until the shock and wonder of his kiss had worn off. She wouldn't sleep with the memory of that wonderful disaster refusing to be dismissed all night long. Might as well make good use of the time, then, and try to track down his wild goose, despite her conviction there was nothing worth finding out about Miss Court, governess, or at least nothing he was ever going to hear.

Fergus rubbed a weary hand over his eyes and shook his head at his brother's offer to pass more bacon.

'If I had to ride about the place all day long, I'd eat enough to keep several bears alive before I started, but if you want to fall off your horse for lack of food halfway through the day that's your problem,' Brendan told him. 'And speaking of bears, you're like one with a sore head yourself this morning.'

'You talk too much,' Fergus replied, wishing

he'd taken to the bottle last night since he had such a head today he might as well have drunk himself into a stupor anyway. Of course, enduring a sleepless night tossing and turning and feeling guilty about Miss Court as frustration racked him was guaranteed to make him short-tempered, but that was understandable.

'Quite an achievement given I currently share a house with you, Brother dear,' Brendan told him with enough edge on his insult to make Fergus wonder if he'd been unusually terse with his little brother and he'd missed the boy like the devil all the years he was far away.

'Don't call me that here,' he said gruffly, 'servants have ears as well.'

'As well as what? A fine feminine figure and large brown eyes a man could drown in if he let himself?' Brendan said with a knowing look that made Fergus want to punch him for noticing Miss Court's more obvious assets when why wouldn't he?

'Attempt to explore that particular servant's worst-kept secrets and I'll make sure you can't walk upright for a week,' he warned his brother so softly Brendan nearly choked on his vast breakfast and looked truly horrified for a moment.

'Ah, so that's how it is, is it?' he finally recovered enough to reply sagely and Fergus could almost see the cogs turning in his brother's busy head.

'Of course it isn't. You know I wouldn't foul my own nest.'

'How would I? You were never in it before and even now you're pretending to be your own steward.'

'Well, I won't,' Fergus said shortly. Of course the very idea was repulsive, but an image of Miss Court breathless, warm and heavy eyed in his arms last night still tore holes in his certainty he'd be a villain to teach her more about lovemaking than a virtuous governess could afford to find out.

'The truth is you can't see straight about this place or the Selford half of your family. Those old men made you so furious about their precious succession and the way they hated Ma for being a fine and lovely creature your father insisted on marrying that you can't see past what they did.'

'What can't I see, then?' Fergus asked disagreeably, wishing he didn't fear Brendan was right.

'What a mess they left behind them?' Brendan said frankly, looking about the ramshackle room with a frown.

Eyeing the ancient roof and chimneys of Berry Brampton House from the morning-room windows, Fergus couldn't help but agree there was a great deal wrong here and he'd done nothing much to put it right yet. 'What would you do in my shoes, then?' he asked gruffly.

'Send those girls to school, give your precious governess a good reference and go back to Ireland, but that's what I'd do, Fergus, not what you want to do.'

'How do you know?'

'You don't love the land there like I do, so why would you turn your back on all this and go back to being the nobody in particular you've pretended to be these last ten years? You didn't find peace thousands of miles away, so how do you expect to feel it wandering about your own country? You belong here, Fergus, whether you want to or not. Fight the idea until the truth seeps through your thick skull if you like, but you feel something for this place I couldn't if I lived here the rest of my life.'

'I was never wanted here,' Fergus said gruffly.

'Not by a pack of dead men, but they're all gone now, aren't they? You're alive and the Earl in possession, despite all they did to stop you inheriting. Time you learnt to live with who you are and where you come from, my lord.'

Fergus grimaced. 'No, thank you,' he said abruptly, threw down his napkin and stamped out of the room in an even worse mood than the one he came in with.

Riding off to view the next old-fashioned and under-capitalised farm on his list, he thought about the effort it would cost him to live here and make the changes needed to drag this ancient estate into the nineteenth century. He could find a substitute Mr Moss to do it for him, he supposed, but the original one proved to be a broken reed. Since everything his forefathers had left him so reluctantly was entailed he couldn't sell any of it, but he could rent the whole place to a nabob with more ruthless ideas about progress than he had. Or he could stay here and try to be a good master of this grand old house and all the estates he'd never wanted to inherit. He could build the schools and encourage the trades and businesses that might make this place more secure and prosperous for those who lived here than it was as a simple agricultural system unchanged for a hundred years or more. He saw the benefits of shared labour and common land, but growing up in Ireland had taught him a few lessons about holdings that were too small to weather a series of bad harvests or a glut on the market. Yes, Berry Brampton would be challenge enough even without his four wards and the hard task of finding a replacement governess they wouldn't loathe on sight— so could he truly be Lord Barberry for the first time in his life and make suitable arrangements for them as Brendan suggested?

With his true family living in Ireland and no wife at his side it would be lonely sort of enterprise without the girls and their governess here to make it an adventure though, wouldn't it? No, Brendan was right; they would be far better at a good school. Here the fact they were born female and unable to inherit was flung at them at every turn, even more so when he took up residence as his true self. They were as much victims of the Selfords' single-minded determination to keep the son of an actress out of the succession as he was. He was protected from their obsession by a loving mother and stepfather. Not just protected, doted on, he recalled with a guilty glance at those venerable chimneys under which four orphaned girls had lived virtually alone for so long. Gifted with a brother he liked better than any Selford ever did one of theirs, and two half-sisters a man could be proud of, he knew now that he had so much and they had very little. How could he ever have resented them for being living proof of how little his father's family wanted him?

His deception sat heavy on his shoulders this morning and he was tempted to turn about, ride up to the main house and openly declare himself the Earl of Barberry. His mouth lifted in a wry grin for the first time this morning at the thought of the response he would get. Even Brendan's word wouldn't be enough to convince Miss Court in her role as temporary guardian and protector of the Selford girls that he was exactly who he said he was. She would probably refuse to believe him and who could blame her? No, if he was going to do this, he must plan better and wait until he had this mysterious stranger after Miss Court's private papers in his sights. The Earl's arrival might cause a sensation and scare the woman off, so he could forget unmasking Moss for another day and concentrate on the next farm on his list, and the puzzle of reasoning out why anyone wanted to know even more about Miss Court than he did.

'What are you reading, Miss Court?'

'A private letter, Lavinia,' Nell said repressively. Trust her eldest pupil to see the dark shadows under her governess's eyes and try to take advantage.

'It hasn't arrived recently from the look of it. Either you take no care of your mail, or it's quite old and worn out with reading already.'

'I do expect a properly argued, fair copy of that essay by the end of the day and what I choose to read and the state of my letters is none of your business, Lavinia,' she managed to say sternly before she pointedly went back to her reading.

'I hate history,' her eldest pupil mumbled rebelliously.

'We know. Most eligible gentlemen have expectations of a house of some sort though, and not all of them are newly built, so won't you look a fool if a young man you admire has an ancient house and you are ignorant about every age it had to survive to be the place it is today?'

'I suppose so, but it's so very stuffy,' Lavinia said with a mighty sigh.

'Everything a young lady needs to learn is stuffy, useless or boring as far as you're concerned, but the sooner you learn, the sooner you will be a young lady and escape it all at last. Now, kindly get on with your work and leave me to study some slightly less ancient history in peace.'

Lavinia grimaced, tried to distract her cousins from their own work for a moment or two, then went back to the Tudor monarchs with an even louder sigh. Nell fought a strong urge to close her eyes and nod off in the now-peaceful room and forced herself to carry on reading the letters she had set aside last night to read more carefully when she could find time. The ones her brother Colm wrote when they were children, then on his very active service in Spain and France had been read and re-read so many times she was certain there was nothing hidden in them, apart from as lively an account of how it felt to be a schoolboy and then a soldier in extraordinary times as she had ever come across. Maybe one day they could be edited and published to give a colourful picture of how it felt to be a young officer in the Duke of Wellington's army. Then schoolgirls far in the future could sigh to their teachers and moan about how stuffy it all was, until they read what Colm had to say about Portugal and Spain and the makeshift Allied Army who faced the great Napoleon across a muddy field last summer and changed the fate of Europe. Except Colm had been too ill from his wounds to write anything after Waterloo and Nell saw far too much on that battlefield herself the next day to want any reminders of such terrible slaughter.

She shuddered and made herself focus on the letters in front of her to divert herself from memories that would probably haunt her to her grave. Most of her school friends were faithful and often funny correspondents, but their letters were no different from those of any other group of like-minded people who once lived under the same roof. It was good to go over them again and value them as true friends, but otherwise their letters had nothing secret or startling in them.

She kept aside some letters between her mother and father that had found their way into her trunk when she left Linaire House for school. Maybe someone put them in with her things to stop her wicked uncle destroying them. Disappointed in what they had to say to each other and not really wanting another reminder they were both dead, she must have put them back in the box and forgotten all about them. With the eyes of an adult she could see her parents wrote of mundane matters when they were apart, but the easy and affectionate tone of their letters spoke of a far closer marriage than the one she had expected, given what her father did after her mother died. She was three years old when she lost her mother and all she recalled of the years before was a feeling of being warm and loved. So, her parents had been a lot happier than her uncle wanted anyone to think when his brother took up with a notorious woman to try to keep the loneliness away after his wife died. Papa was desperate to satisfy Pamela Verdoyne-Winterley's every whim so Nell had written her parents' marriage off and didn't bother to do more than glance at these letters until today.

What a mistake, she realised now. Her father had learned to love his rich and supposedly plain wife and Nell thought her mother the stronger character of the two, which might explain why Pamela could lead her father by the nose later. Anyway, never mind the old feeling she and Colm had been deserted for a ruthless siren, mutual affection came off the page in every letter and she wished she'd read them properly years ago. She had taken the late Duke of Linaire's word that her parents had a miserable arranged marriage. Instead it must have seemed to him that Lord Chris and his upstart wife had everything he deserved and they didn't. Her nabob Grandfather Lambury's fabled riches, Papa's famous good looks and charm, and, worst of all for a childless duke, children. Her eldest uncle was jealous of handsome, heedless Lord Chris Hancourt who had love dropped into his lap and a son he didn't even need, as fourth son of their noble father.

All this might be a revelation, but there was nothing here anyone would pay handsomely for. Her father might have been all but broken by the loss of his wife and perhaps he'd chased some sort of solace with a noble doxy, but it was an old scandal. Her possession of the letters gave away her true birth and her brother's latest ones spoke of restored fortunes, but how could that benefit anyone else but her? The bare thought of kidnap and forced marriage shook her badly. She managed to turn her gasp of shock into a sneeze and shook her head and apologised before waving her pupils back to their work with a severe look to tell Lavinia not to make it an excuse to disrupt her cousins.

No, she would have known if hard, speculative eyes dwelt on her when she ventured out. Shivering in the stuffy room, she tried to feel safe at Berry Brampton and as anonymous as ever. At least here in this high old schoolroom nobody could see in, unless they could learn how to sit on a cloud and not fall through. Maybe she ought to arm herself whenever she was out and about with the girls? She considered purloining one of the deadly looking duelling pistols locked up in the gun room and shook her head at the very idea. It almost made her smile to imagine herself armed to the teeth like a bandit whenever she took a step outside this room, then she looked at the row of dutifully bent heads in front of her and decided the Selford girls would seem a much finer catch for a kidnapper. It would be an absurd scheme, considering the wrath of the Earl of Barberry if he was forced to come here and meet his obligations for once. The Selford girls had a reluctant but powerful guardian to protect them. And why would a kidnapper want to look at Nell's letters anyway? Even with Mr Moss's fearsome frown and gruff impatience with her to contend with, she couldn't take that threat seriously.

Her letters were important to her alone, but for the small secret of her identity, so she laid them down and stared out of the window. Lavinia shifted in her seat and threatened to do the same if Nell didn't at least pretend to be occupied, so she turned to the only paper left in the pile she had brought into the schoolroom to puzzle over. This odd piece of doggerel seemed senseless, but nothing else would cause a stranger to spend a vast sum of money to get hold of it, so it must be looked at. She hadn't even found it until Colm was away at school and it never seemed important enough to tell him their father had left a message behind for her and none for him. It wasn't as if it made sense and he would have been hurt to be forgotten by the father he once adored.

For years the paper must have been at the bottom of her writing box, forgotten as her parents' letters had been. She had to rack her brains to re-member where it came from until it came to her— she found it a few weeks after she and Colm were parted. The paper was a little tattered even when it fell from the roof of her doll's house after her nursery governess kicked it in a fit of pique. Ap-parently Nell had been paying more attention to her doll family than her lessons and she almost wished the Selford girls had to spend a week with the old dragon to realise they had quite an ami-able sort of governess most of the time.

The few servants kept at Linaire House in the Duke's absence came running when Nell screamed, then burst into loud sobs at the sight of her imaginary home broken open and every-thing inside it flung far and wide. Miss Pitch was obviously in the wrong and not Nell, so her little house was picked up and reassembled as well as it could be. The delicate little figures inside were taken off to be mended by the night watchman and Nell comforted by a scullery maid not much older than she was. And this sheet of paper was left on the floor when everything else had been gathered up. It must have been hidden under the roof or between floors. Nell had never seen it before and felt sad now because she hadn't even rec- ognised her father's writing at the time.

Thanks to his obsession with Pamela, Papa was a stranger to his children even before he died. It never occurred to Nell that it might be painful for Lord Chris to live in the home he'd shared with his wife until today. When it was closed and his children went to Linaire House and Uncle Augus- tus's less-than-tender care, Nell couldn't recall receiving a single letter from her father. Perhaps their uncle kept them back, of maybe Lord Chris really forgot his family and that other life in his lover's arms. Reading those letters between her parents made Nell doubt if her father would turn his back on their children so completely.

She frowned down at the rather dog-eared parchment in front of her. Whether he loved her or not, Lord Chris's scribbles made no sense. Per- haps she ought to show Colm this paper and see if he understood it better, but trusting it to the post made her feel uneasy for the first time in her life. If someone valued her letters so highly she was willing to pay poor Faith to steal them, what else would she do to get hold of one that contained the only mystery Nell had, besides her true identity?

She could show it to Mr Moss, she argued with herself, as she sat here feeling muzzy headed and weary after a sleepless night caused by the confounded man in the first place. Very likely it would make even less sense to him than it did to her, so she re-read the greeting at the beginning instead. No, it was too precious to share with a man so austere and aloof from her, despite the earth-shaking kiss they exchanged last night. He wasn't ready to trust her with *his* innermost thoughts and dreams, so why should she strip her thoughts and memories bare to appease him? Feeling vaguely guilty at wasting good teaching time on this nonsense, she began to doodle notes and questions about her father's odd little drawings and the series of numbers she'd never really tried to work out before.

'Finished, Miss Court,' Penny said cheerfully before she could get very far with that project and Nell looked up to find all four girls watching her expectantly.

'Excellent. Hand in your books and I will mark them tonight. Now it's nearly time for your luncheon, so please go and scrub the ink off your fingers, Georgiana. Lavinia, I hope you will oblige me by helping your Cousin Penelope tidy herself up before we eat.'

'I can do it myself, Miss Court,' her littlest pupil protested.

'You always skip the hairbrush and the washing bit of the list whenever you think you might be able to get away with it, Penelope.'

'Horrid brat,' Lavinia said mildly and Nell thought her eldest pupil seemed ready to be fond of her cousins at last, although she was still a challenge to teach and be responsible for on a day to day basis.

After they had eaten the rather plain luncheon Cook thought fit for growing girls, the cousins were free to play for an hour or so and Nell drifted down to the library with her father's latest mystery because it seemed the most peaceful place to think. The numbers didn't have a logical sequence, but maybe it was some sort of code—if so, she didn't know how her father expected a three-year-old child to work it out and it occurred to her he meant it as some sort of insurance against the chance he would not come home when he hid it. He took a chance then, didn't he?

Betting on the possibility she would even find that piece of paper he'd slipped between the cleverly made attic rooms of her beloved dolls' house was almost as huge a chance as him being able to survive a wild drive in an Alpine blizzard. If Miss Pitch hadn't lashed out at Nell's favourite toy his message might still be there now, or destroyed when the battered and much-mended toy was finally thrown on the bonfire. Still, he had gambled with his life; why shouldn't he take a chance his daughter would find his last message against the odds?

Nell shuddered at the memory of how terribly he'd lost the bet on his own life and his lover's. What a legacy for his children, she thought bitterly; an appalling image of her father lying broken and dying by his lover's side so many hundreds of miles away and beyond help as darkness fell and nobody came.

No, she refused to revisit the nightmares of her childhood. Lord Christopher Hancourt chose to take that risk; he was an adult who ran away to live only in the moment of his own free will. Nell blinked away the memories of how it felt to be less important than the woman her father adored and frowned at the paper in her hand. The numbers made little sense, so what about the odd shapes her father drew around the sequence he set her? Surely he didn't expect a three-year-old child to unravel the numbers, but drawings would be a better bet. She tried to think of it as she might have done back then, if she had paid it this much attention. Perhaps it was something to do with their home at the time? No good, she couldn't even remember what the houses they once had in London and Brighton looked like. She had a sense of warmth and colour and an image of a wide sparkling sea on a lovely day, but that was all. Eyeing his squiggles from every angle, Nell decided whatever talents her father might have had, drawing wasn't one of them.

'Ah, so there you are,' a very different man from the late Lord Christopher Hancourt growled impatiently from the doorway.

'As if I would bother to hide,' she replied coldly.

'You might have; I came to apologise for all my sins last night,' Mr Moss said, sounding so like a schoolboy caught doing something he didn't regret at all that her heart almost softened towards him, despite every resolution she'd made last night to resist his unique sort of charm next time they met.

She nodded coolly to discourage any more folly and raised her eyebrows in what she hoped was a haughty invitation to expand on that gruff statement.

'I also wondered if you found a solution to the puzzle Faith set us yesterday. From the look of that paper you might have done,' he said stiffly, as if only the direst necessity had dragged him in here to confront her once again and he didn't really think he had anything to apologise for because it was as much her fault as his he'd kissed her last night and they both knew it.

Chapter Thirteen

Tempted to hide the battered old document behind her back, since it was some sort of contact with her long-dead father, Nell wondered if it was safe to let Moss see it. It didn't make sense and there was no salutation other than the brief direction *To Nell* on the other side. He couldn't find anything much out about her from a few bad drawings and a senseless series of numbers, not when she had puzzled over them all morning and still felt none the wiser.

'I doubt it,' she replied flatly and held out the dog-eared sheet of hot pressed paper to invite him to see for himself how little sense it made.

'Hmm…' was all he said in reply as he did just that.

He walked over to the window with it to take advantage of what little light there was from the leaden sky on yet another day without sun. Feeling bereft and a little bit piqued at his inattention to her, Nell was free to study him instead of her father's nonsense, since he seemed to be totally absorbed and wouldn't even notice her eyes were on him.

He still wasn't classically handsome, was he? With the clear eyes of a critic she assessed his long-limbed frame with an almost-smile that worried her every bit as much as it would have him if he looked up and saw her grinning at nothing. Resetting her expression to governess-like blankness, she looked away and thought despairingly that she would never need a fine miniature or book full of sketches to recall how Moss looked in his prime.

Staring at the exquisitely carved mantel some long-dead Selford had commissioned for his splendid new library instead of his descendant's land steward this time, she went over her private images of the man still frowning at Lord Chris Hancourt's hieroglyphs because she couldn't seem to help herself. He had those acute and improbably clear blue eyes, of course, they were the first thing you noticed about him, after the general impression of a tall man with power and fitness in every line and sinew of his body. It wasn't just the surprisingly pure colour of his irises that held her attention whenever he was in a room, it was the glimpse into his acute and restless mind they gave her whenever he wasn't wary enough to shield his every thought. Once she had wrenched her gaze away from his azure gaze, she told herself the rest of his face was just a mix of arrogant cheek bones and mismatched features. His nose was craggy, even his own mother would have to admit that. Having been broken once upon a time did little for its patrician haughtiness. His mouth was… well, it was simply his. Nell couldn't even think about it without wanting to feel it burn and need on hers again, so she moved on as rapidly as she could. His chin—now that was firm to the point of stubbornness.

So how did such a man fare as third son of a country squire? Take those features and quirks one by one and Moss was a mixture of iron determination and secrets, put it together the whole added up to more. Nell doubted he took to being the second spare to his eldest brother very well as a boy. His boyhood must have been challenging for all concerned, she decided as she imagined him a clever and argumentative boy with a stubborn streak a mile wide and had to aim another of those almost tender smiles into mid-air. Never mind how he fitted into his allotted place in his father's family then, he was an adult now and somehow she doubted he'd wanted to be a nobleman's land steward since he was in his cradle. As a man he was compelling and unique and she defied a sentient female to forget he was in a room full of his supposed lords and masters and pay them proper attention when he was by, so perhaps he ought to consider a different future before those lords and masters learnt to envy him that quality?

'Where did you get this?' he barked as if he had every right to demand the information, but at least he'd interrupted her wayward thoughts.

'I have always had it,' she exaggerated slightly, to prove to herself he didn't have that right at all.

'Then you must know who it's from.'

'True, but that's my business.'

'Not when someone is trying to get hold of your papers it isn't.'

'I can't see how an old piece of paper that makes

no sense can have any bearing on the matter,' she said defensively.

He sighed and looked as if he wished she was Penny's age so she could be dealt with accordingly. 'I know you are angry with me, but could we at least try to be cool and rational about this problem? What I did last night must have made you hate me, I do understand,' he said with the sort of weary patience she used when Lavinia was at her most rebellious.

'No, you don't, you don't understand at all,' she said bitterly, feeling as if she might break if he didn't stop looking at her as if she was a promise he didn't dare make himself. Anyway, he didn't understand, not when he had no idea who she really was. Lord Chris Hancourt's daughter was the least suitable wife a hard-working man could find himself saddled with if they weren't very careful, heiress or not. They could afford one another in the strictest definition of the word, but would he be able to live off his wife's fortune and not learn to despise himself and her while he did so?

'Mr Moss and Miss Court can't afford to marry so burning for each other is wrong. It was cruel of me to kiss a woman I cannot wed,' he said rather starkly.

Nell supposed she couldn't have put it better herself, in reverse. Except of course they *could* afford a house and estate twice the size of his father's, with her dowry.

And what of his pride, Eleanor Hancourt? she asked herself and stamped on the tiny spark of hope the look in *his* tired eyes lit as they met hers.

He looked as if he was saying goodbye to a dream he couldn't afford to have. The daughter of one of the most scandalous men of his generation wasn't a fit wife for Mr Moss. There, if she told herself that often enough it might even sound impossible. Her fortune would be a bitter pill for such a proud, contrary man to swallow; the scandal of her father's wild life and death with his infamous mistress hanging over their heads all the time would suffocate him. She ought to tell him, perhaps make them both feel better about the heartache that would dog her footsteps, whether she stayed here or went to London to admit she was Miss Hancourt.

'I am…' she began. Too late when he turned away from her impatiently and began to pace the room. How could she shout something so crucial after his retreating back across half the width of the room?

'I am a clumsy idiot,' he told her from the furthest corner of the room. Any further away and they would have to yell and she wasn't prepared to proclaim her identity to anyone within earshot just yet.

He was, of course, but what if he was her idiot? Her heart lurched at the notion she might let the only man she could dream of marrying go because of a silly fancy about money and her father's black reputation. They were rational adults, weren't they? No problem could be insurmountable if there was a chance they might manage to love each other for life.

'True,' she mouthed, smiled sweetly and waited for him to come close enough for them to speak softly and not be overheard.

Too late, with the warning of another set of hasty male footsteps sounding overloud in the tacked-on enfilade that Mr Rivers was here and why the devil must the handsome great fool interrupt them right now? Nell glared at the man and wondered if she dared tell him to go away.

He was the brother of Moss's employer and even a rich woman's husband might want to work to feel better about her fortune, so she stayed silent with an effort it was as well he didn't know about.

'What's this Mrs Winch tells me about one of the maids being paid to steal your papers, Miss Court?' the Earl's brother demanded before he noticed Moss standing stiffly in the opposite corner with a start, as if he sensed something more between them being on opposite sides of the room suggested.

'The work of a madwoman,' Nell said dismissively. Even if it wasn't it didn't seem important next to what might have been said, if not for Mr Rivers's arrival.

'Not necessarily,' Moss argued with a frown in her direction.

'What else can she be but mad to offer so much for so little?'

'In search of something you don't know you have?' Moss replied impatiently and whatever possessed her to think he was struggling to hide deep and tender feelings for her under a gruff manner? He obviously didn't care about her at all, he was just interested in the problem she'd presented him with.

'And what do I have that could be of any interest to anyone but me?' she sparked back at him.

'This,' he said baldly and held up the worn and battered paper she didn't understand when she found it all those years ago and still didn't understand now.

'It's nothing,' she said, shaking her head at the very idea it was worth five pounds to anyone.

'We won't know that until we've at least tried to work out what it means.'

'It's a meaningless series of numbers and doodles done to amuse a child.'

'And someone seems to think it worth a maidservant's wage for an entire year, so we would be foolish to disregard it so lightly, don't you think?'

'Well, *I* have no idea what it means and if I can't understand it, why would anyone else?'

Moss turned the paper over and read the shortened form of her name on the back. 'You are Nell then, Miss Court?' he asked with raised eyebrows.

They had kissed passionately and risked far too much in the candlelit intimacy of Mrs Winch's room last night and still they were Mr and Miss to one another. Nell was used as a short form of Helen and she didn't want to confess who she was with her employer's brother listening, so she waited warily for the next question.

'Who sent it?' he persisted, of course, and that was the next question she didn't want to answer. A plain Mr Court couldn't have secrets because he didn't exist. The idea of untangling lies and half-truths when she had never bothered to create a Mr Court to lie about kept her silent for a long moment as she tried to decide if she had the ingenuity left to invent one right now.

'A friend of my mother,' she prevaricated instead.

'One who knew you very well,' he said, as if he suspected her mama of conduct unbecoming a lady.

'Or perhaps he only thought he did,' she lied, crossing her fingers behind her back because it felt wrong to deny her parents when she'd only just rediscovered them through their letters to each other.

'I suspect this is meant to mean something to you, however well or poorly this man knew you as a child. You need to think harder about who he was and why he left you a coded message you won't take seriously.'

'He must have had more faith in me than he should have done,' she said crossly, because this really was none of his business. Disappointment was gnawing away at her good manners with every moment Mr Rivers stood listening to their argument with that knowing look on his face.

'Perhaps there's a reason you refuse to look more deeply into this puzzle?' Moss said as if he could read her mind. 'And why don't you write and ask him what it means?'

'He's dead,' she said flatly.

'Then you have even more reason to solve the problem he left you, in the mistaken belief you would bother to decipher it.'

'You are very rude, sir. Both the problem and solution are my business and not yours.'

'When it intrudes on Berry Brampton House and the safety of Lord Barberry's wards it is mine and his lordship's,' he said with an impatient glare at Mr Rivers, who was listening attentively but leaving him to ask all the awkward questions. 'The welfare of four vulnerable young girls trumps your privacy, Miss Court.'

'As if I haven't been putting them first for the last two years when you didn't even know they existed,' she snapped back sharply, near the end of her tether now he was intent on solving this puzzle rather than the bigger one of how a steward and a governess could find a way to love each other after all.

'I do now and it's my duty to safeguard them if some fool is trying to prise this away from you and they might get in the way.'

He was right, she decided reluctantly. It seemed insane anyone would want that hasty note from her father, but there was nothing else in her papers to explain why someone had such a burning desire to read them.

'I don't understand it at all,' she admitted with a shrug because she still couldn't see any sense in random numbers and squiggles.

'Then try harder. How old were you when this was written?'

'Three or four years old, I suppose.'

'Why don't you know precisely?'

'Why do I have to, Mr Moss?'

'You think I'm being rude again?' he said impatiently.

'I know you are.'

'Then I need not worry about losing your good opinion, need I?'

Nell wanted to slap his arrogant face, but somehow controlled herself and shot a glare at Mr Rivers, standing with his hands in his pockets as if he hadn't been this well entertained for months. 'No, but the girls are likely to realise I've been gone too long at any moment and come to find out what's going on,' she warned with a frown for both of them this time.

'Then we'd best hurry up and find out what this is about before they get here. Where did you find it?'

'Hidden in the roof of my dolls' house. I only found that slipped under the roof when it was damaged and I have no idea when it was put there,' Nell lied again, because she could probably find out if she wanted to.

'When did this eccentric gentleman of yours die, then?' Mr Rivers chimed in as if feeling it was time he took a part in this odd comedy.

Ah, that was the question she'd been dreading, but why should they connect her with Lord Christopher Hancourt's and the first Viscountess Farenze's scandalous and tragic death in the same year?

'1799?' she said, as if she didn't know all too well.

'Why would anyone wait so long to chase this down?' Mr Rivers asked them as if they ought to know.

Nell shrugged and Moss began to pace the room again with that odd missive in his hand, staring at it as if he might wrench Papa's secrets off the page by willpower alone. 'These drawings are trying to tell a story. If the man had any skill with a pencil it would be a damn sight easier to work out what they're meant to be.'

'Don't swear and give it back to me,' Nell demanded, suddenly desperate for another look. 'Come, Mr Moss, you said yourself I alone can solve this problem—you must return it if I'm to stand any chance of doing so.'

'Yes, give it back to her, Moss,' Mr Rivers prompted with a laugh in his grey eyes Nell didn't even begin to understand and he seemed to be taunting Moss with some secret of his own.

'Very well, but don't forget someone else wants

this puzzle solved more than you seem to, Miss Court.'

'Yes, you do,' she snapped and saw the sudden revulsion in his blue gaze that she could even think he was behind this. 'I didn't mean I think you so devious you might pay an intermediary to find this,' she said hastily. 'Not that your insistence I look hard for its meaning when I might not want to isn't both intrusive and annoying of you.'

'We'll take that as a given then, shall we? I seem to have been annoying you since the very first moment I set foot on Selford land.'

'Perhaps you're a very annoying man,' she said softly, looking up at him almost fondly as she forgot Mr Rivers's presence for a moment.

'Or maybe you are a pernickety female, overprotective of her charges and suspicious of anyone who comes within their orbit?'

'Arguing about which of you is most unsociable is going to help us solve this then, is it?' Mr Rivers asked with the wave of an elegant hand at the parchment in Moss's more work-worn one.

'No, but it might stop worse things if we work

hard enough,' Moss muttered as he passed her in one of those restless lopes up and down the room.

'Don't,' she whispered so softly she hoped Mr Rivers couldn't hear and how badly she wanted him to go away. 'We can't,' she murmured when he turned not far away and began his pass back to that remote corner.

'Then think, woman, before frustration gets the better of one of us,' he muttered as if he was only managing to keep his hands off her because he had something else to do, even with the Earl's half-brother watching them as if fascinated by the spectacle they made as they almost quarrelled in his presence.

Comforted by the passion almost under control in Moss's intent gaze, the quirk of his firm mouth and the stern control he was trying to keep it under, Nell tried to think about quirks on paper instead and failed. He wanted her; the heat and promise of being feminine and desirable to him, despite her repressive gown and spinster's cap, burnt deep inside and made her breath come short. For a long moment he paused instead of passing her by and they both seemed spellbound by the chances of it, the possibility land steward and governess could make a life together if they tried hard enough. Then he handed the paper back to her and the crackle of expensive paper even after all the mistreatment it had been subjected to over the years reminded her how many lies and barriers still stood between them.

Stepping back, she stared unseeingly at her father's message for a moment. It was looking at them with only half her attention that must have let her eyes see the funny little stick figures Papa used to draw come to life again. Of course, he used to laugh and tell her their drawing talent was about equal back then, didn't he? She must have blocked the memory out, along with so much else about a man who left his children alone for the sake of a woman like Pamela Verdoyne-Winterley. Feeling the stirrings of what could be wild passion for a man for the first time, maybe she could understand what drove Lord Chris a little better, or perhaps those letters between her parents unlocked something too painful to remember until now. Whatever the reason, her favourite tale from *Aesop's Fables* was suddenly there—rendered in Papa's uniquely awful stick figures of two very familiar animals he'd danced around the edge of his message as if she was sure to understand him. Stuck in an echoing nursery with her elderly and embittered nursery governess, she must have made herself forget the life that went before. She spared a thought for that bereft little girl, but felt she had the father she'd once adored back at long last. He drew this direly executed message still loving her; this message said his every thought had not been of Pamela after all.

'It's meant to be the Tale of the Stork and the Fox, it was my favourite,' she said, delight softening her voice as she remembered him reading it to her night after night when he must have been bored by it even the first time.

'What tale; where is it from?' Moss demanded.

'I can't imagine how I missed seeing it all these years now. *Aesop's Fables,* of course,' she said and made for the stacks to find a copy. '*Mr Dodsley's Select Fables,* to be exact, as I suppose we must be if those numbers relate to the pages of a book.'

'Which they must do, or why leave a clue only you could understand?' Mr Rivers said as he got caught up in the mystery after all and followed them both to find a copy as fast as possible between the three of them.

'But what is it a clue to?' Nell mused.

She felt almost guilty for not telling either man she came from a far wealthier home than her current occupation argued. Even so, what could Papa have left her but some little present she was supposed to find while he was away? He had probably planned it as a diversion to keep her from pining, then forgot to tell her when he came back and she hadn't discovered it. Yes, that made sense. He must have done this when she was quite a small girl, before he dreamt of running away to France with his scandalous mistress and died there with her when Nell was not quite six years old.

'We won't know until we find it,' Moss said impatiently. He didn't deserve her guilt about deceiving him when he adopted his lord-of-all-I-survey manner, as if he'd taken on Lord Barberry's role as well as his own when he came here.

'He probably only hid a box of sweets or a toy at the end of a treasure hunt that doesn't exist any more,' she warned him anyway.

'Since you didn't find anything else to explain why this stranger wants your papers, this is the only clue we have.'

'Very well, but you'd best prepare to be disappointed,' she said to Mr Rivers and moved away from Moss to find the small children's section of Lord Barberry's neglected library. 'The girls have a newer copy than any in here, but I don't want them drawn into this,' she said in her best governess manner.

Unimpressed, Moss raised his eyebrows as if to remind her how un-governess-like she could be. 'Here it is, although I can't see how a series of page numbers will help us.'

'Neither can I,' she said, but her heartbeat speeded up anyway.

Tense now as he picked out the volume and turned to her favourite tale, she read it again over his shoulder and had to fight memories of being held safe in her father's arms as he read it to her with a catch in his voice she must have been too young to take in at the time. For a while he had tried hard to be father and mother to her when Mama and the baby died. Instead of feeling too little for his children, did Lord Chris feel too much? She cursed Pamela anew for taking him away and blinked back a tear for what might have been. Wrong to blame only her when Lord Chris fell under the woman's witchy spell and blithely walked away from any reminders of his late wife of his own free will.

'What else can these numbers mean?' she mused out loud, sure now that this was a wild goose chase.

'You might as well look at the pages and see if they mean anything to you,' Mr Rivers suggested helpfully.

'Very well, but I don't see how,' she agreed with a sigh, wondering what the girls were up to and if that hour she gave them to read or, more likely, gossip was up.

'Nothing ventured, nothing gained.'

Nell didn't even grace that cliché with a reply and signalled impatiently at the book so both men could see what a waste of time this was. Reading each page carefully, she got to the end of the list and tried hard not to say *I told you so.*

'Are you sure there's nothing in any of your other papers this mystery woman might pay for?' Moss said after a few moments of frustrated silence.

'Very sure.'

'You could always let me see your letters and papers and judge for myself?'

'They are private,' she said primly.

'Then we'd best hope this means something after all. Have you got your own copy of *The Fables*?'

'Yes, but it's very battered and there are quite a few pages missing. I used to get upset about some of the tales when animals ate each other so my mother decided to cut out all the pages that made me cry.'

'Then your numbers are different from this one,' Mr Rivers said triumphantly and, of course, he was right. 'You must send for it immediately,' he added, now so caught up in the thrill of the chase he had forgotten to be amused by the foibles of his fellow men.

'No need, I always have it with me. It may seem foolish of me, but my brother coloured in many of Mr Bewick's illustrations as carefully as he could for me before our guardian sent him to school, so I treasure it even now.'

'That doesn't seem foolish at all,' Moss said gently and here was the man she had been so terribly tempted by last night again and she had to remind herself Mr Rivers was still here to make herself turn away.

'I will try to steal upstairs without the girls

knowing,' she said to get out of my lord's library before she disgraced herself.

Upstairs she glanced at the small square of mirror provided for a governess. The flush on her cheeks and the slight breathlessness she seemed to be suffering from lately could be explained by a rushed search for her book. She tucked a stray curl back into her cap and nodded sternly at herself before going back to the library.

How tempting to stand and stare at Moss's straight back, broad shoulders and narrow hips without him knowing, but Mr Rivers's grey eyes saw more than she would like them to if he turned and caught her at it, so she nobly resisted. 'Here it is,' she said brightly to interrupt their murmured conversation in the far corner of the room where she couldn't hear a word of it.

'Good, maybe we can get to the bottom of this strange business at last,' Moss said as if he had a hundred better things to do this morning.

'I'm sure I can work it out for myself now, gentlemen,' Nell said with an inviting glance at the grey sky outside they wilfully ignored.

'You won't get rid of us that easily,' Mr Rivers said with a mocking grin.

'Like a couple of burrs,' she mumbled disagreeably, but handed over her precious book all the same, before she could give herself time to think about not being rid of Mr Moss ever again and liking it all too well.

'Very like,' he agreed and seemed almost as jarred as she was by the flare of something bright and hot flashing between them when their fingers touched on the worn leather binding. He cleared his throat as if that might help. 'Read out that list of numbers, if you please, and we'll soon see if this makes more sense,' he ordered as if he had every right.

'How will we know?' she asked lamely.

'I suppose we must have faith in this friend of your mother's, since there's no other explanation for Faith's rich stranger taking such an interest in you,' he said.

'I suppose you're right.'

'Even if you don't want me to be?'

There was compassion as well as curiosity in his acute blue eyes this time. Eleanor Hancourt, who braved the world alone, felt something aloof and a little bit frozen inside her threaten to melt.

'Even then,' she replied softly and never mind their unwanted listener.

'Why not tell me about him?' he invited, laying the book he had been in such haste to see on the window seat behind them. 'You can trust me, I promise you.'

'I know I can,' she said.

'And Mr Rivers will give you his word as a gentleman not to tattle if you don't want him to, won't you, sir?'

Rivers nodded obediently, 'Word of honour, Miss Court.'

'I have managed for myself for almost as long as I can remember,' she said as if that explained everything, and perhaps it did.

'Poor little girl,' Moss said softly.

'I was well enough and never hungry or in need,' she argued half-heartedly.

'You sound lonely as the man in the moon,' he replied.

'My brother loved me and I was very happy at school,' she said, unable to look away from his blue, blue gaze this time and never mind if Mr Rivers was watching them with a worried frown.

Here was the magic and promise of last night

almost within reach again. Her breath caught in a strange sigh that stuttered out between her parted lips as if they wanted to invite him to breathe with her, kiss her, be part of her and whatever else it meant for two people drawn to be more than the world saw when it looked at them.

'Miss Court, there you are at last. Georgie stole my book and now she won't give it back. I was almost at the end of it as well, so she only had to wait an hour or so and I would have given it to her,' Lavinia informed her from the doorway.

Nell jumped as soon as she heard her voice and stepped away from Moss and Mr Rivers as if she'd been scalded. She had nearly been caught kissing Lord Barberry's steward, in front of his lordship's uneasy and embarrassed brother, by one of her pupils. That would have almost rivalled her late father's sins if the story of what Miss Hancourt got up to before she met the critical gaze of the *ton* ever got around.

Ordering her inner demons back into their box, she raised a hand and found her cap disappointingly straight and proper. Wrong to be frustrated and cross because she was missing a chance to repeat her bad behaviour of last night, so she did her best to pretend he wasn't here and talked to Lavinia instead, because she usually understood her and Moss was a brooding mystery right now.

'It's high time we got back to our lessons, but I wish you two wouldn't quarrel like fishwives whenever my back is turned.'

'It wasn't my fault.'

'I didn't say it was. I will get your book back for you and make Georgiana apologise, but you two are setting the younger girls a bad example.'

'They don't need any help,' Lavinia muttered as if there were things she could say about Penny and Caro, but didn't want to be accused of tattle-mongering.

'Excuse me, Mr Rivers, Mr Moss. I must get back to my duties,' Nell said and swept her eldest pupil out of the room before they could argue.

Chapter Fourteen

Fergus stood looking at the worn and obviously much-loved book in his hand and wondered why he thought the key to Miss Court herself might lie inside it, as well as a solution to her latest mystery. He heard her and Lavinia's voices fading as they went up the intricately carved oak staircase and wondered why he'd spent so long listening to a woman walk away from him of late. He tried to shrug off an uneasy feeling it would be impossible not to listen for her step long after he escaped from this ridiculous position and made sure she was employed a long way away.

'We had best do this without her, Fergus,' his brother said uneasily.

Because Brendan had said nothing about what had almost happened just now Fergus knew how bad it was as his heart sank into his work-worn boots. The Earl of Barberry had been about to misbehave so spectacularly even his little brother couldn't find the words to say what a selfish fool he was. Unable to find the words to explain what was in his heart, because he didn't understand it himself, he opened the book in his hands and froze stiff as a statue as he took in the name so proudly written on the first page he could almost imagine a tiny version of the woman claiming her book with the deep concentration of a girl who had only just learned how. Damnation take the woman; she was in danger of charming him even as his inner man was screaming at her for what she'd done—how could she have lied to him so heinously it felt like the worst betrayal he'd ever suffered to stare down at the words as if they'd been written by the devil himself?

'This Book Belongs to Miss Eleanor Hancourt of Lambury House, Hanover Square, London, England, Great Britain', it stated in childishly self-important capital letters.

My God, Fergus, she's not only your equal, she could easily be your superior in both birth and *fortune,* his inner Earl whispered with a snarl of noble temper.

Fergus felt the pain of her deception sear through him and down to his very toes—how could she have deceived him so brazenly? She'd kissed him as if she meant it last night; left him racked with guilt and sleepless as he fantasied about promises he couldn't make to a governess and hated himself for breaking her heart. Clearly she didn't have one to break or she wouldn't have let a mere Mr Moss hope for a future he could never have with her. A marriage between the impoverished younger son of a country squire and Miss Eleanor Hancourt, granddaughter of a duke on one side and the richest nabob of his generation on the other? The very idea was laughable, but oddly enough he didn't feel like laughing. Crying and beating his breast was out for a hardened nobleman of one and thirty, so that only left him with fury, didn't it? Good, he felt the vigour of it sweeping past the desolation of knowing he'd been taken for a fool by a woman he'd come perilously close to loving.

Even in Ireland he'd heard the fuss this last winter when her brother inherited the huge fortune everyone thought lost by his notorious father on his twenty-fifth birthday. Hancourt's sister must have been an heiress in her own right when she wrote this inscription as a child and to think he'd been feeling sorry for her until he read that childish assertion and realised she meant something in the world.

Tempted to throw the book into the darkest and most dusty corner of the room and march away from this place without a word of explanation, he let his imagination get to work on what might happen if he did and frowned fiercely at the battered old tome instead. If Moss vanished like a thief in the night, Fergus's young cousins would be caught up in any misadventure the lying jade stumbled into because of her determination to stay here and brazen things out. If he had to stay as he was until he got rid of the confounded woman, he didn't dare risk seeing her right now. He might let out something crucial as he raged at her for not being humble Miss Court at all. He might even be tempted to forgive her and that would never do, would it?

Fergus scooped up the now rather battered beaver hat from where he'd flung it when he entered the room, so eager to see Miss Court again he had almost forgotten the gulf between the lord of all this and a mere governess. Sneering at himself in the watery old mirror over the fireplace, he gave a wordless shrug of apology to Brendan, then waved the inscription under his brother's nose to explain his silent fury. With Miss Hancourt's book under his arm he marched out of the house without another word to anyone. Never mind if it was uncivil of Moss to ignore his fellow servants as he stormed through the kitchens and out of the back door, he felt uncivil.

More than that, he discovered as he strode back to the land steward's house as if his feet were on fire, he felt furious and hurt and outraged all at once. A terrible anger salted his regret for a life he could never have with a woman who didn't exist. It didn't make a grain of sense, but that didn't matter—she'd lied to him. The fact she'd deceived everyone else here for a lot longer didn't matter right now. Once he had unwrapped this last mystery and made sure his wards were safe he was going to make sure the whole neighbourhood knew who had really been living under his roof all these years, so they couldn't condemn him as an arrogant beast when he sent Miss Court to the right about the moment he was his true self again. The fine Irish temper he'd got from his mother, mixed dangerously with her first husband's English certainty he was always right, and now flared into full, fearsome life because Miss Court's betrayal felt so very personal it hurt. With all those fierce emotions rattling in his head Fergus managed to ignore the voice of reason that whispered, even if Eleanor Hancourt neatly deceived him and everyone else at Berry Brampton, he was just as guilty of double dealing as she was. When this didn't hurt any more he might listen. For now, being in a raging temper felt a lot better than the raw feeling underneath it that he'd been on the edge of something deep and dangerous with Miss Eleanor Hancourt, until he found out who she really was and jumped back from a precipice he hadn't even realised he was on the edge of until Miss Court vanished into it like the wraith she truly was.

'Mr Rivers wishes to see you, Miss Court,' Parkins the butler informed Nell disapprovingly later in the day. 'The gentleman is in the library.'

'Very well, I will come down as soon as I can be sure the Misses Selford are usefully occupied.'

'I will inform the gentleman,' Parkins said

stiffly, distancing himself from the whole sorry business.

'What do you suppose he wants?' Caro asked, still a little bit infatuated with her guardian's brother, even though he treated her as the child she still was and that had taken the fervour out of her girlish crush.

'No doubt I shall find out shortly, Caroline,' Nell said repressively, wondering how she was to preach propriety at her charges when the Earl's brother ordered her to meet him alone in the middle of a working day. 'Now, Lavinia, you will read this passage out for me and the rest of you must do your best to understand it, girls. I want to hear your explanation of the ideas it contains when I return and you will do as your cousin tells you to, or I shall have to be very cross with you indeed when I get back and there will be no sweet course at dinner tonight if that happens.'

With many assurances they would be good as gold echoing in her ears, Nell went to see what Mr Rivers wanted with an odd feeling of dread deep in her belly.

'Ah, Miss *Court*,' the gentleman greeted with undue emphasis, so she wasn't as surprised as she might have been when Mr Moss appeared out of the shadows to snap the door closed behind her and stand glaring at the floor, his face like thunder and her copy of *Aesop's Fables* held out accusingly in his hand.

How stupid of her to have forgotten her real name was written all over the frontispiece. She was so proud she could write her name and address back then that she'd scrawled it anywhere she could find space until even Colm protested. All sorts of contrary emotions threatened as she tried to take in the fact Mr Moss knew who she really was and Miss Hancourt couldn't wed a steward without making him a laughing stock. Since he was far too busy frowning into the middle distance now to even look at her, she had no intention of letting him know she cared how he felt about her true identity.

'This meeting is rather singular, gentlemen,' she said with a nod at the closed door to let them know it was improper as well.

'Do you want the entire household to know your secrets?' Moss asked as if he had every right to be furious with her.

He almost had, since she kissed him back last

night as if they were equals. Six months ago they would have been on a par for poverty, if not rank, and it felt unfair that he should cast their differing fortunes at her as if it was her fault. Why should she be made to feel ashamed of being her true self again? She would have to disown her brother and the rest of her family to do that and not even the almost magic she had spun about in when locked in Moss's arms last night could make her do that. It had only been an air dream though; he couldn't feel anything enduring for her if he could stand there glowering at her like the sternest judge in the land and not a hint of softer emotions in his hard blue gaze.

'I suspect they soon will, whether I like it or not,' she replied as lightly as she could to his harsh query.

'I'm no rattle-pate,' he said shortly and why was the Earl's brother letting him take the lead in this embarrassing meeting?

'Neither am I, so your secret is as safe as you want it to be, Miss Hancourt,' Mr Rivers said quietly, with a hard look at Moss to say he might be wondering the same thing himself.

'Why? Why did you pretend to be Miss Court

when you are a lady of high birth and fortune?' Moss burst out, as if not even his employer's brother had a right to silence him on the subject of her crimes.

'I'd rather not tell you, sir,' she said haughtily as if he had no right to question her and even good manners told her she was right as he backed away from her as if she'd turned into the Medusa. 'I had a living to earn and a strong dislike of those who are always so curious about my late father's exploits that I would have got very little peace here if I admitted being his daughter.'

'You certainly don't need to earn a living now,' Moss muttered darkly.

'Yet the Misses Selford still need a governess and I didn't want to desert them. I am sorry to be blunt, but your brother did that when he refused to come here and meet them, Mr Rivers, so how could I abandon them as well when my fortunes took a sudden turn for the better?'

'I still can't see why you didn't confide all this to me when I came here in his lordly lordship's stead,' Mr Rivers said quietly, exchanging a complicated look with Moss that Nell didn't even want to understand right now.

'If you or your brother only had a lady I could have told her and trusted her to find a suitable replacement,' she said stiffly instead. 'A single gentleman cannot ask the same questions as a lady can of a potential governess.'

'*You* certainly took a wily lawyer in without much trouble,' Moss interrupted as if he had the right to sneer at her in front of their employer's brother.

'If this was any of your business, Mr Moss, I could point out I never lied about my education, teaching experience or willingness to work as hard as I can to help the Misses Selford learn what they need to know to live a useful life as ladies of rank and fortune one day. Lord Barberry's lawyers seem to have a great deal of practice at hiring his upper servants, don't they? So I doubt they are easily deceived by those they must trust to run the household and keep his lordship's wards happy and usefully employed in his absence after all those years of putting his wishes into place by proxy, do you?' she countered. He must have fooled them he was a patient and calm land steward and he didn't look anything of the sort right now.

'I'm trying not to think them a pack of fools,' he said through gritted teeth.

'I don't believe you have the right when you must have fooled them you a quiet and biddable soul, sir. And it makes no difference who I am; I am here and I'm ready, willing and able to carry out my duties, just as I have been for the last two years. You are not in any position to object to my presence, Mr Moss, any more than I can have *you* hired or dismissed on a whim. I leave it to you, Mr Rivers, to decide what you will tell your brother about me. I doubt very much that he cares much who instructs his wards, since he's avoided being a stand-in father to them for a decade.'

For some reason that not very tactful reminder seemed to have more effect on Moss than it did on his lordship's half-brother. He grunted something furious under his breath and went back to pacing the book stacks again, as if he might find his lost serenity hidden down one if he looked hard enough.

'True, if not very diplomatic, Miss Hancourt,' Mr Rivers said mildly.

If he could seem almost amused by her forthright criticism of the absent Earl, why must Moss take it so badly when he'd never even met him? Because he felt betrayed by her lie in a way he couldn't express in front of his employer's brother, Nell supposed, with a sinking feeling he had some right to resent her position in society when she'd matched him kiss for kiss and never said a word about her recently returned wealth. If only Mr Rivers hadn't interrupted them before she could get that crucial explanation out, how very differently Moss might feel about her now.

'You're a coward, Miss Hancourt,' Moss accused as he paced back towards them again. 'Instead of playing out this pantomime of a dutiful governess at Berry Brampton House you should be in London with your brother and his new wife, making a much-delayed debut in the world where you truly belong. You have no right to risk bringing trouble down on your pupils by continuing to lie about who you are. By staying here in such a guise you made yourself a target for kidnappers and fortune hunters. Either breed will exploit your ridiculous charade if they can and you set yourself up for it by refusing to re-join your family.'

Nell gasped in shock at the notion of being abducted and forced into marriage. Somehow even the thought of such wickedness tarnished her life here as the very real possibility he was right sank in and made her shiver. 'You think that's why someone wanted my papers?' she asked him before she could stop herself.

'It seems an obvious answer to me.'

'Yet you doubt it?' she asked as he frowned at the very plainness of it.

'Yes, your father's conundrum can't be designed to make you tell the truth to your employer, since he didn't know what a clever little liar he'd sired when he wrote it,' Moss said, waving the old paper Nell wished he'd put away and forget, now there were more important matters to discuss.

'How do you know my father wrote it?'

'Who else could have done so? The current Duke of Linaire was in the Americas by the time you were born and the last one was well known to have no time for *his* wards. Rumour has it the late Duke actively hated you and your brother, so your father is the obvious man to be sending coded messages to his daughter.'

'My brother might have done so,' she said defensively. It seemed cruel of him to point out how bereft she and Colm were when Papa died in that stupid accident somehow, despite the hurt she had obviously dealt him with what he must see as her lack of trust and dishonesty in not telling him who she really was last night, when it might have been said and got around if only he loved her.

Which he obviously does not, Eleanor, her inner realist pointed out rather unhelpfully when she felt as if a chasm had opened up between them and she was swaying on the edge of it, not wanting to look down and see a bleak future as Aunt Eleanor, bluestocking spinster of the Hancourt family, stretching ahead of her.

'This isn't the work of a child,' Moss pointed out implacably and why did she still long to be on his side of that divide when he was being such a steely judge of her sins?

'It might as well be for all the sense it makes,' she said sulkily, sounding very much like Lavinia did when she was confronted by something she didn't want to do.

'Then look it up yourself,' he ordered her impatiently. 'Find those references in your copy of *the Fables*, then tell me the riddle isn't serious.'

'Give my book back then,' she demanded and waited for him to hand it over with what she hoped was chilly dignity, because she felt as if a part of her had been ripped away and the hurt might not heal for a very long time.

'I wrote the solution down in my pocketbook, for all the help it is.'

'There you are then; it *is* only nonsense,' she said as he handed over her book and Papa's scrap of paper. She drew back as if he'd burned her when he went to hand over his leather-bound notebook as well.

'Oh, do it yourself, then,' he said bitterly and went back to his pacing.

'Do you mind if *I* join you, Miss Hancourt?' Mr Rivers said with a polite gesture towards the map table by the window where they could see what they were reading a lot better.

'Certainly not, your help will be very welcome, Mr Rivers,' Nell said sweetly.

The tension in the room was almost thick enough to slice when Moss let out a curse he should keep to himself in feminine company and paced harder. Let him think she was doing her best to flirt with the handsome brother of an earl if he liked. Now her true rank and fortune were out in the open, why shouldn't she? She couldn't let the bad-tempered bear see he'd hurt her.

Mr Rivers calmly wrote down the series of words she read out as she found them underlined after counting her quota of pages instead of the numbers they began life with. It sounded as if the riddle made a sentence, but Moss was right, it still didn't make much sense. Nell took the paper Mr Rivers handed her at the end of it all and frowned.

'I don't know what he meant,' she told him.

'Your father had faith in your intelligence when you were too small to know half what you do today. Not that you seem inclined to make use of the brains I suppose you must have been born with,' Moss pointed out unhelpfully when he came to another halt beside them.

'Now that's going too far—in fact, it's downright uncivil of you, Moss,' Mr Rivers said sharply.

It sounded as if his gentlemanly soul could bear no more, even if there was a frustrated love affair to account for Moss's fury with the unmasked heiress in their midst and almost justify him being so rude. Nell flinched at the idea their feelings were on show for even one member of the aristocracy to see. She truly hoped the Earl's brother would keep the chance she might love his lord-ship's steward to himself.

'I apologise, Miss Hancourt,' Moss said with a cool bow, as if that might make his bitter hostility feel better as he shot her a dark look to say they were only words.

'Thank you, Mr Moss. Perhaps we can be a lit-tle less childish about this business from now on.'

'Maybe that's it,' Mr Rivers broke in as if her words had sparked off a solution to all this in his head.

'Maybe that's what?' Moss barked gruffly, ob-viously forgetting his faux humility the moment a chance to take over again hove into view.

'We are looking at this through adult eyes and he was showing a child,' Mr Rivers said, almost as if this man taking over was something he ex-pected and Nell wondered about the younger man's spinelessness even as she let half her mind think about his theory and wonder if he might not be right.

'Hmm,' Moss said thoughtfully, as if it was his secret to uncover. 'Let's see what he said again,' he went on, leafing through his book to find the page she had rejected just now. 'Through the eyes of a grandfather clock everything that is hidden will be found again,' he read out and Nell gasped as an image of the slow-ticking clock in the smallest drawing room of Linaire House came into her mind for the first time in years. 'You know what he means, don't you?' Moss asked.

'I may have some idea, but the clock he means is in London.'

'Then you must go there and find what he hid for you to find, must you not?'

'I am still responsible for four girls. I cannot order a carriage, jump into it and blithely demand the horses gallop headlong for the capital on a whim, sir.'

'Maybe not, but I could,' Mr Rivers intervened before his brother's steward could argue as if he had some right to dictate all their actions.

'Even if you ordered it so, Mr Rivers, I can't leave the girls here unprotected with this strange woman probably still in the neighbourhood,' Nell protested. She didn't want to leave the Selford girls—for all the trouble they gave her she was fond of them. And she was a coward, of course, so she would far rather stay here as the governess than be Lord Christopher Hancourt's daughter again under the critical gaze of the *ton*.

'You could take them with you, if you feel you cannot go unless they do. From what I could see last time I was in London, your aunt and uncle are not the sort of people who would turn them away if that's the only way you can be convinced they are safe,' Mr Rivers said, as if he was trying to find logical solutions to problems she wasn't sure she wanted solved. Moss's brooding impatience for her to leave here was too heavy a presence in the room for her to want to oblige him as well. She shot him an impatient glance and got ready to argue with Lord Barberry's little brother as well.

'According to Winch, you went dashing off to Brussels with your uncle a few days before your brother was injured at Waterloo. You can hardly claim the current Duke doesn't look kindly on you both after that, Miss Hancourt,' Moss pointed out and chopped even more ground from under her feet.

'Do you think the Earl will want to be rid of me?' she asked Mr Rivers, since he was more likely to know than anyone else.

Mr Rivers shot Moss a sidelong glance, as if

he might offer him inspiration, but the man was staring at the Selford coat of arms at the centre of the elaborate carved over-mantel and didn't even look their way.

'Now an outsider knows you're here I expect he would say you are safer in London with your family, Miss Hancourt,' Mr Rivers said at last.

'Aye, and you'll be confoundedly in the way if you stay,' Moss growled even as his employer's brother glared at him, as if he might just dismiss him for being so rude to a lady and risk his elder brother's displeasure at being robbed of such a perfect land agent when he needed him most.

'And how will I get there without being way-laid?' Nothing could make her want to stay more than being told to go by this rude barbarian.

'Easy enough,' Mr Rivers went on as if she and Moss weren't still frowning darkly at each other from opposite corners of the room. 'Winch can chaperon you and the girls, whilst Moss and I act as outriders. I'm sure we'll terrify law-abiding citizens going about their rightful business, let alone any villains you manage to attract, Miss Hancourt.'

'You're determined to unmask me?' she asked.

'What else can he do?' Moss barked impatiently. 'You can hardly pitch up in Grosvenor Square and announce your identity at the last possible moment. You're the one who claims to care so much about them, but I suppose you'd have an uncomfortable time if you were shut up in a carriage with the Selford girls once they know about your deception and you wish to avoid such a tense journey.'

The girls would indeed be shocked, but how dare he imply she had such a selfish reason for keeping them in the dark for a few more days? 'How long have I got?' she asked Mr Rivers, who seemed rather young and helpless in the face of Moss's unyielding fury at her for flying under false colours.

'You can pack tonight and be ready at dawn,' Moss said brusquely.

'Luckily I don't take my orders from you, Mr Moss. Mr Rivers?' she questioned with as much steely dignity as possible when she had to clasp her hands into fists at her sides to stop them visibly shaking.

'It would be the best way out of this muddle,' the Earl's younger brother said with an apologetic shrug and Nell turned on her heel to leave the room in disgust.

'Don't say anything about Faith or your father's puzzle,' Moss ordered before she could open the door.

'Good day, Mr Rivers,' she said coolly and left before she lowered herself to throw something at the infuriating man and rage at him for being such a mannerless and unforgiving great oaf.

Chapter Fifteen

'**W**hat the devil did you rip up at her so stiffly for?' Brendan demanded before the echoes of a door being closed painfully softly could die.

'She's a liar, why shouldn't I?'

'Because you aren't Moss any more than she is Miss Court?'

'That's got nothing to do with it.'

'If you truly think that, I'd hate to be in your shoes when she finds out who *you* really are.'

'That's different.'

'Is it now?'

'Yes, I had to find out what was going on and it all turned out to be her fault.'

Brendan shook his head and looked as if he didn't know where to start arguing with that statement. He knew Fergus's hot temper of old, though, and seemed ready to let him stew, since he murmured something about warning the coachman and grooms of the hasty journey they must make to the capital tomorrow.

Fergus still paced the neglected old library. Why the devil *did* he feel as if this was the worst betrayal of his vulnerable inner self ever committed?

'Or maybe it's because I'm a damned fool and cool, vulnerable Miss Court was a fiction I almost fell for,' he added, paused in his hasty march and considered Miss Hancourt's life as a governess and the blight her father's sooty reputation would have cast over it. 'I ought to pity her for the scandal that wound itself into every strand of Lord Christopher Hancourt's life when he set up another man's wife as his mistress, I suppose,' he said as he set off again and his brother lounged back against the library table and listened with an infuriatingly knowing smile on his face.

'If she didn't inherit a fortune the day her brother turned five and twenty I might be able to forgive her, but she chose to stay here and draw poor Edward Moss into her web of deception.'

'Lucky you're not Moss, then,' his brother pointed out laconically.

Fergus snorted rudely and went back to his pacing. To think he had even considered the wild notion of wedding an upper servant for her sake and all the time she must have been laughing at him behind his back.

'You know how hard her so-called betters were to Ma when she wed above what they considered her place in life, Brendan. She's worth a hundred of the idlers who look down their long noses at her, but how could I subject a woman I almost let myself fall in love with to what she's had to endure since before I was born?'

'Hmm, see what you mean, but Miss Hancourt's not really a governess.'

'She's not the woman I thought her though either, is she? She played me for a fool, Brendan. How can I forgive her for that?'

'With difficulty, I should imagine, since you're a pretty big fool without her help.'

'Moss was her primer for finding a husband. She's had no chance to try out her wiles until I came along. A lady of her breeding, looks and fortune will have a whole troop of suitors falling over themselves to win her during the next London Season if she did but know it, but they're welcome to her.'

'Are they now?' Brendan asked with a sly grin Fergus might have been tempted to wipe off his handsome face if they were a decade younger.

'Yes,' he said between set teeth, 'they damned well are.'

Brendan held his right hand up as if conceding the argument, but Fergus knew him a little too well for that and glared at him for good measure.

'Perhaps I'll remind you of that when we see her engagement announced in the London papers,' Brendan said as he inspected his already immaculate fingernails for hidden damage.

'If you want your teeth rearranged, you do just that,' Fergus snapped and felt his much-tried temper tug a little harder at its tethers.

'Pistols or swords?' Brendan challenged with a dare to beat him at either in his laughing grey eyes he knew Fergus wouldn't be able to resist.

'Pistols,' he agreed with a glance out of the windows to see if the usual grey clouds were about to produce rain, but, no, it was fine enough for what they needed.

'Best of ten?'

'A hundred might make my head ache enough to distract me,' he said with the barest hint of rueful humour breaking through his own personal thunder clouds.

'Fifty and I hope your bad temper about Miss Hancourt will distract you, so I can get my revenge for you beating me hollow last time.'

'Best of fifty, then,' Fergus said and they went to fetch the best of his late lordship's guns and enough ball and powder to keep their contest going.

It had helped, he decided, when they declared it a draw and resorted to the gunroom again to clean and put the weapons away again, until tomorrow.

'Are you going to forgive her then, Fergus?' Brendan asked at last.

'No,' he said baldly and even now the white heat of his fury was dying down a little he couldn't see a day coming when he would. She had almost been a dream the Earl of Barberry was never going to let himself have before he met Miss Court in the gloom that first day. Miss Hancourt had turned that dream into a nightmare and why should he forgive her for it when she could only have been playing with Moss? He wasn't Moss, but he might have been. No, she had shown him the true meaning of betrayal so why would he ever forgive her for putting another layer of cynicism around Lord Barberry's already frosty heart?

'I still can't believe it's true,' Caroline said as their carriage finally rolled its weary way through the outskirts of London and even the novelty of it all couldn't distract her from her former governess's sins for very long.

'Nor can I, but Miss Court seems quite certain she is really an heiress and a niece of the Duke of Linaire, so who are we to argue with her when we spent two years trying to believe every word she's told us?'

'Thank you, Lavinia,' Nell said as firmly as she could when her eldest pupil was subtly calling her a liar and she really couldn't argue, 'but you must get used to calling me Miss Hancourt if you truly want to stay at Linaire House and not with your own aunt and uncle in Cavendish Square.'

'Oh, no, they wouldn't want me even if I wanted to go there.'

'I'm sure that's not true,' Nell argued, although if Lavinia's maternal relatives had a scrap of love in their aristocratic hearts for their niece they would have taken an interest in her happiness before now.

'And I want to see how you behave when you're not pretending to be a governess, of course,' Lavinia said, as if she was looking forward to watching her former teacher feel uncomfortable in own her skin for once, instead of the other way about.

Nell wondered if she'd made a rod for her own back when she insisted the Selford girls come to London. Too late to regret it now, the mud-spattered carriage was turning into the broad streets of Mayfair and they were nearly at their destination. Far too late to argue again with the stiff, aloof man riding alongside the Earl's travelling coach as if he didn't trust her to go unmolested in the most exclusive area of the capital city.

'So do I,' Penelope said with a stern nod at her one-time teacher.

Georgiana said nothing; she had refused to speak to Nell since she'd confessed she wasn't Miss Court but a well-connected heiress. At least she hadn't stopped talking altogether, Nell reflected philosophically. It would be awkward to introduce a girl who refused to speak at all into her uncle's home. The Selford cousin who had always seemed most damaged by her family's folly and neglect was Lavinia, but Nell was beginning to wonder if Georgiana hadn't been hiding her hurts under a quieter manner. It felt wrong not to find out why she was using silence like a weapon, but she wasn't the girls' governess any longer and had lost some of the natural authority a grown-up held over a girl by admitting she'd lied to them all. Perhaps Aunt Barbara or Eve could break through the silent defiance Georgiana had put up against her former governess.

'Now this house really is grand,' Penelope said when the horses turned into Grosvenor Square and the coachman halted at Linaire House.

'Yes,' Nell agreed hollowly, 'it really is.'

As a child she was convinced the mansion had a stiff and disapproving soul and saw her as an unwanted interloper. It was Uncle Augustus's house then—cold and austere and the perfect reflection of his dour personality. Nell shivered; even on the hottest days of summer coming back here had felt like stepping into an icehouse. It was a wonder she didn't freeze during the two years she'd spent alone here.

'Nell! Oh, you darling, stubborn girl. It's so

lovely to see you again,' the Duchess of Linaire exclaimed as she bustled down the grand steps of her latest home as if she wasn't a duchess at all and took Nell's dread of coming here clean away.

By the time she had been hugged and scolded and exclaimed over and her four companions made welcome, Nell felt this grand classical mansion could be home after all. It was a lesson in not blaming a place for the temper of its owner and even Georgiana's stony silence hadn't survived long in the face of Aunt Barbara's warm interest in her guests.

'Now I must thank you two gentlemen for escorting my niece and her charges here safely,' the Duchess of Linaire said when she could spare the two men the time of day. Nell felt unworthily smug about her aunt's priorities and hoped it would put surly Mr Moss, her judge and jury, firmly in his place.

'My name is Rivers, Your Grace, and this is…'

'He is Mr Moss, Lord Barberry's land steward…' Nell heard herself introduce the wretch at the same time as Mr Rivers and stopped. She flushed and waved a hand at that gentleman to continue, but this time her aunt beat them both to it.

'Nonsense, Eleanor, this young man is quite obviously Mr Rivers's brother,' Aunt Barbara said, seeing the fugitive likenesses between the two men Nell ought to have spotted the first time she'd laid eyes on Mr Rivers.

With her piercing artist's eye Aunt Barbara saw more than any person Nell knew—when she chose to truly look at a person with it, instead of letting her gaze drift over their head to something more interesting. Was Nell glad or sorry the Duchess had come out of her artist's studio long enough to welcome her here and subject the Earl of Barberry to an eagle-eyed scrutiny? Hard to tell with the truth still ringing in her ears as if they'd been boxed by an angry hand.

'Of course he is,' Nell heard herself say numbly.

'Don't you *dare* faint,' she heard her aunt whisper as the possibility occurred to Nell as well and pride ordered her not to give him the satisfaction.

The Selford girls had gasped, then clung together on hearing this latest betrayal of their trust. Who could blame them for only relying on each other after the two huge lies Nell and

Lord Barberry had told them? And she'd been doing penance for much lesser sins for the last two days. Nell glared icily into the middle distance instead of lowering herself to look at the lying toad.

'I won't,' she whispered fiercely.

The similarities between the brothers outranked the differences when she finally managed to glance disdainfully at his lordship instead of ranting at him for what he'd done. Mr Rivers was fair and his eyes were grey rather than blue; his handsome features had some of the softness of youth that his brother's emphatically lacked, but standing side by side on the carriage sweep in front of Linaire House with the reins of their weary horses in their gloved hands, it was so obvious they were brothers she had no idea how she'd managed to miss seeing it for so long.

'You had best come inside and talk about it without any onlookers,' the Duchess said with a glance at the grooms and coachmen as well as the bland, blank windows of the other grand houses in the square.

'But we're still in our dirt, Your Grace,' Mr Rivers protested half-heartedly.

'We have more important things to worry about than a little mud and the odour of horse, young man,' Aunt Barbara said magnificently and ordered their mounts to the mews to be pampered until their owners were ready to take them away.

Nell saw the brothers exchange glances as if assessing their chances of escape, then shrug, as if resigned to a scene and resolved to get it over with. How had she missed the cool devilment in the so-called steward's blue eyes, the imperious nature betrayed by his haughty Roman nose, not to mention his arrogant stance that said no man was his master? Fool, she chided herself as she followed her aunt inside the grand Palladian mansion and reminded herself it was still her duty to put the Selford girls' feelings first, but how she wanted to rage at the man for kissing her so passionately he woke up a Nell Hancourt even she hadn't recognised and how he'd condemned her for it when he found out she wasn't a poor little dependent governess after all. He was the Earl of Barberry and a far bigger liar than she was, but perhaps he'd hoped to set her up as his mistress? What a lucky escape they'd both had, then. But if she felt betrayed by the false rogue, how must his wards be feeling? First their governess hid her true self for two years. Now the Earl of Barberry was unmasked as a man who had skulked about Berry Brampton acting as his own land steward, instead of finally shouldering the responsibility he'd dodged for so long.

'What a shame my nephew and his wife are spending a few days at Darkmere to celebrate the arrival of Eve's new half-sister. Colm will be so annoyed that he's missed you, my lord,' Aunt Barbara informed the Earl with a regal irony that made Nell want to hug her, even as she shuddered at the idea of her brother meeting this brute at dawn to shoot him for her sake.

She had no doubt Colm could put a bullet in the Earl's sorry hide wherever he chose, for he was a famous marksman under his other name. Her shiver was for her brother's horror if he had to fire in anger once again. Colm would suffer if he hurt another human being after the endless carnage of Waterloo and all the battles he'd somehow survived before it.

'Mr Hancourt will find me at Barberry House in a week or two if he still wishes to make my acquaintance,' Lord Barberry said, as if quite ready to be challenged when he had the leisure to spare for such a minor matter as his improper intentions towards Colm's little sister when he'd thought of her as a mere governess.

As if she would tell Colm exactly what they had got up to at Berry Brampton when his lordship thought her fair game. Nell felt so furious on Miss Court's behalf she wanted to slap the wretch, then rage at him for his sins, but it would take too long to list them and lower her to his level, so she decided a sniff of chilly disdain would have to do instead.

'You intend to stay at Barberry House and grace polite society with your presence at last then, my lord? The *beau monde* will be so delighted I dare say you'll be nigh crushed in the stampede,' Aunt Barbara said, as if she routed pretenders like him every day before breakfast. 'Meanwhile, here is my husband; he might be eager to bid you welcome as well, my lord.' The words *if you're very good* sat unspoken in the air as if he was a small boy who hadn't washed his neck.

'Were we expecting visitors, my love?' the Duke of Linaire asked amiably.

Nell smiled warmly at her eccentric scholar

uncle, even with the Earl of Barberry looking on as if at a play. She was too fond of her Uncle Horace to pretend not to be in front of strangers and Lord Barberry was one of those, wasn't he?

'I'm sure you're as delighted as I am to welcome our dearest Nell home, Horry,' the Duchess said with a fond smile at her husband.

'What, you're actually going to grant us your company despite all the past rebuffs, are you, miss?' the Duke asked and hugged her.

'I am, and these are my former charges, Uncle Horace,' Nell explained. She managed a smile, despite the Earl's stormy glower. The girls were his wards, but Nell beckoned them forward to be introduced, despite his lordship's silent disapproval. 'This is Miss Lavinia Selford, Uncle Horace. Miss Georgiana, Miss Caroline and Miss Penelope Selford are doing their best to hide behind her for some reason best known to themselves.'

'No need, my dears, you're very welcome here *and* you managed to bring my stubborn niece with you. That's something the Duchess and I haven't managed this last year and more, so we're very grateful,' the Duke said and made Penny laugh at the idea they had brought Nell here rather than the other way about.

'We must contain our joy for now, my dear,' the Duchess intervened, 'the Earl of Barberry and Mr Rivers are waiting to be noticed.'

'Pleased to meet you, Rivers, I knew your father at Eton.'

'I doubt he learned very much there, Your Grace. I hear he was as wild as a mountain pony until my mother tamed him as best she could.'

'True, but he lacked patience rather than kindness or good humour. I dare say time has taught him that.'

Mr Rivers chuckled. 'He hasn't changed very much from the sound of it.'

'Then be sure to tell him I'll be delighted to see him if he ever feels like crossing his beloved Irish Sea for a week or two.'

'I'll be sure to do that, Your Grace,' Mr Rivers said, a coolness coming into his eyes as they rested on his half-brother, perhaps recalling why Sir Graham Rivers stayed away from London after he wed the widow of the last Lord Barberry's youngest son.

'So you're the elusive Earl of Barberry, are you,

young man?' the Duke said as if Moss's worn riding coat and breeches were in no way remarkable on an earl.

Seeing the fine cut and expensive fabric of the old and slightly outdated clothes he must have sent for after she christened him Mr Moss, Nell wondered how she could have deceived herself he was the man and not the master. She recalled the way she'd behaved in his arms only a few nights ago and shuddered at the idea of him smirking at her as he walked away to share her silly, willing vulnerability with his younger brother and perhaps laugh at her in his cups.

'I am indeed,' the wretch admitted coolly.

'Then whilst you may have had a hard journey escorting my niece and these delightful young ladies here and are currently a guest under my roof, I have a good many quarrels to pick with you, sir. The first is why you have let our Nell take your responsibilities on her shoulders for so long? My wife and I have been pleading with her to live with us ever since we got back to England, but, no, she must stay with your wards because nobody else cared tuppence about their happiness and well-being. Now I've met you all I can see why our girl here refused to abandon you, but it defeats me why she didn't bring you here a year ago. There's room enough for twice as many girls to stay and still leave room to billet an army.'

'I would not have permitted such an arrangement,' Lord Barberry argued.

'Everyone knows you ignored your cousins from the day you inherited Berry Brampton House,' Nell said hotly. 'If you have a scrap of feeling in you, then you'll stay out of their lives now and send them to a good school so they can make friends their own age and learn to enjoy life, instead of always being conscious they were born female so you are the Earl of Barberry and not one of them. It's far too late to pretend you care about anyone but yourself, *my lord*,' she finished with a regal glare she hoped would cinder any memory he might have of her eagerly returning his kisses as if he was a good and decent man.

'It's never too late to put things right,' he snapped.

'That's up to your wards. Affection and respect cannot be demanded like a ton of coal or a baron of beef from a tradesman,' she said so coldly even she shivered.

'If the Duke and Duchess will have us, I would

like to stay here with Miss Hancourt,' Lavinia surprised Nell by saying, then moving to stand at her side. The other three girls looked at each other and Penny went to her eldest cousin's other side while Caroline and Georgiana took Nell's and their loyalty brought tears to her eyes.

'I should be delighted to welcome your wards to Linaire House until an acceptable compromise can be reached about their future, Lord Barberry,' Aunt Barbara said blandly, prepared to be diplomatic now she'd got what she wanted. 'Barberry House has been rented out for a decade, I believe, and must need a great deal of work before it's ready to house four young ladies and their maids, plus a governess to continue their education *and* a suitable chaperon for you all.'

The stubborn line of the Earl's mouth looked set as worked stone now. Nell was sure he would refuse, however sweetly the Duchess of Linaire pointed out he was ill prepared to house four growing girls. They'd resented Nell's authority when she arrived at Berry Brampton House— how much worse would they be with the guardian who had wanted nothing to do with them for a decade? She was tempted to stand back and let him try, but she loved the girls too much to inflict it on them if there was any chance they could stay here instead.

'The Duchess is right, Fergus,' Mr Rivers said rather apologetically.

Nell wanted to shout at him for pacifying the stubborn liar instead of telling him not to be an arrogant fool. Yet her inner idiot treasured the gift of his true name and silently tried it out on her tongue. *Fergus.* Foolish Nell felt every syllable on her tongue as if it was unique.

'Barberry House must be threadbare and out of fashion by now,' Mr Rivers went on. Maybe he was used to finding ways around impasses for his arrogant brother and no longer even realised he was doing it. 'We have no lady with us to make all right either.'

'We're not related to the Hancourts—what reason can there be for them to take the Selford girls into their home, even if I were to allow it?'

'The world knows my niece had to earn her living before the blind trust her father set up matured on the day her brother was five and twenty. At the moment it's considered a fine and romantic tale: a poor orphaned girl forced out into the world penniless by her own wicked guardian, my late brother,' the Duke said in a shrewd summary of the whispers going about the *ton*. 'All *you* need do is go and live at Berry Brampton House for a few weeks, my lord. No more explanation of why your wards are living under my roof instead of your own will be needed. You will seem like a kind guardian and my niece a right-minded and careful lady to come here the moment you put in an appearance there at long last. You could thank her for her care of the girls she has grown so fond of by allowing them to take a holiday here while arrangements are made for their future. That would show how wrong everyone is to call you a care-for-nobody, wouldn't it?'

'I seem to have very little choice in the matter,' Lord Barberry said. 'As well I don't want to stay at Barberry House until the upholsterers have been in for a month or two. If we go now we'll be back at Berry Brampton House by tomorrow evening and you can spread this unlikely story while I catch up with my sins and omissions of the last ten years.'

'And what a thankless task that will be,' Mr Rivers said. 'I can hardly wait to be back in the saddle after our long and uneventful journey here,' he added ruefully and Nell silently blessed him for trying to lighten the mood.

'Needs must when Miss Hancourt drives,' the Earl said disagreeably.

If they hadn't managed to stop making love in his housekeeper's sitting room she might be planning their wedding right now. Feeling sick at the very thought of enduring such a hasty and hollow marriage, Nell got through the next few minutes by pretending this was all happening to someone else.

'And thank goodness *we* don't have to make that awful journey again today,' Caroline said as she watched from one of the drawing-room windows as the half-brothers waved goodbye to the Duke and rode out of sight on lively new mounts provided by the ducal stables.

'Would you rather have gone home with Lord Barberry?' Nell asked guiltily, wondering if she had robbed the girls of a chance to know their guardian.

'No, he doesn't want us and we'll have far more fun here,' Penny said happily.

When the Duke came back in with a procession of footmen bearing food, Penny sat down to toast a muffin by the fire and never mind if she hadn't had her hair brushed or her travelling dress changed yet. As the Duchess pointed out, they had come a long way and there hadn't been children at Linaire House for far too long.

'Plenty of time to sort things out when his lordship has his feet under the table at Berry Brampton and these young ladies aren't cold and hungry after a long journey, Nell. Sit for a while now and stop fussing, my dear,' the Duke said and took over toasting duties when Penny almost dropped a muffin in the fire. 'Ring the bell and tell Biggins we're not at home to visitors for the rest of the day would you, my love?' he asked his wife, 'We're far too busy to entertain this afternoon.'

Uncle Horace would have made a wonderful father, Nell decided, as she finally took off her bonnet with a sigh of relief. Between the fire and hot tea and muffins she should be warm, but part of her felt cut off from the lively scene around the ducal fireplace. Maybe that bit of her would always feel chilled now the rightful owner of Berry Brampton hated Miss Eleanor Hancourt with such stern passion.

Chapter Sixteen

'**W**hat, the chit is in London with her confounded family now and you're no nearer to finding out where those damned jewels are?' Lord Derneley whispered furiously and he could fit a lot of fury into a mere whisper.

'They suddenly packed, upped and left, Derneley. I could hardly stop them,' his lady said and looked as if she preferred his room to his company for the first time in their joint lives. 'It *was* quite pleasant to get out of this horrid house for a few days, though,' she added sulkily.

'You'll be stuck here for good if we don't get hold of those jewels. One day even those fools on my tail will get in and find me and I'll be hauled off to the Fleet.'

'Oh, no, Derneley, we can't stay here. It's not at all what we're used to.'

'And I can't rot in a debtors' prison, woman, so you'll have to do better next time, won't you? What did you do to find those papers I wanted?'

'I found a maid servant willing to search her room and bring them to me.'

Her lord's eyes narrowed against the dim light of a single tallow candle that was all the nip-farthing old lady allowed her niece when she thought the best use for darkness was to sleep. 'Why didn't she do so, then?'

'I don't know, Derneley. She didn't come to the place we were to meet and I waited for hours. Next thing I heard the Selford brats and that silly chit of Chris's were off to town and Barberry's brother and some manservant escorted them all the way here. Even if I could catch up, I could hardly pretend to be a highwayman and hold them up, could I?'

Derneley brooded on her tale for a few moments, then seemed to untangle the gist of it and arched over the weak candle light so he could look straight into her eyes. 'To guard them that closely, they must have been suspicious,' he told her harshly. 'You did something stupid, didn't you?'

'No, I was quite clever to find a girl whose family are even more miserable and in debt than we are.'

'Hmm, what did you offer her for the Hancourt girl's papers?'

'Oh, only five pounds,' Lady Derneley told him proudly. 'Just enough to tempt her and not enough to seem desperate.'

'Five pounds,' he echoed as if he could hardly believe his ears.

'Yes, she wouldn't do it for less.'

'You negotiated,' he said flatly, frowning so fiercely he looked as if he was only managing not to shout with a huge effort of will. 'You offered this cunning little doxy all she might earn in a year for one trivial task and expected her to keep quiet about it?'

'Yes,' Lady Derneley said, sounding a little uncertain now.

'You damned fool,' he said and she flinched away, looking terrified of the fury in his eyes as they glinted back at her in the semi-darkness. 'You brainless, feckless, stupid woman,' he managed with angry despair. 'What the devil are we going to do now?'

'Find that paper some other way?' she said with

a desperate sort of helpfulness that somehow didn't look to be very helpful to her once-dashing lord.

'No, they know we're after it now,' he said and turned his back on her as if he could brood better on the misfortunes dogging him without the sight of her defensive, sulky face distracting him.

'Then we must stay here for ever?' she asked as his despondency made her realise they might be penniless for the rest of their lives. The sound of despair in her voice instead of her usual shallow optimism seemed to make even selfish and spoilt Lord Derneley consider someone else's miseries for once in his life.

'No, we'll find another way, Lexie, don't you worry your pretty head about it,' he said and she smiled brilliantly and he seemed to forget his ill temper. 'I'm not staying in the old cat's cellar for the rest of my life,' he went on. 'If they're on the hunt for the Lambury Jewels I could always let them find them, then snatch them out from under their noses at the last minute.'

'You're so clever, Derneley,' his lady said admiringly.

'Lucky one of us is, then,' he muttered under his breath.

* * *

'You're a success, Nell,' the Duchess of Linaire told her husband's niece as they travelled back to Linaire House one night with the dawn.

'My fortune has cast a wonderful gilt over me.'

'Nonsense, now you're dressed as befits Miss Hancourt everyone can see what a lovely, lively young lady you are at last. You are a refreshing change from the usual empty-headed young miss launched straight out of the schoolroom into the *ton*.'

'Fine feathers make fine birds,' Nell said, because somehow her success in the wider world meant far too little. She had been shut up in a large old house in the country with four girls for so long she should be eager for every new experience, but instead she felt as if she was acting in a play about someone who wasn't the real Nell Hancourt at all.

'That really is the most ridiculous saying. Not even a fine gown like that one would make you appear as you did tonight if you were not a very pretty young woman to start with. No, don't dismiss what I say as partial because you're Horace's beloved niece. Remember I aspire to be an artist and don't argue with me because I don't flatter, I simply report what I see.'

'Affection can distort even the clearest vision.'

'And false modesty can infuriate the most patient of souls. I am not one of those, Nell, so please don't try me any further tonight.'

'Very well, I shall accept all praise as my due from now on.'

'Hah! That's about as likely as Horace becoming prime minister.'

Nell chuckled at the idea of her uncle's face if such an invitation came his way. 'He would drag you on to the next ship sailing to America and refuse to come back, however much we missed you, lest they ask him again,' she said.

'And now we've come all this way to be a duke and duchess it would be wrong of us to run away. These things have to be faced, as your Lord Barberry finally seems to have accepted, since he's firmly settled at Berry Brampton.'

'He does, doesn't he?' Nell said sweetly, refusing to rise to her aunt's bait and reveal her still-raw feelings for the stubborn great idiot.

'As well there are so many personable young men in town for you to choose from and you danced twice with Mr Rivers tonight, didn't you? Now he really is an Adonis and a knowing young rogue with it.'

'And very young and not in the least bit inclined to marry and settle down yet. I wonder Lord Barberry can spare him, though.'

'Perhaps he can't,' Aunt Barbara said and Nell could think of nothing to say in reply to such a cryptic comment.

For a while there was silence inside the luxurious coach and Nell wondered if her aunt had nodded off. Not so, she felt the Duchess's acute gaze on her face as they rattled over the cobblestones and surely they would be home soon, so she could go to bed and try not to dream of a man who certainly didn't want to marry her. Aunt Barbara smiled in the strengthening light with too much understanding in her eyes and Nell felt a wave of love for this strong, loving and clever woman who had taken her to her heart and given the Selford girls a temporary home as well.

'I have enjoyed the last few weeks, Nell dear, but I'll be glad if Eve or one of Lady Farenze's friends can chaperon you now you are properly launched and a success. I shall be far too tired to do aught but sleep in the morning, not that it isn't already morning and I'm far too old to be out half the night.'

'You know I'm always glad of your company, Aunt Barbara, but now Colm and Eve are back in town you can get some painting done at last.'

'Especially as they brought Eve's old governess with them. Now that scamp Verity is back at school while her father and stepmama sail the seven seas for a while, I'm glad Miss York has agreed to keep your girls occupied while Lord Barberry makes up his mind what to do with them, despite the fact she must be in need of a long holiday. The best thing Lord Barberry could do is consult you, of course, since nobody knows as much about his wards as you do.'

Nell was so tired after dancing all evening and trying hard to pretend she was happy she felt as if she'd smiled until her face ached. She had to blink her weary eyes several times to stop herself crying. It was ridiculous to let the wretched man affect her this way when he'd been back at Berry Brampton for a month and obviously didn't care about her. He'd certainly found it easier to forget her than she had him. Nothing seemed to erase the way he made her feel when they were close. 'I have no wish to speak with him ever again,' she said as soon as she could steady her voice.

'Do you not, my love? Well, hasn't the world changed since your uncle and I were courting? I longed for the next time we could speak and hated every event my mother dragged me along to if he wasn't there.'

'You and Uncle Horace were in love.'

'Yes, and it's wonderful to find the man you can be happy with for life, Nell. Are you sure you haven't met that man yet?'

'Very sure, I think I danced with half the young men in London tonight and my heart only beat faster because I needed to get my breath back,' Nell said lightly, telling herself it was stupid to feel so disappointed not one of her partners had outshone a man she hadn't danced with and now never would.

Fergus would have laughed, cynically and rather hollowly, if he'd been able to read Nell's thoughts. He'd spent three weeks camped out in his rather shabby London mansion with nothing much to do but think about Miss Eleanor Hancourt and how not to miss her as if half of him had been cut away. Of course, the contrary, stubborn, confoundedly popular female was never still long enough to pine for him. On the other hand, he had hours on end to watch her new home through the best spyglasses money could buy by day and lurk about the Square at night in the hope whoever was after her letters at Berry Brampton would try again. He was in the ideal position to know Miss Hancourt was so much in demand among the younger gentlemen of polite society that she was rarely at home for very long unless she was asleep. He caught glimpses of her dressed in the first stare of fashion and groomed to perfection as she stepped out of a fashionable town coach with some eligible man's sister or mother, or climbed the dizzy heights up to a dashing curricle. He frowned at the house across the Square and watched her being handed up into one so ridiculous the coachmaker ought to be shot for selling such a vehicle to a mere whipster. Tempted to run across and mill the flash young fool down, he hit the nearest wall to relieve his outraged feelings instead.

He was the best man to watch out for any mysterious strangers haunting Grosvenor Square because nobody here knew him, but he was slowly going insane while he pretended not to be here and Eleanor Hancourt ran about town pursued by eager suitors. And what would Miss Hancourt make of the fact her nearest and dearest were deceiving her for her own good as well this time? No doubt she would be furious and declare she could look after herself, thank you very much, and it was all his fault. Which was exactly why he was stuck here, trying to pretend he was nowhere near the capital, so she couldn't take a pet and ruin the whole enterprise, then insist on going about alone to frustrate him. Fear for Nell and his cousins' safety goaded him into coming back here to watch over them in case whoever was after her secrets got desperate enough to kidnap one of them. And life was devilish flat and empty at Berry Brampton House now anyway.

He'd been watching from the eyrie he'd made in one of the top-floor rooms overlooking Linaire House when Brendan arrived to escort Miss Hancourt and her aunt or sister-in-law to any events Hancourt or the Duke could not attend. At least his brother was welcome at Linaire House, but suspicion such dangerous proximity might make a

marriage between his little brother and Miss Hancourt had got Fergus so desperately overwound
with frustration and fury that he wanted to hit
something very hard until his fists were as numb
as the rest of him. He couldn't risk that because he
might need them to protect her and the girls one
day soon, but Nell wouldn't let him escort her if
he begged on bended knee. If he came out into the
open she would be more stubborn and uncooper-
ative than ever just to prove she didn't need him,
so he had to stay here and watch for her enemy
to make a move and somehow he'd find a way to
contain all this raw emotion and keep his temper
before he punched his way out on to the roof and
could watch her from out there as the rain dripped
into his fine London house.

He glanced down at his latest less-than-aristo-
cratic outfit. Whose idea had it been for him to
pretend to be a down-at-heel footman? Surely he
wasn't fool enough to want to spend his days in
a shabby and mismatched set of livery in case he
had to fool someone he was a willing conspirator
in whatever mischief they had planned this time?
So far he might as well have spent the time at his
tailor's and strutted about the place in new clothes

for all the good it had done him not to. He hadn't been entirely idle, though, and was beginning to get information from Poulson's sources now he'd put the right feelers out. As well to be certain before he moved against the man he suspected was behind this nonsense, so he waited and watched. At last his patience was rewarded when his most likely quarry left his lair in the depths of the darkest night Fergus had lurked in since he'd got home. Now it was time to bait his trap and wait for the desperate idiot to walk into it. He just hoped the man would leave his wife at home this time.

'Are you sure about this, my boy?' the Duke of Linaire asked his nephew a few nights later.

'No, but Barberry says Derneley is desperate for the Lambury Jewels and he might hurt Nell or Eve if they get in his way,' Colm Hancourt said grimly.

'Miss Hancourt won't be safe until we smoke the fool out,' Fergus confirmed.

'And he was behind that odd business at Berry Brampton?' the Duke asked.

'He seems to think that because his sister-in-law was given paste copies of the Lambury sapphires and emeralds he was defrauded of the fortune they should have been worth when she died and he found out they weren't real.'

'He's mad, then,' Colm said impatiently.

'No, he's selfish and vain and ridiculous, but he's not mad,' the Duke said before Fergus could argue it didn't matter.

'He's desperate enough to be dangerous and we need to contain him before he does any more damage.'

'Well then, we must do so, but he's no gentleman.'

'After what he tried to do to Eve last year we know he's nothing of the sort, Uncle Horace, and don't forget Lady Derneley fooled me into writing to Nell so they could find out her address,' Colm pointed out irritably.

'And she was the female who offered to pay my servant to steal your sister's papers,' Fergus pointed out.

'Is that why you're taking such an interest in my sister's affairs, Barberry?' Colm challenged.

'My wards seem to love her and this business did start under my roof,' Fergus said defensively, avoiding his gaze because somehow he didn't want to ask for Nell's hand with this farce hanging over them. He wanted her free and clear of danger and misunderstandings before he dared try to court her, because it would be hard enough to get her to believe a word he said without a shabby villain trying to steal the jewels she was so indifferent about and distracting him at every turn.

'No, it started here, more years ago than I care to recall,' the Duke said as if all this was his fault though he wasn't even in the country when Lord Chris set his little girl a funny little puzzle.

'Then why tonight?' Colm Hancourt asked as if he didn't care about the jewels either and they were a minor inconvenience he could have done without.

'Since I found him loitering outside your house one dark night it's taken me a while to wriggle into the man's confidence as your disgruntled former employee, Your Grace,' Fergus told the Duke. 'I told him I'd persuade my sweetheart to leave the garden door unlocked tonight, if he gave me the silver inkstand from your study as my share of his ill-gotten gains.'

'My grandmother gave me that,' the Duke said

indignantly. 'It's the only thing I took to America and back again, apart from the Duchess, of course.'

'Just as well I don't really want it then,' Fergus said.

'Or my aunt, I hope?' Colm muttered.

Fergus had to muffle a surprised laugh at that wry comment and wondered if he and Hancourt had something in common after all, apart from Miss Eleanor Hancourt, of course.

'So he will get in once most of the servants are in bed and the light goes out in your study, Your Grace. Mr Hancourt is rumoured to be out tonight and the ladies are from home. I told him he would just have to risk the younger ladies all being asleep and I hope they don't hear anything from the schoolroom floor and come creeping downstairs to find out what's going on. That's why I needed you both on hand, in case we have to contend with more than Derneley tonight.'

'Hmm, that's wise, I suppose,' the Duke said. 'Just as well the ladies are out, though, or we would certainly have to contend with them.'

'True, now perhaps you could check the servants are all abed except the footman on duty downstairs, Hancourt? We need to get on lest the man gives up and goes home and it's all to do again.'

'Heaven forbid,' Colm Hancourt said, rolling his eyes at the elaborately plastered ceiling at the very thought of lying to his wife for much longer.

He'd told her he was meeting some old army comrades tonight and even Fergus could see how much it pained him to lie to her. How must it feel to love a woman that strongly? he wondered, then assured himself he wasn't the kind for such overwhelming emotions, even if a goodly part of him didn't believe it.

'And what happens once we blow the candles out in this room, my boy?' the Duke asked genially.

'We wait for Derneley, confront him with his sins and send him packing across the Channel where he can do less damage. Until he's in we only have Faith's word that it was Lady Derneley who offered to pay her for your sister's private papers and a lot of vague suspicions he's after the Lambury Jewels.'

'Not much to prosecute him with, then, even if we wanted to.'

'So long as he goes away for good that'll be enough for me,' Fergus agreed.

'I'm not a vengeful man and they'll be miserable enough with nothing in their pockets but what they can earn for once in their lives.'

'Are you sure your niece hasn't already worked this riddle out, Your Grace?' Fergus asked, wondering if it might be cause to hope if she was too distracted to search for the jewels because she ached for him as much as he did for her.

'She would have told us if she had.'

'Yet her father's words seemed to mean something to her at the time.'

'Will you show me?' the older man asked.

Fergus opened his pocket book to the page where he'd scribbled the words so angrily when he'd discovered Nell Hancourt's secret, then lost his temper so spectacularly he'd lost her as well before he'd finally cooled down and realised what he'd done.

'Through the eyes of a grandfather clock everything that is hidden will be found again,' he read out.

'The clock in the red drawing room looks as if it has eyes,' the Duke said with a visible shudder. 'Our father used to make us explain our sins in there and Chris always used to say the clock shared Papa's low opinion of us both.'

'Is it still there?'

'Yes, although I've been meaning to have it taken down and stored in a dark cellar ever since we got back to England, I haven't got around to doing it yet.'

'Perhaps we should see if we can make sense of it while we wait,' Fergus suggested.

'My brother did leave that clue for Nell,' the Duke argued uneasily.

'She hasn't pursued it though, has she? Hush, did you hear that? And we haven't even put out the light,' Fergus whispered, puzzled because the soft steps outside the Duke's study sounded too light for a man of Derneley's build and former habits. Surely the man hadn't sent his wife again?

'I knew you were all up to something,' an all-too-familiar feminine voice exclaimed and how the devil had she got wind of this?

'Nell, m'dear, whatever are you doing here? You're supposed to be dancing away at some ball with your aunt and sister-in-law until the sun comes up.'

'Colm is a terrible liar and we thought we ought to know what was going on here before one of you got hurt. If I don't send word within half an hour, Aunt Barbara and Eve will send Eve's Uncle James and half-a-dozen grandees to rescue us, so don't look at me as if I've run mad.'

'You'll drive me to Bedlam then, even if you don't end up there yourself,' Fergus told her in a furious undertone.

'And what are *you* doing here?' she said haughtily, the only female he knew who could manage it dressed in a governess's dull plumage and when had she found time and chance to put that absurd get up on again?

'Tracking down your family treasures, since you're obviously too busy to bother,' he told her and wasn't it satisfying to get under her skin again? 'You're a woman of so much substance you obviously can't spare the time to worry about it,' he told her with an ironic bow in the hope of doing it again. He hadn't wanted her to march into danger with her nose in the air, but his whole world felt wider and more vital with her nearby. God save them both, but he'd missed her.

'You look like a derelict,' she said with a disdainful look at his down-on-my-luck servant's garb.

'And you look like a governess,' he said with a humble bow, as if he really was the Duke's footman, before he did something disgraceful and was dismissed.

'Half an hour, you say, m'dear?' the Duke said with a glance at his watch to remind them time was a-wasting.

'You're not planning to go on with this now your niece is here, are you, sir?' Fergus only just managed not to yell as fear for her nearly felled him.

'If not tonight, Nell will get involved in some other way, when we're not by to stop her getting hurt. The Lambury Jewels were left to her as well as Colm.'

'But…' Fergus began to protest, but the Duke calmly went about snuffing candles before he could find words powerful enough to forbid it.

'My wife is a lady of iron resolution as well, so you might as well get used to it, Barberry,' the Duke told him kindly.

'I don't see why I should,' he managed to mutter grumpily before Miss Hancourt elbowed him in the ribs and he decided to save his breath, not sure if he wanted to kiss her senseless or leave her to find the Lambury Jewels without him, but very sure the idea of her being in danger made him afraid as he'd never been before.

'You're supposed to be at Berry Brampton,' she told him in an irritated whisper.

'And you're supposed to be at a ball,' he retaliated.

'Hah! A ruse to get us out of the way that a five-year-old child could see through,' she told him softly.

'Will you two be quiet?' Colm demanded irritably.

'I wasn't making a noise,' Nell muttered darkly and Fergus recovered his sense of humour and his delight at being close to her again at the same time as terror for her made his heartbeat gallop in his ears.

'And crows aren't black and fish don't swim in the sea,' he parried and this time it was his turn to nudge her in the ribs and surely it wasn't right to feel such joy at being shut up in a dark room with her and her closest male relatives? She *was* speaking to him again, even if it was in insults though, wasn't she? 'I missed you,' he informed her softly and somehow he knew she was smiling rather smugly about that, even in the stuffy darkness of this closed-up room.

'You two can croon at each other later, someone's coming,' Colm whispered sharply.

Fergus decided nothing about this evening was going to plan, but he might as well learn to reshape them, because Nell would never be a predictable female if they both lived to be ninety. He wouldn't want to spend all those years with her if she was, but he very much wanted all that time with her and they were in the middle of a dangerous muddle that could go horribly wrong. He listened for their quarry and wondered if it was too late to kick up enough row to make an intruder jump out of the window and dash back into the night. Anything rather than endanger Nell and her otherworldly uncle, although Colm Hancourt could obviously look after himself. The whole untidy business might still have gone smoothly enough if the Duke hadn't sneezed at exactly the wrong moment.

'There you are, Lexie, didn't I say it could be a trap?' Derneley observed as he uncovered the dark lantern he carried in his other hand and saw the

Duke and two pretend servants plus the Duke's nephew not even trying to hide from the cocked pistols he had stolen from Lady Derneley's aunt. 'Keep Hancourt covered, my dear, but don't get close enough for him to get hold of your gun. He's tricky, that one,' he observed coolly, taking a closer look at the smaller servant as he put the lantern where it cast the best light to watch them all by, 'just like his sister.'

Somehow Colm managed to look amused by the fact he was being held at gunpoint by Lady Derneley. Fergus cursed himself for not taking this threat more seriously and getting the Bow Street Runners involved, whatever Hancourt and his uncle had to say about keeping it in the family. He wondered if it was worth trying to overpower the couple before they settled.

'I may not be clever or accomplished, but I am an excellent shot,' the lady boasted as if she could read his mind and he decided it wasn't worth the risk.

'It's true,' Derneley told them proudly. 'Once won me a pony by shooting the pip out of an ace at fifty paces. Wish I'd bet a monkey; I could do with it now.'

Fergus could imagine the wild and rather dashing couple they must have been thirty years ago, but look what all that fizz and sparkle dulled to after years of headlong pleasure seeking. 'Which brings us to business,' he said laconically.

'Who are you really, then?' Derneley asked, his long-barrelled and over-decorated old pistol aimed at him, and Fergus bit back a sigh of relief. If the fool shot Nell he'd rather die himself than endure seeing her hurt in any way.

'The Earl of Barberry's land steward,' Fergus lied. If he could keep the man talking long enough James Winterley and his cohorts would rescue them. On the other hand, the more people there were here, the more chance there was that someone might be hurt.

'What the devil are you doing here, interfering in my business, then?'

'My lord asked me to; his wards live here,' he said and watched the weight of the clumsy old pistols taking its toll. Another few minutes and Lady Derneley would need a flat surface and her other hand to keep her gun level. Derneley didn't look in very good shape after hiding from his creditors and a lifetime of dissolute living either.

'Tell me where the Lambury Diamonds are or I shoot the wench,' his lordship said as if he'd noticed that, too, drat him.

Lady Derneley narrowed her eyes at Colm as if she had a suspicion he was up to something she wouldn't like. 'And the rest of the jewels are here somewhere,' she reminded her husband.

'Nonsense, of course they're not. Do you really think a fortune in diamonds could be been hidden in a public room for so long without them being found long ago by the servants?' Nell asked scornfully.

'He must have hidden them very well,' Lady Derneley said with a shrug.

'So well that no maid, clock-winder or upholsterer has found them in all these years?'

'Even a fence couldn't hide having so many stones to cut up and as your father managed to fool Pamela with his tricks he'll have hidden them cunningly,' Lord Derneley told Nell, as if Lord Chris was the one at fault instead of him.

'My sister had the rubies inspected and cleaned. They were the real thing, so why would we have doubted them when he gave her the sapphires and emeralds as well?' Lady Derneley said indignantly.

'You stole them when she died, didn't you?' Nell accused with such bitter contempt Fergus was afraid Derneley might shoot her anyway and tensed to jump in front of her if the man's finger tightened even a shade on that heavy old trigger.

'I had to wait until that useless treaty in '02 and I searched for nearly three days up and down those mountains before I found them both lying at the bottom of a valley nobody thought they ought to be anywhere near. Finest stones I ever laid eyes on, netted us a fortune, didn't they, my lady?' Derneley boasted. 'How your sister would have cursed Chris for tricking us out of the rest if she'd known.'

'He was my father,' Nell said through clenched teeth.

'Left you behind for Augustus to neglect though, didn't he? Can't have loved you very much to do that,' Lord Derneley taunted and Fergus felt any mercy he'd been inclined to grant the worm seep away.

'This thing is heavy, Derneley, how much longer must we stand here talking?' Lady Derneley asked querulously, bracing her gun hand on the back of a chair this time and looked ready to wilt into it if he didn't hurry up.

'Until we get what we came for,' he said impatiently. 'So where are they, wench?' he asked Nell. Fergus stiffened as the pistol in Derneley's hand swerved away from him to aim straight at her heart and fear froze every inch of his body for a long and terrible moment.

'I don't know. We only found his message when your wife came looking for it and I've been too busy to work it out,' Nell explained impatiently.

'Too busy for a fortune in jewels?' Lady Derneley sounded so incredulous her gun wavered from her own target until she caught Derneley's glare and steadied it on Colm Hancourt again.

'She don't need a fortune, she's got one, Lexie. You, steward—read me this riddle and if you've got a pistol I'd wonder if you can get it out and shoot me before I shoot her if I were you,' Derneley ordered.

'Which clock does he mean?' the man asked after Fergus did as he was bid.

'It's the biggest one in the small drawing room,'

the Duke said mildly and Fergus hoped the man was a lot cannier than Derneley thought him.

'They're not in the clock,' Nell said wearily when they got to the old-fashioned room that looked as if it was rarely used even by family.

'Why does it say it is, then?'

'"Through the eyes of the clock…"' she quoted the puzzle Lord Chris left behind as if they were slow infants and she was an impatient governess again.

'Clocks don't have eyes,' Derneley argued and swung about to look hard at every dial he could see.

That was enough of a chance for Fergus. Every muscle and sinew must work to get him to that pistol in time, so he sprang and prayed at the same time. Almost, he thought in a daze, as the confounded thing fired anyway. He waited for the terrible reality of the bullet to strike him and hoped he'd expire in Nell's arms if that was all they were going to be allowed.

'Stupid great idiot,' his love all but shouted in his ears. He marvelled she'd got her breath back and could speak so abruptly to a dying man who had only just realised he loved her with everything he was when it was too late.

'Don't you love me, then?' he asked in a bewildered voice even he hardly recognised.

'Why the devil should I after you nearly got yourself shot like that?' she demanded furiously. 'And I don't know why the rest of you are standing there grinning,' she went on to accuse the Duke and her brother, who were now holding the Derneleys at bay with Lady Derneley's pistol.

'Would you rather we let them go then, Sis?' Colm Hancourt asked with a shrug that told Fergus he no longer figured in the man's list of enemies he must have banished to a dark corner of the earth.

'No, but I don't know how we're going to explain this to the rest of the world,' she said a little more reasonably.

'Explain, my dear? Why would we Hancourts lower ourselves to enlighten the curious?' her uncle asked haughtily.

'Ah, I see,' Fergus heard Nell say and groaned.

'You need to marry me,' he argued. 'Before I die.'

'We'll have time to sort you two out later,' the Duke said soothingly.

'You're not going to die, you idiot,' Nell said once she finished poking and prodding his helpless form as if he was related to the sofa he had refused to lie on. 'The bullet went through your coat sleeve,' she pointed out as she helpfully pushed her index finger through the hole it left behind it to demonstrate. 'You're not even grazed,' she added kindly, as if she was humouring a half-wit.

'You need to marry me anyway,' he said gruffly as he got to his feet feeling very sheepish, but determined not to let her off that easily again.

'No, she doesn't,' the Duke argued calmly. 'Unless you want to of course, my dear?'

'Not if he can't do better than that,' Nell said grumpily and Fergus wished everyone else would go away so he could kiss her breathless and persuade her he loved her with everything he was, Earl or not.

'Ah, well, that's sorted out then. We'd best get these two turned over to the Runners and go to bed, I suppose,' the Duke said as if nothing very much out of the way had happened tonight.

'On what charges?' Derneley managed to ask gloomily.

'Breaking and entering, being a greedy worm who never did a decent hour's work in his life let alone a day of it? Owing your creditors a fortune will do if nothing else sticks,' Colm Hancourt said briskly.

'And don't you ever even think about stealing the Lambury Jewels again,' Fergus said, feeling as if he ought to assert himself after making such a monumental fool of himself just now.

'We're still ruined, then?' Lady Derneley said wistfully.

'The diamonds aren't here anyway,' Nell said comfortingly.

'Why don't you give them a pat on the head and invite them to supper?' Fergus demanded caustically.

'Don't be rude,' she told him with a militant look in that made Fergus groan out loud as he sensed her spotting a cause in Lady Derneley that the foolish and heartless creature did not deserve to be.

From the sound of it Mr Winterley and his bevy of powerful friends had just arrived and Fergus wished he cared enough to find out what they were going to do with Derneley and his wife as the Duke and his nephew shepherded them out of the room and at least now they were out of Nell's orbit and they could concentrate on more important things.

Chapter Seventeen

Before anyone else could come in Nell stood in front of the clock and stooped far enough to make her eyes on the same level as the holes where the key went in. 'If Papa left something for me to find it must be in there,' she said as she eyed the case where an automata a past Hancourt must have brought back from his travels stood. It represented a czarina in full coronation regalia and she had never found time to study it closely before, but the incredible detail and opulence of it almost distracted her from the quieter beauty that finally gave her father's mystery away. 'There,' she said softly at last and felt her smile wobble and tears threaten at the thought of Lord Chris hiding it for her before some trip he was about to make, knowing how much she would miss him and hoping to distract her.

'The belt?' Lord Barberry asked.

'Yes, or at least what looks like a clasp on it— it's my mother's locket,' she said reverently. 'I thought I'd forgotten her, but now I see it I remember how she always wore it. Of course he couldn't take it with him on an adventure with Pamela, she would have thrown it in the nearest midden.'

'It's very fine piece of workmanship,' he said as he came up beside her to peer at it through the glass and Nell shivered at the image of them reflected in the polished glass. They looked right, she decided and never mind clothes, lies or rank.

'Can we take it out?' she whispered, feeling as if she hardly dared breathe on the case lest it shatter and take her newly discovered memories with it.

'Do you know where your uncle hides the key?' Fergus asked and how could she think of him as a stiff and stubborn earl when he was standing by her looking as if he wasn't fit to clean his own steps, and he'd just made such a fool of himself in front of Colm and Uncle Horace surely he felt something out of the ordinary for her? They had told each other so many lies she wasn't sure she trusted words any more, but this time maybe his actions spoke for him and they were saying

something silly and un-Moss-like and quite wonderful. This lurch of heat, tenderness and awe
she felt when she thought of a possible future for
them must wait a few more minutes though, so
they could finally admit it to each other without
someone interrupting.

Uncle Horace eventually found the key to the
czarina's cabinet in a puzzle box he and Chris used
to play with as boys. 'Racked my brains to think
where he might have hidden it as soon as I realised
where that villainous old clock was pointing us,'
he said as he watched Nell unlock the cabinet.

A small gilt pin held the belt in place at the back
and it was the work of moments to tug it out and
there, at last, it was in Nell's hand. 'He used to
show me the trick of it until I could undo it,' she
said softly and pressed the neat mechanism that
held the clever thing together and there were her
parents; young and happy and as full of life as if
it had been painted yesterday.

No need for tears this time, not with Fergus at
one side and Uncle Horace holding a candle aloft
at the other so she could study the finely painted
images more closely. Aunt Barbara was warming
her toes on the hastily lit fire and Eve had gone

to bed, since Colm was still busy arranging the Derneleys' future with the lords of creation who had marched them off to some anonymous place they kept for awkward problems before they were quietly exported somewhere more convenient.

'You are very like them,' Fergus said.

'Hmm, my father was accounted very handsome and my mother quite plain.'

'Then account was wrong,' he argued, his gaze steady as he met hers to assure her that her mother certainly wasn't plain and nor was she. 'The very fine artist who painted this took the trouble to see her as she was, instead of listening to such jealous nonsense.'

'Yes, it's very like,' Uncle Horace said, 'Come and look, Barb.'

'It is,' her aunt said as she joined them, finally warm after an anxious wait to find out if all was well with her nearest and dearest. 'And Barberry is right, you do have a strong look of her.'

'I'm glad then; he loved her back, didn't he?' Nell said. 'And I suppose he was terribly lonely after he lost her,' she added with a shake of her head to say it seemed a very small excuse for his obsession with Pamela.

'I wouldn't do that,' Fergus protested as if she'd accused him of a betrayal beyond even his record of them so far.

'No, you're too strong to need anyone that much, Lord Barberry,' she told him sharply and why must she snap at him when most of her only wanted to coo words of love and melt in his arms?

'Not strong, just stubborn, and I need you end-lessly, my torment,' he whispered in her ear and it took a cough from Aunt Barbara to remind them they still weren't alone.

'Aren't you going to take a closer look at what Chris left behind?' the Duke asked as if he knew she and Fergus were too busy with one another to worry about jewels right now.

'Do you think there could be more than this then, Uncle Horace?' she asked half-heartedly and followed her uncle's gaze over the magnificent-looking czarina. 'Oh, heavens above, you mean the jewels in her regalia are *real*?'

'Are they?' Fergus asked and wrenched his gaze from her face to see for himself. 'If those are your mother's diamonds, please promise never to wear them in public without a private army on hand to protect you,' he added as if such a vast fortune in jewels was a liability, which looked very close to the mark, she decided, as the cold glitter of them made her shudder with disquiet.

'I'd sooner have this locket than all the Lambury Jewels put together,' she said at last.

'Truly?' Fergus said, one eye on the large stones that could outfit several countesses.

'They seem gaudy and rather soulless to me,' she said truthfully.

'From the look of them in the family portraits I have had nothing else to do but get acquainted with these last few weeks, the Barberry jewels can't hold a candle to these,' he warned softly, 'but you might like them better.'

'Never mind what you're going to do with them right now, let's lock the cabinet up until we can get a jeweller in to remove them and put them in a bank vault while you and Colm decide their fate,' Uncle Horace said with an expectant look at his duchess to say it was time to be tactful. Nell silently agreed with him and waited impatiently for them both to leave the room.

'And you will make sure Colm doesn't come after us with a horsewhip, won't you, Auntie dear?' she murmured as the Duchess was on her way to the door.

'Of course, my love, a lady should always be left in peace to dictate terms to the love of her life,' Aunt Barbara whispered back and sailed off to bed as if there was no single Earl standing in the red drawing room and staring down at their niece as if he couldn't get enough of the sight of her.

'Do you expect me to thank you for interfering in my affairs and nearly getting yourself shot?' Nell asked when they were alone at last.

'Not unless you've changed out of all recognition since you took up your new life, Miss *Hancourt*,' he said with a frown at her workaday old gown.

'I could have managed very well without you,' she said crossly and shot him one of Miss Court's best frowns because this wasn't the most romantic of interludes so far and even Miss Court had her dreams.

'Are you as rude as this to all your suitors?'

'No, only you,' she said grumpily.

'And I recall you being so to poor Moss on more than one occasion as well.'

'I would never have been so discourteous if you hadn't goaded me into it,' Nell defended herself.

'You saved that for your noble employers, then?'

She snorted inelegantly at the description of my Lord Barberry as a noble in anything other than fact. 'Noble indeed, and it's just as well I don't intend to have any more of them, since you put me off the whole breed.'

'And your days of acting the governess are well and truly over, madam.'

'Perhaps I shall take to the stage instead,' Nell managed to say airily. He was holding her at a distance again, as if they had only ever been impossible together, whatever rank they were pretending to have at the time, and she didn't like it one little bit.

'My mother became an actress to save her family from want and went back to it to keep me fed and healthy. She's worth a dozen of any duchess I ever met except your aunt and I refuse to be ashamed of her even for your sake.'

Nell's heart thumped a fluttering, hard beat. He had just said *even* for her sake, hadn't he? So maybe he did love her. She stared up at him as if she might read the truth in his eyes and gasped in a great breath because she might faint if she didn't and this wasn't the time for such missishness. 'I truly admire Lady Rivers for doing as she did. She is obviously a lady of spirit and resource; why wouldn't you be proud of her?'

'You really mean that, don't you?'

'Of course I do; why would I say it if I didn't?'

'Forthright as ever, Miss Court?' he said with a rueful smile she almost took as a compliment. 'I'm not ashamed of my mother and never will be,' he added as if he intended setting out rules for the future when this was all about trust for her.

'Lord Chris's daughter wouldn't have a leg to stand on if she wanted to condemn Lady Rivers because she once had to work for a living,' she said steadily and met his eyes with a challenge to stop judging her by polite society's rules when it had done neither of them many favours in the past.

'It's not your fault your father loved unwisely, Nell,' he said earnestly.

There it was; that real, true love and trust in his eyes and voice that she wanted so badly this felt like the most crucial conversation of her entire life. Of course, his rock-like determination to keep her safe came from the true heart of him. She could excuse it because he'd watched his beloved mother be sneered at and looked down on because she didn't fit the exact mould of a nobleman's wife, but she didn't intend to let him protect her until she was stifled. She had been an independent woman too long to meekly submit to being cosseted for her own good and put in a glass cabinet like the imitation czarina.

'My father would have done far better to love a lady who deserved his devotion,' Nell said absently because Fergus Selford was far more interesting right now.

'He ruined your life.'

'No, he ruined his own life and Colm and I had to become stronger than he was as a consequence.'

'Too strong to think the world well lost for love like he did?' he asked huskily.

'Too strong not to love anyway. We know we can live outside the tight limits of polite society because we've done it most of our lives. How many of our kind could say that, Lord Barberry?'

'I can,' he said rather unsteadily, as if this was another caveat they had to get out of the way before they admitted their feelings to one another and he was getting as impatient with them as she was. 'I made it my mission to live without my title and the trappings of an English earl when

I went to Canada and stayed there although my little cousins needed me. Beware of a man with a mission, Miss Hancourt; he tramples on innocents to get what he wants.'

'I don't think your cousins are that easily downtrodden, my lord.'

'What about you, Miss Court?'

'Didn't I just finish telling you how hard I am to cast out and bring low?'

'So you did, then please will you finally agree to marry me?' he said. He looked caught between horror she might say no and hope she would agree as he stared down at her with so many complex emotions in his fascinating blue eyes she felt as if she could stare into them like a bewitched idiot for hours on end.

'Why?' she asked at last.

'I love you.'

'Hmmm, I wonder,' she said, forcing the words past her galloping heartbeat and a vast, dangerous hope that was making her clench her hands into fists at her sides so she wouldn't throw herself into his arms and agree to anything if he'd only keep saying it.

'How can you doubt it? I have just made such

a fool of myself when I thought he was going to shoot you that I suspect even your brother has to know I love you more than life itself by now.'

'You were either furious or mocking most of the time I was Miss Court and not much different since I owned up to being my true self,' she argued.

'You always were your true self, isn't that what you just told me?' he said impatiently. 'And you don't look that different to me, if you're dressed in Bond Street's finest or that gown you wore back at Berry Brampton.'

'I look completely different when I'm dressed up in all my finery,' she said defensively.

'Your hair is beautiful, but it always was,' he said coming to stand behind her and looking at the only traces of the new, fashionable Nell available tonight.

She felt the heat and proximity of him and forgot what they were talking about, until he cocked his head on one side as if eyeing up a masterpiece in need of some restoration. 'I would like it a lot better if it was down about your shoulders, of course. I've always wanted to run my hands through it and find out if it feels as soft and seductive as it looks.'

'I'm not beautiful, Fergus,' she said stiffly.

'You are to me; I can't look at any other woman and think her anything but pallid and uninteresting next to you and I want you endlessly, Nell. You're lucky my mother knows a bit too much about lusty young gentlemen and taught me to control my urges and burn in duchesses' drawing rooms. I want to throw you down on the *chaise* over there and teach you how bitterly a man can long for you and you alone right now, so be more careful what you say because I'm too close to proving how lovely you are to me by actions if you won't believe the words.'

'Oh, you idiot,' she said, with a soft sound between a laugh and a sob. 'I want you so much I feel as if every inch of me is screaming for your touch. I don't know how to say it more politely, but if you really mean to love me I wish you would just get on with it, Lord Barberry.'

'What, here and now?' he said as if startled the notion could enter her head.

Nell turned away from the shadowy look of them in a nearby mirror the wrong way around and felt Miss Court was being left behind in that fine old Venetian glass, frowning with disapproval as Nell's inner demon boldly stared up at the Earl of Barberry and considered the idea very seriously indeed.

'Best not, perhaps, Colm might not take to you as I want him to if he catches us being very improper indeed on one of my uncle's fine couches.'

'Come and be improper on one of mine then, Nell?' he breathed as if one of them might shatter soon if she didn't.

'Haven't you got the upholsterers in? That's what you told my aunt and uncle just now.'

'One or two of them are still serviceable and I seem to have slept on most of the ones that are this last fortnight, so at least I know which will not shoot a spring out of place at the worst possible moment.'

'Arrange it then, my lord,' she demanded boldly, still not quite sure why she still hadn't admitted she loved him and felt truly desperate to marry him now she knew he loved her back.

'I ought to demand you wed me first.'

'I dare say you ought,' she said, examining her highly polished fingernails as if it didn't matter very much if he refused to be scandalous with her tonight or not.

'Meet me at the side gate in half an hour and don't forget to bring keys, because you'll have to creep in and get yourself into the right bed on your own tonight. I'm not inclined to let your brother shoot me if I have to break into your uncle's house to let you back in with the dawn.'

'An hour,' she challenged, because it would take her that long to wash, pretend to take to her bed then redress as soon as her maid had gone to bed herself.

'Three-quarters,' he argued as if that was the outside limit of his patience.

Nell wanted him so urgently and was beginning to read his darkest frowns and grimmest glowers as the sign of the controlled emotion they truly were. She nodded and agreed to their first compromise as lovers, then went off to get ready to seduce and be seduced by the first and last one of those she ever intended to have.

Chapter Eighteen

'At last,' Fergus murmured in Nell's ear and drew her close for the brief tiptoe across the square and up the steps to his own nearly splendid again mansion.

Nell caught her breath and wondered nobody could hear the thunder of her heartbeat as they crept through this merciful, cloudy darkness to the side door of Barberry House. She didn't dare speak, but felt him move next to her and her breath caught with the hugeness of what they were doing. If she lost her nerve he would let her turn tail and say *no* to such a final commitment between lovers, but she refused to damage this wondrous feeling at the outset. So there was no stumble of maidenly hesitation for her and Fergus had to stop her running up the side steps to get herself ruined all the faster and giving them away.

'Have all your servants gone to bed?' she managed to whisper softly when he had the door open, at last, then locked it hastily behind them.

'The few I have left here are enjoying a holiday at my expense,' he managed to murmur in a fairly normal voice, although it was rasped by powerful emotion as she snuggled against his side as if there was nowhere else she longed to be and wasn't that the truth?

'How convenient,' she said coolly as a woman could when she was plastered against her man's torso so tightly he might as well wear her as a shirt.

'It won't seem so when you have to live among the debris.'

'Why would I do that?'

'Because you're not going to get away with a splendid marriage in Hanover Square and a six-month viscount after tonight, my lady,' he said a little bit too seriously even as he lit a branch of candles waiting on a dusty side-table and turned to meet her hot eyes as if even now he'd say them nay, if she wouldn't agree to wed him as fast as they could obtain a special licence.

'I might like being the most notorious Hancourt since my father,' she objected half-seriously.

'You might, but I wouldn't and you haven't met my mother yet. I doubt she would speak to either of us until after the babe was born if we disgraced her like that,' he said with a warm chuckle that changed into a groan as even the thought of bearing his child made Nell forget they were standing in a chilly hallway in a dusty and deserted mansion and writhe her body against his in a silent demand they start the project right now.

'Are you certain it's me you really want as a wife, Fergus?' Nell made herself ask and even managed to set a few fractions of an inch of space between them against all her instincts never to let him go again.

'Certain of myself, Miss Eleanor Hancourt, not quite as sure of you,' he said unsteadily and led her into the little sitting room he must have been using as his base to watch over her these past weeks, when she'd thought he was long gone and forgetting her.

'Even when I'm behaving like a wanton *houri* in your arms, my lord?'

'Even then,' he said seriously.

'I'm sorry,' she said and felt him flinch, then cursed herself for making him even think it could be a refusal. 'No, sorry I find it so hard to admit I need anyone, not sorry about you and I'll just creep back to my lonely bed, thank you very much, my lord. I spent so long telling myself it was better not to rely on anyone it seems nigh impossible to admit I need you so desperately now. For most of my childhood and adult life I have had to walk my own path, you see?'

'So you need me, do you?' he said and his soft sigh at her intransigence spurred her into saying what she meant at last, because it sounded as if he was trying not to hurt and that was the last thing she wanted.

'Need wouldn't be enough. What I feel for you is fierce and hungry and far more powerful than anything I ever expected to feel. I always thought I was cold and immune to loving to the edge of reason, but I wouldn't be here now if I didn't love you to distraction, you great fool.'

'You would make me wait until after the wedding, then?'

'No, I wouldn't marry you at all.'

'Thank heaven you love me, then,' he said with another of those heartfelt sighs she felt guilty about wringing out of him. 'And why not you?

You deserve to be happy,' he added as if the rest of her words had taken that long to get past his relief at her final, life-changing admission she loved him.

'But I'm Lord Christopher Hancourt's daughter.'

'An aristocrat who shouldn't love Kitty Graham's son?'

'No, she loves him beyond her wildest dreams, but my father really did disgrace the Hancourt strawberry leaves—trust my eldest uncle to make sure I knew that every day of my younger life.'

'Ah, but he's dead and done with and we're alive, with a lifetime of proving him wrong in front of us. Don't let him win, Nell.'

'Only if you promise to forget your grandfather and uncles' foolishness as well, my love,' Nell said and finally gave into the desperation she'd been fighting since she saw him again, frowning back at her as if he was daring her to hate him for being there.

She rose on her toes to meet his hungry mouth with hers and to the devil with propriety and maidenly modesty. Their kiss was even more hot and urgent than the ones they exchanged at Berry Brampton, but this time there was a confidence, a sweetness behind the passion that made Nell's toes curl into her kid slippers, then flex with sensual pleasure. She locked her arms about his powerful neck and pulled him closer.

'I can't stand up,' she whispered when he raised his head to breathe.

'Do you want to?' he demanded hoarsely and walked them to the nearest flat surface as if he couldn't wait to get there either.

'This *chaise is* up to our weight, isn't it?' Nell asked with a hint of a breathless giggle in her voice that sounded girlish and giddy and delight shot through her like champagne bubbles because this was real and he was here and how very much she loved this man.

Fergus took her attack of giddiness in his stride. There was a lightness, almost a boyishness in his deep chuckle that made her realise how much of himself he'd been holding back since they met as well.

'It's far too uncomfortable to get worn out,' he told her as he found time to reach blindly for a tumble of cushions and a softly expensive blanket to guard them against stiff old leather and horse-hair stuffing.

'Let's try anyway,' she murmured and pulled his head back down so he could kiss her into forgetting their surroundings altogether. 'Oh, yes, I think we should start as we mean to go on,' she murmured into his ear, then explored it with her curious tongue while she was up there. She felt him twitch with a shock of manly desire, so of course she did it again.

'You'll unman me if you're not careful,' he warned unsteadily when he'd got enough breath back to speak.

'I'm tired of being careful,' Nell murmured. Fumbling the knot in his frayed neckcloth undone and throwing it into a corner, she was glad he wasn't in full gentlemanly fig. She knelt upright on the unyielding old couch to try out what kissing her way down the intriguing chord of tension in his neck and down to the hollows at the base of it might do. Luckily he remembered what his hands were for before she got there and he found the laces of her gown and undid her even more completely while she was so busy undoing him.

'Shift,' he demanded and she was delirious with love and delight and anticipation and frowned in puzzlement that he was troubling to name her garments at a time like this.

'Yes, I know,' she said blankly, sparing her fingers long enough to smooth the fine silken stuff of her very expensive underwear with absentminded approval.

'No, shift your knees, unless you would like me to rip this very respectable gown off you right now and ruin it, Miss Hancourt. We need to get you home before the house is stirring, don't forget, and it'll be a lot easier to do that if you're not naked,' he said, laughing as she hastily did as he said and let him slide the mundane stuff gown out from under her then it was off and over her head in one smooth move.

'Are you sure you're not a rake?' she said, frowning at the very thought of him doing this with anyone else.

'If I ever was I would have met my match in you,' he said with only half his attention on what they were saying. His hot blue gaze was intent on the whisper of silk that made up her new shift and her rather exotic short corset, rich with satin and lace and shaped by a mistress of the art. Eve had insisted such a fast garment would make her feel as well as look a very different female from sternly practical Miss Court and she was so right. 'Whoever made that ought to be locked in a tower and ordered to make one in every colour under the sun only for you, since I doubt this one will survive the night,' he said hoarsely.

'I like it,' she protested and wriggled about to undo it before he could rip the delicate laces open.

'Did I say I didn't?'

'No, and why are we arguing about my corset?'

'Because that's what we do; I doubt we'll give it up simply because we love one another,' he replied and somehow made himself tug the bow undone and loosened the laces so she could wriggle out of it although his wonderful eyes were blazing with need and something close to desperation as he watched ever more of her emerge from its rather sensuous embrace.

'We might get bored with each other if we lived in sweet harmony,' she agreed absently, revelling in the feel of his work-hardened palms abrading her tightly needy breasts with only this whisper of silk left between them now. 'Oh, please, give me more, Fergus,' she managed to gasp as the absolute pleasure of his touch there shot flames of merciless need right through her. 'Please?' she asked as he lowered his dark head and suckled on her frantically needy nipples until she keened with desire. In the shadowy gloom of one branch of candles and the fire she watched his dear, dark head as he feasted on her blatantly aroused breasts as if he was desperate for the taste of her. Even as she felt the flick of his wicked tongue on her wet, silk-veiled nipple she gloried in the chance to know his powerful neck and the sensitive curves of his head and brow by touch. He felt as if he was hers every bit as surely as she was his. He felt hot and passionate and possessive as he gave her tightly demanding breasts one last, lingering caress and worked his way back up, meeting her gaze with a rather self-satisfied grin.

'Is that it?' she teased as if she didn't know there must still be a banquet of some sort waiting for them. She couldn't be this tense and hot and needy for something even more incredible if this was all men and women did together in a bed.

'It should be until we're wed,' he said with a frown and she cursed herself for finding words instead of kisses at such a time.

'Don't be silly, my lord,' she said brusquely and

decided it was high time she satisfied her curiosity about the intriguing differences between him and her. 'I am three and twenty and know my own mind, and my mind wants you nigh as much as my body does right now,' she said, as if he didn't already know.

'Soon you will be my lady and you won't be able to throw my title in my face like an insult,' he said even as his mighty body quivered when she ran a curious, exploring finger over his tightly muscled torso and down over his own tiny nipples to linger briefly and see him tighten with desire as well. Too intrigued to linger for now, she moved on and felt his breath hitch. She felt satiny skin shift under her touch, as if the almost not there sensitivity of her touch made him more of everything. More aroused, more delighted they were here together like this, more Fergus Selford than ever before and he was *her* lover.

Even as she thought he couldn't be more than he already was, her wandering finger slid further down and the stark evidence she was wrong reared rigidly against his flat belly. He was mightily aroused and mighty indeed, it felt as if every muscle and sinew he possessed in this very impressive body of his was clenched with driven need for something very intimate indeed with her.

'Do you know how a man and woman mate, my love?' he whispered into her gasped open lips as he leaned his forehead against hers to look the question into her love-dazed eyes.

'Like the wild animals, I suppose,' she said, having long ago decided the more fanciful of her fellow pupils at Miss Thibett's School had to be wrong about husbands and wives for the human race to have lasted as long as it had.

'Not entirely,' he qualified with a tender, secretive smile that promised a great deal more than the simple urge to mate and a few harsh grunts.

'Like tame ones, then?' she whispered provocatively.

'Why not let me show you? Telling is much less fun,' he murmured against her mouth and kissed her so deeply and passionately she forgot what the question had been.

Heat was pulsing through her in ever stronger waves and she wondered if she might faint from the sheer, edgy pleasure of it as her body seemed to know what it wanted better than she did. It rose against her lover, back bowed so his rigid sex was emphatic against her roused core, the feel of him there sending shivers of hot anticipation through her until she felt as if she'd been half-tortured, half-pleasured as the knot at the heart of her got ever tighter and hungrier to be unknotted by him.

'Careful, my love,' he whispered and she was impressed he still could.

Lost for words herself, she gasped open her mouth to try and moan out some sort of question as he stroked his index finger over parts of her she never knew wanted his caress so badly until this very moment. Even as he brought her to the edge of wonder he seized her mouth with his and plunged his tongue inside it, setting up a beat as strong as life itself. She shifted, smoothed out her cramped legs to fall back against the silk and velvet cushions until she was open to whatever came next because she trusted him that much. Her breath coming in gasps now, she heard it hitch even more as he followed her down and his sex butted against hers. If not for the fact she could hear his lungs labouring to get breath into his body against the power of wanting her so much, she might have hesitated and learnt to fear, but his desperation rekindled her own after that moment of wondering how she could endure sharing any more of herself even with him. There, now, he was inside her. Gentling as best he could as he tried his hardest to let her grow accustomed to having a man inside her for the first time; her man inside her for the first time, she amended smugly somewhere in her head.

A flood of warmth, a softening she couldn't quite describe and he was even further in and she purred and raised her knees beside his paused flanks to demand yet more of him. Still for a long moment, taking his weight on his elbows and caressing her hungry mouth with his busy tongue and lips, he seemed almost reluctant to go on until she bit his upper lip gently and licked it better with a sensuous satisfaction that seemed to snap his last tether. Still bowing back his head in an effort for self-control, he broke through the fragile barrier of her maidenhead and she knew why he had hesitated, why he seemed almost on the edge of keeping her out of the land beyond it until their wedding night for a long, desperate moment. Glad he wasn't as gallant as he wanted to be, for both their sakes, she rode the wave of a brief pain that subsided to soreness as her inner and most sensitive Nell adjusted to not being alone any more. She felt him holding his breath, waiting for any sign she didn't want him to go on. He would stop even now, whatever it cost him; she knew that as surely as if he'd sworn it on paper and signed it in blood before they began.

'Idiot,' she muttered into his dark, sweat-dampened curls and made him lift his head to face her gaze by gently cupping his chin as if he was the one new to all this and not her. 'How could I not want you?' she asked huskily.

'I'm told it hurts.'

'Who by?' she asked, almost sharpened out of pleasure by the most acute jealousy she could ever imagine before he became her one and only lover.

'One of my sisters,' he said flatly, 'but don't you dare tell her I said so.'

'I won't,' she said and lay back on her seducer's shabby old couch again and gave him a heavy-eyed gaze of what she hoped was sensuous encouragement.

Seeing him frown as if he still wasn't sure if he ought to stop right now anyway, she managed an experimental wriggle and contracted her internal muscles about his rigid manhood. It jerked inside her as if it had a life of its own and she heard him groan with need with a very self-satisfied smile on her face.

'Show me everything,' she demanded.

'That will take years, love,' he protested with a chuckle that felt wonderful as his muscular torso shifted against her pertly demanding nipples and reawakened another wild need inside her.

'Then show me some more,' she whispered with the wild lure of all those years to come making her catch her breath and yearn even more.

He withdrew almost all the way out of her and flexed his tight buttocks to thrust all the way back in again and this time she knew there was nothing in the way of their driven exploration of each other. Feeling him fully engaged inside her for the first time as he rocked all the way into her, she let herself believe this was really happening with the love of her life and opened herself up to him completely. She felt her muscles contract and relax around him and she forgot questions and murmured words and let her body have its head. It knew how to rise and fall to the tune he set for them, it felt the pulse and glory of life itself draw her on and, most of all, it cherished and trusted this mighty man who took so much care for her pleasure he was using every muscle and breath he had to make this good for her. At last his mouth was set with effort, his breath rasping as he used every ounce of self-control he had left to hold himself back from some goal she could sense but not know. She reached an unsteady hand to smooth the frown from his fierce brow and it seemed to break his chains. On a gasp of manly protest, then he bucked and moaned even as she felt the first almost fearsome contractions of something strange and new threaten to drown her.

'Go with it, love, don't fight us,' he ground out between clenched teeth and how could she *not* trust him to know what was coming and cherish her through every beat of it?

'I will, I do,' she whispered on a gasp of wonder and trusted him and her body to know what to do, even if this felt too enormous to cope with on top of all the other novelties he'd shown her tonight for an awed moment. Such power, such light, such uncanny warmth and *oh, oh, ooh*, this was way beyond any words she could conjure up as she flew in his arms.

Nell reached for her lover and clasped his strong shoulders since she seemed about to drown in endless pleasure while her body bowed and jerked in time to his. Wave after wave of it swept through her like the force of life itself and with any man but him it would have been so lonely. Instead it was joy and love and their soft moans of exquisite pleasure sounded right in the intimate warmth of this half-dismantled room. Just when she thought she was drained of all wonder, his sex seemed to harden even more as he surged into her ever more powerfully, until she wrapped her slender legs about his hips and hung on to his shoulders as he thrust into her with a huge, driven groan and she felt the surge of his seed inside her for the first time while ecstasy finally wrapped them both in a long, hot glory that went on and on and was over all too quickly at the same time. Now their gasps were of sated wonder, hers almost a whimper of protest as she felt the last echo of absolute pleasure and unity fade. Still surprised by the occasional spasm of ecstasy, she sucked in air as if she had just run from here to Berry Brampton and yet suddenly she felt absurdly shy as she met his gaze in the fading firelight.

'I, well… I don't know what to say,' she managed to say at last.

'Miss Court silenced? Isn't that a marvel?' he whispered teasingly and she laughed even as she felt a little bit sorry for that poor, lonely governess.

'You'd best ask my pupils.'

'I'd best not, I hardly think it's a guardian's lot to tell his wards what a fraud their teacher has proved herself to be, in so many ways,' he said and raised a wicked eyebrow to encourage her to ask the question she was too wise to say out loud. 'You never were cold or restrained or wrapped up in icy propriety, were you, my love?'

'No, and I always wanted you,' she said with a contented sigh and tried not to regret it when he withdrew from her body and she was one and a little bit lonely again after that triumphant coupling with this man she never wanted to live without. 'Miss Court was horribly lonely at times, my lord,' she added with a frown, 'but she nearly drove herself mad with wanting you and knowing it would it would be seen as a sad misalliance and damage his pride if she stole into Mr Moss's rickety bed one night.'

'Would that you had then; my ancient bed was

rendered hideous by the lack of you in it most of the time I stayed at the steward's house.'

'Would my lord have been able to take Miss Court's hungry heart and trample on it like that, though?' she asked, almost offended by the idea that the woman she was not might have been seduced by a man he wasn't either, if they hadn't been so wary of each other.

'No, and my lord wouldn't have been so bad tempered and gruff if he hadn't wondered if he could and come up with a firm *no* every time he wanted to.'

'Good, I don't want the man I love seducing any more virgins.'

'I'll never love any other virago but you, my darling,' he said and shifted her to lie across his torso where she could feel him breathe under her for a luxurious few minutes before she had to go home and pretend none of this had happened somehow or another.

'If anything ever happens to me, promise me you'll not love a heartless jade and put our children through the loneliness Colm and I endured, Fergus?'

'Hard to imagine anything worse than being

caught in the toils of a Viscountess Pamela, but the best way to make sure our children live happy lives is for you to live them with us. Don't expect any such promises from me, Miss Hancourt. You're going to have to be here to look after them yourself because I'm not willing to do any of it without you and my wards can't spare you either.'

'Be serious, love.'

'I am,' he said implacably and Nell let herself know this wasn't going to be a conventional marriage and who would want one of those when she could have him as her husband instead?

'Very well then; I won't accept you leaving me alone and bereft and with a son to bring up alone as your father did your mother either.'

'If I decide to sail the Irish Sea in the teeth of a gale I promise to take you and our offspring with me,' he conceded and kissed her disordered curls, then sighed with such total contentment it brought hot tears to Nell's eyes.

'Better still, don't set out so recklessly in the first place,' she ordered him as sternly as she could when she was lying in his arms and appreciating every vibrant inch of him.

'And welcome back, Miss Court,' he said with

a mock sigh and shake of the head to argue he didn't enjoy the idea of having two strong-minded ladies in his bed when it was very obvious to her that he liked it very much.

'Hmm, shall we keep Mr Moss as well d'you think?' she asked with a delighted shiver at the idea of that short-tempered son of the soil making the odd guest appearance in her wildest fantasies once again.

'At your own risk,' he growled and ungallantly pushed her off his chest and on to the rather threadbare hearth rug when she purred a long moan of anticipation at the very idea of risking it right now. 'Home with you, woman, there's too much to do for us to have the time to undo you all over again right now,' he said as if he wasn't on fire again as well and she knew perfectly well that he was.

'A man is at a distinct disadvantage with his lover, isn't he?' she said smugly at the sight now as well as the feel of all that masculine fire and need blatantly wanting her all over again against her bare body. He was being gallant, despite all that fire and need, and she was torn between feeling touched and frustrated.

'Yes, now stop talking and keep dressing, it's nearly morning.'

'Would you mind if I gave them away, Fergus?' she asked seriously this time as she reluctantly did as he asked.

'Gave what away?' he asked absently, his eyes hungry on her still near-naked body and she almost gave up and encouraged him to be even more absorbed in it and forget the daylight beginning to steal around the shutters and chase away the night.

'The diamonds,' she explained instead, since she didn't want to be caught stealing home by the servants either, or for Colm to catch them and kick up some silly masculine fuss because his sister had chosen the man she wanted to spend a lifetime with and couldn't wait to begin it.

'They're worth a fortune,' he cautioned and why wouldn't she love him when he seemed more concerned she might not have grasped their worth than he was by the fact she wanted to give them away?

'I know; one day our children might curse me for doing it, but there are even harder times than usual coming for the poor, are there not?'

He nodded and frowned at the thought of the

terrible prospects for the harvest after such a wet, cold and cheerless summer. 'Aye,' he said seriously, 'it's been bad enough for them since the French wars ended, but this winter will be terrible with so little grain to be gathered in and not a lot else to take its place. Even the Lambury Diamonds couldn't fill that mighty a gap though, love.'

'But they might help,' she argued and it felt right to put the chilly, dangerous things to good use at long last. 'I don't want them and I don't want our children to be burdened with them either. There's something wrong with them, they only ever cause bloodshed and tears to those who own them. It's time they did some good in the world. Maybe they can lie easy in some princess's crown because I really don't want them.'

'Your brother says they're yours to do with as you wish, love, and I won't argue with bidding goodbye to them if that's what you truly want.'

'I think I shall like you as a husband nearly as much as I do as my lover, Lord Barberry,' she said with a come-hither smile.

'No, stop it, you witch; your brother might kill me if he catches you coming home after the dawn.'

'Or he might be asleep and you're worrying about nothing.'

'In three weeks we'll have every right to sleep in the same bed, but right now I'm not willing to be compromised by you or shot by your brother. No kindly get yourself dressed and back in your own bed before he finds out where you've been tonight.'

'Very well, my lord,' Nell said meekly and thought three weeks a devilishly long time for them to make love on the most uncomfortable couch in Britain. 'You won't ever get rid of this monstrosity, will you?' she asked with a sentimental sigh.

'Never,' he breathed, with a long look back at the nest they'd made to love each other on for the first night of a lifetime as lovers and a very fond smile.

* * * * *

If you enjoyed this story,
you won't want to miss Elizabeth Beacon's
A YEAR OF SCANDAL *miniseries*

THE VISCOUNT'S FROZEN HEART
THE MARQUIS'S AWAKENING
LORD LAUGHRAINE'S SUMMER PROMISE
REDEMPTION OF THE RAKE
and
THE WINTERLEY SCANDAL